The Devil

Paul Doherty was born in Middlesbrough in 1946. He was admitted to Liverpool University where he gained a First Class Honours Degree in History and won a state scholarship to Exeter College, Oxford. While there he met his wife, Carla.

Paul worked in Ascot, Newark and Crawley, before being appointed as Headmaster to Trinity Catholic High School, Essex, in 1981. The school has been described as one of the leading comprehensives in the U.K. and has been awarded 'Outstanding' in four consecutive OFSTED inspections. All seven of Paul and Carla's children have been educated at Trinity.

Paul has written over 100 books and has published a series of outstanding historical mysteries set in the Middle Ages, Classical Greece, Ancient Egypt and elsewhere. His books have been translated into more than twenty languages.

Also by Paul Doherty

The Brother Athelstan Mysteries

The Nightingale Gallery
The House of the Red Slayer
Murder Most Holy
The Anger of God
By Murder's Bright Light
The House of Crows
The Assassin's Riddle
The Devil's Domain
The Field of Blood
The House of Shadows
Bloodstone
The Straw Men
Candle Flame
The Book of Fires
The Herald of Hell
The Great Revolt
A Pilgrimage to Murder

PAUL DOHERTY

The Devil's Domain

CANELO

First published in Great Britain in 1998 by Headline Book Publishing, a division of Hodder Headline PLC

This edition published in the United Kingdom in 2022 by

Canelo
Unit 9, 5th Floor
Cargo Works, 1-2 Hatfields
London, SE1 9PG
United Kingdom

A CIP catalogue record for this book is available from the British Library.

Print ISBN 978 1 80032 872 3
Ebook ISBN 978 1 80032 141 0

Look for more great books at www.canelo.co

Printed and bound in Great Britain by Clays Ltd, Elcograf S.p.A.

I

Chapter 1

'A time of bloody tribulation! Of horrid sights! The season of murder and subtle trickery!' is how the chronicler of Westminster described the late summer of 1380. The old monk sat in his carrel overlooking the cloister garth, scratching the edge of his quill against his unshaven cheek. How could he truly describe these times? The King was only a boy; the Regent, his uncle John of Gaunt, that bloody man of war, ruled the kingdom. Some even whispered he wanted it for himself. The French were at sea, their war fleets attacking the English galleys and cogs along the sea lanes from Bordeaux to Calais. At home, the summer harvest had been good; prices, however, still climbed out of the reach of the poor who swarmed along the highways over Southwark Bridge and into the city.

The kingdom was waiting! All the signs and portents were there. A coffin had been seen in the skies above St Paul's: draped in a ghostly pall, it had moved from east to west before disappearing into the low, threatening clouds to the north of the city. Many said that was where the danger would arise, from the fields and villages north of Cripplegate. The men of the soil, the earthworms, who laboured and spun so the great ones could clothe themselves in silk and ride great destriers, drink deep of the blood-red claret and count their silver and gold coins. In the streets of London, sepulchral voices were heard crying woe, prophesying disaster. Black-draped barges, rowed by ghostly hands, were glimpsed on the river shooting the turbulence under London Bridge. Were these, the gossips chattered, the ghosts of men who had defied the Regent and lost their heads which, salted and pickled, decorated pikes along the rail of that same London Bridge?

The chronicler's brothers and monks at Westminster said such signs were mere trickery and foolish chatter. The peasants, now well organised and calling themselves the 'Great Community of the Realm', were despatching troublemakers, traitors, inciters to rebellion and treason into the city, stirring up trouble along its foul alleyways and runnels. Others, less worldly, shook their heads. These signs, surely, were warning of horrors yet to come? Had not a holy man, who claimed to have wandered in the deserts of Palestine, had visions which he preached, at a penny a time, from the cross of St Paul's? How God was planning to sweep London with fire? To bring it as low as hell, to leave not one stone upon another?

In the cemetery of St Erconwald's, Pike the ditcher and Watkin the dung-collector reflected on these rumours. They sat beneath the old yew tree sharing a wineskin and staring up at the starlit sky. They were both drunk as hogs. They should have gone home. However, a few blackjacks of ale in the Piebald Tavern, followed by a cup of canary, a gift from Joscelyn the one-armed taverner, and Pike and Watkin had rolled out into the streets feeling like great lords of the land. They shared their pennies and, before they'd left, bought a bulging wineskin.

'Be careful,' the taverner had warned, watching these two fellow parishioners sway backwards and forwards on their feet. 'You've drunk enough. You should go home and sleep it off!'

'We are not thrunk!' Watkin scoffed. 'I just wisth your bloody floor would stay still. This is a tavern, not one of your bloody cogs of war!'

Joscelyn had sighed in exasperation. The two men had wished him good night.

'Where are you going to?' Joscelyn called curiously as he followed them to the doorway.

He smiled at Cecily the courtesan who, arm in arm with a young fop, was strolling down towards the fields south of the Bishop of Winchester's inn: a famous trysting place for the likes of Cecily and her customers. Cecily waved her fingers. Pike the ditcher watched her go and licked his lips even though his wife had warned him off.

'If I catch you with that trollop again,' she'd screeched, 'you'll be nothing more than a gelding!'

Pike swayed and put one mud-covered hand on Watkin's shoulder.

'We'd best be going,' he slurred.

'Go where?' Joscelyn repeated.

Watkin tapped his fleshy nose and winked. 'Secrets,' he slurred. 'Great secrets.'

Joscelyn stepped back and glanced round nervously. Were the rumours true, he wondered? Were these two rapscallions members of the Great Community of the Realm? Plotting treason and rebellion against John of Gaunt? If that was the case he wanted no more of it! Gaunt had a way of dealing with traitors: hanged like rats on the gallows at Smithfield or on the other side of London Bridge. Spies abounded in Southwark, more than fleas on a mongrel's back.

'Take care!' he warned. Joscelyn retreated into his taproom closing the door firmly behind him.

Watkin and Pike had stumbled along to the church, gone through the lych gate and taken up residence beneath the yew tree at the far end of God's acre, the broad cemetery which bounded the old church of St Erconwald's. They had drunk and waited, watching the sun set and the stars come out. Then they had seen it, on the top of the church tower, a slight glow from a charcoal brazier.

'He's up there,' Pike said, referring to their parish priest the Dominican Brother Athelstan. 'He's up there watching his bloody stars! Him and that cat of his. What's its name? Eh? Benedicta?'

'Benedicta!' Watkin laughed. 'That's the widow woman, you know, dark-faced and dark-eyed with a softness for Brother Athelstan.' He leaned conspiratorially closer. 'The name of his one-eyed cat is Bonaventura.'

'Do you think it's true?' Pike continued.

'What is?'

'That he left St Erconwald's…'

Watkin felt a chill of apprehension, which almost sobered him up. Such rumours and stories had been rife in the parish, fiercely discussed on the church steps or in the Piebald Tavern. Watkin knew he was a sinner. He drank too much, he swore, he fought, he lusted after other men's wives. Nevertheless, he feared God in heaven and the Lord Jesus; but Watkin loved their small parish priest with his olive-skinned face, dark, soulful eyes and brain as sharp as a razor. Athelstan made Watkin feel good about himself. Every so often, the Dominican would pat the fat dung-collector on the shoulder.

'What you do, Watkin, cleaning the muck in filthy alleyways, is loved by God. You are like the Holy Ghost.'

Watkin had seen the laughter in the Dominican's eye.

'You make things clean and fresh! Therefore, Watkin, in God's plan, you are very important!'

Watkin had never forgotten that. He had been frightened by the rumours that John of Gaunt had taken a savage dislike to the little friar and arranged for his transference to the Halls of Oxford. They claimed Athelstan had got as far as Cripplegate before Prior Anselm had intervened and sent a message ordering the Dominican back to his parish. Athelstan had never said anything but, there again, he was unlikely to do so, Watkin mused. And Watkin, although leader of the parish council, dare not challenge him. Athelstan had a dark side. If he lost his temper, his tongue was like a lash. Watkin loved him yet he was more frightened of Athelstan than he was of the Regent's men-at-arms or even the great coroner Sir Jack Cranston who'd come swaggering into Southwark, one hand on his sword belt, the other clutching a wineskin.

Watkin often reflected on the relationship between Cranston and his secretarius Athelstan but he couldn't reach any conclusion. Cranston was as big as Athelstan was little. He could, and often did, drink the entire taproom of the Piebald Tavern under the table. He could swear like any soldier. He had the ear of many powerful men in the city. They even said the young King deferred to him but Cranston could do nothing unless Athelstan was by his side.

'How long do you think we'll wait?' Pike broke in.

Watkin stretched out his legs and cursed. The ale in his belly was turning sour. He had seen the warning look in Joscelyn's eyes and quietly cursed his growing involvement in Pike's madcap schemes. All of Southwark knew about the Great Community of the Realm! The Secret Council of peasant leaders and their ruthless agents who slipped like shadows along the wards, bringing in messages and instructions which could not be defied. Once you were part of the Community, you either supported it or you died.

'Do you think this is wise?' Watkin asked. 'I mean to be waiting here? If Athelstan found out he'd lash us with his tongue or worse,' he added morosely. 'Just stare at us so sorrowfully until we confessed everything.'

'I am a part of it,' Pike declared defiantly, looking up at the sky. 'And, Watkin, so are you!'

Watkin moved his great rump and scratched his bulbous nose. He and Pike used to be rivals on the parish council but now Pike had drawn him into these secret matters. Had he done it deliberately? A surety against Brother Athelstan's anger if their parish priest ever found out?

'Remember what happened to Ricaud!' Pike said, enjoying himself.

Watkin shivered. Ricaud was a pedlar who used to sell his gewgaws on Shoemakers Lane. Gossip said he also sold secrets of the Great Community to the Regent's spies: one morning, Ricaud, or rather his head, was found fastened to a pole on the mud flats above the Thames.

'When Adam delved and Eve span,' Pike sang softly, 'who was then the gentleman? Just think of it, Watkin.' Pike stretched out on the grass. 'Think of a kingdom, no princes, no bishops, no great lords of the soil, where the meek truly inherit the earth.'

'Sometimes,' Watkin interjected drily, 'I think all we'll earn, Pike, is what you are lying on. A twisted neck at Smithfield and a shallow grave.'

Pike smacked his lips. Watkin knew this was a sign for one of his speeches.

'I've got to piss,' he grumbled and, staggering to his feet, walked through the grass to the great sycamore tree which stood next to the boundary wall of the cemetery. Watkin undid the points of his breeches. He had relieved himself and was about to turn away when he heard a sound above him.

'Good evening, dung-collector!'

Watkin gaped up into the dark branches.

'My name is Valerian.' The voice was low but harsh. 'With me is Domitian!'

Watkin stumbled backwards.

'You won't recognise those names,' the voice hissed, 'but we bring you fraternal greetings from the Great Community.'

'Don't run away!' Another voice spoke up.

Watkin heard the click of a crossbow.

'Just call your friend across.'

'Pike!' Watkin urged. 'Pike, come over here!'

The ditcher got to his feet and lumbered across, the wineskin still in his hands.

'What's the…?'

'Greetings, Brother Pike.'

The ditcher dropped the wineskin.

'We've been here some time,' the voice continued. 'Listening to you burping and farting. You are still handfast to the Cause, are you not?'

'Of course,' Pike stammered. 'You know we are!'

'Not like Ricaud.' The voice was laughing. 'He squealed like a pig when we took his genitals off. Valerian here wanted to stick them into his mouth after he cut off his head but…'

'What do you want?' Watkin tried to keep his voice steady.

'We want you to dig,' the voice continued. 'Dig and ask no questions.'

'Dig!' Pike exclaimed. 'Where?'

'Why, here.'

'In the cemetery?' Watkin responded.

A click and a crossbow bolt skimmed between him and Pike, thudding into the ground behind them.

'You don't question,' Valerian's voice continued. 'You carry out the orders of the Great Community. Go down on your knees, both of you!'

Watkin and Pike obeyed with alacrity.

'You will dig a ditch nine yards long and three feet deep along the cemetery wall.'

'Brother Athelstan will ask why.'

'Well, you can say it's for draining or you want to ensure the foundations of the wall are strong. That is your problem, not ours.'

'Why a ditch?' Pike asked defiantly.

He stared up into the darkness. He could see two shapes sitting on one of the outstretched branches. Pike turned away in disgust as urine splattered on to his face. Watkin stretched out and grasped his arm.

'We will do what you ask!'

Pike wiped his face on the soiled sleeve of his jerkin.

'You will begin? Well, today is Friday, the feast of St Oswald. So, tomorrow will be soon enough!'

'Do we dig the ditch in its entirety?'

'No, in the evening after work. The following day you will fill it in and dig some more. Do you understand?'

Watkin glanced longingly up at the glow of fire on the church tower.

'Oh, and by the way, Watkin and Pike, you do have lovely children. Now, go back to your wineskin, sit under the yew tree, at least for another hour. By then we'll be gone!'

Hawkmere Manor was a lonely, gloomy dwelling place built, so it was said, in the time of cruel King John. It stood behind its high curtain wall to the east of the Priory of Clerkenwell. Once owned by a robber baron who'd preyed upon travellers on the roads to and from Cripplegate, Hawkmere had fallen on sad times. A doleful, haunted place now used by the Regent John of Gaunt to house French prisoners captured either in France or during the bloody battles waged between English and French ships on the Narrow Seas. For the men who dwelt there it was truly a time of tribulation, even more so for Guillaum Serriem, formerly captain of the French man-of-war the *St Sulpice*, taken off Calais six weeks earlier. Serriem had been brought to Hawkmere as a captive and hostage while his friends in France tried to raise the huge ransom demanded by the English.

Lying in his narrow cot bed, Serriem knew in his heart of hearts that he would never again see his manor house outside Rouen, stroll in its gardens, kiss his wife or play with his sons in that lovely apple orchard which ran down to the river Seine.

Serriem was dying. He could feel the poison coursing through his body yet he had no strength to call out or crawl to the door and scream for help. His body was coated in sweat, the pain in his stomach sending arrows of agony up into his chest and making him twist and turn. He pushed back the dingy sheets and stared helplessly at the barred door. What was the use? The walls were thick, the door was locked and Sir Walter Limbright, his gaoler and custodian, would have retired to his own chambers to drown his sorrows in cup after cup of claret.

Perhaps someone was out there along the gloomy gallery, a guard, a servant? Serriem dragged himself off the bed, rolling on to the dirty rushes. He tried to pull himself towards the door but his strength failed him and he lay gasping. Serriem realised he had been poisoned by some secret, subtle assassin but who, among his companions, would want him dead? And surely the Goddamns, the English, for all their cruelty, would not want to forfeit the ransom money? Serriem's mind wandered. He had always hoped he would die in his own bed, his family around him or, if not there, on his ship at sea like a true warrior, sword in hand with the oriflamme of France fluttering above him. Now he was to die here in this lonely, smelly chamber, a prisoner of the English, forsaken and forgotten even by his own kind.

Serriem rolled over on his back and stared up at the cobwebbed rafters. His mind wandered. The pain was so intense that he slipped in and out of consciousness. He was at home, the windows open, the fragrant scents of the garden filling his chamber. He could hear the cries of his servants and the shouts of his sons as they played in the courtyard below. Serriem opened his eyes. Nothing! Only a foreboding stillness. He tried to move again but he felt as if the floor were shifting under him and his mind went back.

He was on board the *St Sulpice*, its sails billowing above him. He was with the Master at the wheel, watching the prow fall and rise as they raced back to port, away from the four English cogs of war pursuing them as ruthlessly as greyhounds would a deer. Serriem felt the bile at the back of his throat. Over the last few weeks he and the others had discussed how the *St Sulpice*, and its sister ship the *St Denis*, had taken up position on the sea lanes off Calais, eager to snap up the heavily laden English wine ships. Serriem groaned: it had all gone wrong! Instead of wine ships two men-of-war and, when the *St Sulpice* and *St Denis* had turned, they found two others waiting over the horizon. The race had been intense, the consequent battle bloody and ferocious. The *St Denis* had been taken and sunk. The *St Sulpice*, its crew decimated by the archers massed in the stern and prow of the leading English man-of-war, had been trapped and boarded. A bloody hand-to-hand fight ensued but, at last, to save his crew, Serriem had ordered the oriflamme to be lowered and he had surrendered to the English captain. What was his name? That young man with a boyish face and close-cropped hair. Ah yes, Maurice Maltravers. Serriem's body arched in pain, his hands clutching the soiled rushes.

At first he had put the defeat down to the fortunes of war. However, over the last few weeks, he and his companions had discussed how the English ships knew exactly where the *St Sulpice* and *St Denis* would be. Betrayal? Treason? Serriem's head fell sideways. He glanced beseechingly at the stark, black crucifix nailed to the plastered wall. He wished he had a priest to shrive him. He would confess his sins. Outside came a footfall.

'*Aidez moi!* Help me!' Serriem groaned.

The footsteps faded away. What was this poison, Serriem wondered? He had eaten with the rest. Had they all been killed? Their lives wiped out, extinguished like a row of candles in a lonely church? Hadn't they all agreed to be so careful? Serriem turned once more to the crucifix. He tried to lift a hand to wipe his sweat-soaked face but even that was too much. His mouth began to form the words '*Confiteor Deo Omni Potenti*', 'I confess to Almighty God, to Mary ever a virgin...' His breath was coming in short gasps. He couldn't form the words. Serriem recalled Sieur Charles de Fontanel, the French envoy in London.

'Avenge me!' Serriem whispered.

The pain in Serriem's belly grew more intense. He couldn't breathe. Something was closing off his throat as if a noose were tightening around his neck. Serriem's body jerked, legs lashing out, and he died, his sightless eyes staring across at the crucifix on the wall.

Sir Maurice Maltravers, knight banneret in the household of John of Gaunt, waited in the shadows of the Austin Friars church. In the far distance he could see the Abbot of St Albans inn and, along the lane, the main thoroughfare leading down into Cheapside.

The church of Austin Friars was old and crumbling. Its door had long been barred and locked, no candles glowed in the windows. It was night; a time of darkness when stealth and subterfuge were the order of the day. Sir Maurice was ill pleased with this. He was a knight, a warrior. He recalled the words of the Gospel, how men of honour should do things in the light of day and not scurry about in the dark like some felon or housebreaker. Yet what else could he do?

Sir Maurice stepped out of the shadows and, going down the side of the church, pushed open the battered lych gate leading into the cemetery. The two horses, saddled and ready, patiently cropped at the grass. He checked the bulging leather panniers placed behind each saddle. Everything was in order but would she come? Sir Maurice knelt down and stared in the direction of the sanctuary.

'Oh Lord,' he prayed. 'Help me! And, if you do, I will go on pilgrimage to Compostella. I will be the most faithful of husbands. I will dedicate my children to you and your Blessed Mother.'

Sir Maurice opened his eyes. He felt slightly ridiculous kneeling here in the darkness but he had no choice. He loved Angelica, daughter of the great merchant Sir Thomas Parr, with all his mind, heart and soul, more than life itself. Yes, and if he was honest, more than God.

He had met Angelica weeks ago. Since then his life had been changed. He thought of her every second of the day: that beautiful face, the alabaster ivory skin, cornflower-blue eyes, lustrous golden hair. Yes, she was well named Angelica. At seventeen summers old, her beautiful body was vibrant with life – and those eyes! Sir Maurice had never seen a woman's face reflect so clearly her shifting moods. Angelica possessed strong and fierce will coupled with a biting sense of humour and yet a sense of merriment, a wonder at life and all it held.

Sir Maurice had paid court, at first shyly because he was more used to the routine of the camp and the affairs of war. He was frightened of no man living: only twentyfour years of age, he had distinguished himself in battle both in France and at sea. Oh, he had been a clumsy suitor; he knew Angelica was laughing at him. Nevertheless, far from refusing his advances, she had lowered her eyes and, on occasions, dropped, as a token of affection, a piece of silk, a flower she had been carrying and, finally, a small silver ring.

Sir Maurice could not believe his good fortune. He had expected refusal. Sir Thomas Parr was one of the richest men in London yet Angelica had been as smitten by Sir Maurice as he by her.

He had planned his wooing as he would the siege of a castle. Sir Thomas would bring his daughter to court, at Gaunt's palace of the Savoy. Sir Maurice would shyly wait and, sure enough, the occasion would present itself. A few whispered endearments, lingering looks, fingers brushing as they passed, only fanned the flames. Sir Maurice would find himself outside Parr's great half-timbered mansion in Cheapside, staring longingly up at the mullioned glass windows. One night his patience had been rewarded when a red rose had been dropped, a small note tied by a piece of pink silk to its stem.

They had met in the shadowy corners of churches along Cheapside or the Poultry. Angelica's maid, Rosamunda, would stay just beyond earshot though close enough to intervene. At first Sir Maurice thought Angelica was teasing him, full of spite, of malicious glee. He was wrong. Her heart was as pure and as beautiful as her face. Sir Maurice did not think of himself as a fop or a gallant; he was a soldier with a warrior's face and blunt mannerisms. Though tongue-tied he'd confessed to Angelica that she was the love of his life. She had touched his fingers, those blue eyes scrutinising his face and, at last, towards the end of July, she had confessed that her love was as great as his: a fierce flame of passion which would never be extinguished. After that Sir Maurice felt as if he had been walking on air. A few more clandestine meetings and then, armed with letters from John of Gaunt himself, he had presented himself at Sir Thomas' house in Cheapside.

The young knight clambered to his feet. Even now his face went red with embarrassment at what had happened. He had knelt before Sir Thomas Parr and confessed his love. Sir Thomas had gazed speechlessly back, his face turning puce as he gave vent to the most terrible rage.

'How dare you!' he had bellowed, striding up and down the solar, leaving Sir Maurice on his knees. 'How dare you even look at my daughter? What are you but some penniless knight!'

'I have a manor and lands in Berkshire,' Sir Maurice had retorted.

'What! A paltry cottage and a few pigsties!'

Sir Maurice's hand had dropped to the hilt of his sword but Parr had remained unabashed. His henchmen standing in the doorway came forward. A group of city thugs, bully boys led by the squire Ralph Hersham, a mealy-mouthed character with a narrow pointed face and sly eyes. Parr had leaned down, eyes blazing with fury.

'Go on!' he had grated. 'Draw your weapon! Let us end it now!'

Instead, Sir Maurice had scrambled to his feet and, with Parr's strictures ringing in his ears, had fled the mansion. He'd drowned his sorrows in a tavern and, when he returned to the Savoy Palace, summoned up enough courage to see his lord. John of Gaunt had been sympathetic but unhelpful. The Regent had slouched in his chair, his sharp, hard eyes keenly observant. As he listened, he would stroke his silver moustache and goatee beard. Now and again he would nod or intervene with a question.

'But there's nothing I can do,' he concluded sadly.

'My lord, you are the Regent!'

'I am the King's officer,' Gaunt replied with a smile. 'I can command his armies, issue writs, but I have no power over Sir Thomas and what he wishes to do with his daughter.' He held his hand up, emphasising the points on his fingers. 'First, my good knight, our opponents in the Commons would love that. John of Gaunt, the King's evil Regent, forcing one of his knights into the bed of the daughter of a powerful London merchant! How the scurriers and the gossips would relish it! They'd depict me as an even greater tyrant than Nero or Caligula!'

Sir Maurice didn't know who these were but he stared bleakly at Gaunt.

'Secondly,' the Regent continued remorselessly, 'Sir Thomas Parr is a very, very wealthy man. Oh, he comes from nothing but he virtually owns the wool trade to the Low Countries. He has ten ships which he has put at our disposal. Thirdly, the Crown owes him monies. Fourthly, and more importantly, Sir Maurice, so do I. If Sir Thomas called in these loans…' John of Gaunt drummed his fingers on the table-top. 'Well.' He sighed. 'It's best not to think about what might happen.' He got up and grasped the young knight's hands. 'Maurice,' he continued kindly. 'You are my man in peace and war as your father was. In battle I couldn't ask for a better soldier. You took those two ships, the *St Sulpice* and *St Denis* and, for that, you will always have my favour. In time I will grant you lands, manors, fields, meadows but not now. In this matter of Sir Thomas Parr's daughter I can do nothing.'

Crestfallen, Sir Maurice had withdrawn. He had not seen Angelica after his confrontation with her father. He thought his cause was doomed but, a short while later, Rosamunda brought a short letter.

'Are you a lackey to leave the field?' the note had read. 'Is your love so shallow that it breaks at the first obstacle?'

Full of fire, he had returned to his wooing though this time it was more difficult. Nevertheless, thanks to Rosamunda, he and Angelica had met, sworn oaths of love and agreed to elope this very night. He had no real plan. They would ride into Berkshire and hire some hedge-priest to marry them and be their witness when they exchanged vows at the church door.

Sir Maurice stepped back into the lane. Further down, cats fought rats among the ordure piled on either side of the open sewer. A mongrel cur came snarling out, but the cats drove it off. In the pool of light thrown by the sconce torches, Sir Maurice stared in pity at the tarred figure swinging from the makeshift gallows: a house-breaker who had been caught red-handed and executed at the scene of his crime. The gibbeters had coated the body in pitch which gleamed eerily in the dancing torchlight.

Sir Maurice returned to the church path. What would happen to him once Gaunt found out? Would he be favoured or punished? The Regent had a vile temper and those who betrayed him received no forgiveness.

The bells of St Mary-Le-Bow now began to chime the hour of Compline. Sir Maurice tensed. Would Angelica keep her word? He heard the sound of horses and stepped out but the figures who came out of the darkness were not what he expected: no Rosamunda, no Angelica. Instead he recognised Sir Thomas Parr's henchmen led by Ralph Hersham. They left their horses and walked forward, drawing sword and dagger, fanning out in a semi-circle.

'What do you want?'

He felt his heart would break with disappointment.

'Don't be foolish.' Hersham edged forward. 'There are five of us and more coming. We do not wish to cross swords with you, Maltravers. We bring you messages. My master says he knows you and rejects you. You are forbidden to see his daughter again. And do not bother,' Ralph's sly face broke into a smile, 'to come and wheedle beneath the windows of his house. Angelica is now with the holy nuns at Syon on Thames. They have strict orders to keep you at the gates!'

Chapter 2

Sir John Cranston, coroner of the city, lowered his massive body into the high-backed chair in his small chamber at the Guildhall. Simon, his scrivener, thought Sir John looked in fine fettle. He was dressed in a doublet of burgundy, white cambric shirt, hose and soft leather Spanish riding boots. Sir John's hair was swept and oiled back, his moustache and beard fair bristling with expectation.

'Why are we here, Simon?' Sir John patted his stomach. He unhitched his thick leather war belt and threw it over the corner of the chair. 'When I leave make sure I put my sword and dagger in my sheaths. The King's coroner cannot be too careful in this vale of wickedness.'

'Of course, Sir John.' Simon dared not raise his eyes. He fought to keep his face straight at what was coming. Sir John Cranston was not a man of easy temper, though kindly and big-hearted, but, as Simon told his wife, when he was surprised, Sir John's rubicund face was a veritable tapestry of moods and emotions.

'Well!' He leaned his elbows on the arms of the chair. 'Where is Adam Wallace? He said he had something important to tell me. I've heard Mass, broken my fast. I'm just in the mood to listen to a lawyer.'

'I'll fetch him in now.' Simon rose and went down the stairs.

Sir John leaned back in his chair and scratched his head. Wallace had sent him a message yesterday afternoon, saying he had something important to tell Sir John and that he was bringing a bequest of old Widow Blanchard who lived in Eel Pie Lane. Sir John had spent the evening wondering what it could be. Blanchard had been a merry old soul; Sir John had often called in to ensure that all was well with her. Blanchard's husband had fought with Sir John in France. Perhaps she wished to give him some keepsake? Or…? He heard a creaking on the stairs. Simon came back into the chamber at a half-run, hands hanging by his side. Sir John's light-blue eyes blazed. He could always tell when Simon was laughing at him: the scrivener would become all humble, stoop-shouldered, chin tucked in, face down.

'What is it, Simon?'

'You'd best see for yourself, Sir John.'

Wallace waddled into the room, followed by a little goat.

'In heaven's name!' Sir John half-rose out of the chair.

Wallace was a small, self-important man, his hooked nose perpetually dripping, little black eyes ever searching for a fee or a profit. His smile was smug as he hitched his cloak about his shoulders. He held a scroll of parchment in his hand and approached Sir John's desk.

'You are Sir John Cranston, coroner of the city?'

'Of course I am, you bloody idiot! Who do you think I am, the Archangel Gabriel?'

'Now, now, Sir John. I am only performing my duty in accordance with the law, its customs and usages.'

'Shut up! What are you doing in my court with that bloody thing?'

He pointed at the goat and glanced dangerously at his scrivener, hunched over his desk, shoulders shaking, pretending to sharpen his quill.

'I have identified you as Sir John Cranston, coroner of the city,' Wallace continued lugubriously. 'I have brought into your court, in accordance with the law, its customs and usages, the will of one Eleanor Blanchard, widow of this parish. I am her legal executor as approved in the Court of Chancery!'

Sir John pointed a podgy finger in Wallace's face.

'If you don't hurry up, I'm going to have you thrown into the Fleet for contempt!'

'Widow Blanchard's dead,' Wallace gabbled. 'Her will has been approved. She has left this goat as her gift to you. She also asked that the gift be delivered in your court in a formal way according to the law, its customs and...'

'Shut up!' Sir John bellowed. 'Shut up, you little noddle-pate!'

Wallace stood back, head bowed. Sir John could see the smirk on his face. Eleanor Blanchard had a sharp sense of humour. She had often talked of the goat but he had never met it. Now, by having the goat delivered here in court, he had no choice but to accept it.

'I don't want a goat!' The words were out before he could stop them.

'Sir John, Sir John!' Wallace's eyes rounded in mock hurt. 'It is the last wish of that poor woman. If you refuse such a gift delivered in court...'

'Yes, yes, I know,' Sir John mimicked. 'In accordance with the law, its customs and usages, I must decide what happens to it. I could give it away.' He beamed at Simon.

'My lord coroner.' Simon sprang to his feet. 'As you well know, the coroner's court is the King's court. If you refuse the gift here, then the goat belongs to the Crown.'

'And if it belongs to the Crown...' Wallace added maliciously.

Sir John wearily sat back. 'I know, I know.' He waved a hand. 'The Crown will order it to be taken to the slaughterhouse and sold for the highest possible price.' He stared at the goat.

The animal seemed docile and obedient enough. It was a fine, handsome beast; its coat was dappled gold, its small horns pointed and straight, its eyes gentle. It chewed quietly on some victual picked up from the courtyard below.

'Sir John, I wish you well.' Wallace bowed and walked out of the door, his shoulders shaking with merriment.

Sir John followed him and, with his boot, slammed the door shut. He walked back, slouched in his chair and studied the goat.

'What in hell's name am I supposed to do with you?'

'You could take it home, Sir John.'

'Lady Maude has a great fear of goats. By the way, what did that clever bastard call it?'

Simon sifted among some scraps of parchment on his desk.

'Er, Judas, my lord coroner.'

'I beg your pardon!'

'According to this piece of paper, Widow Blanchard called it Judas.' Simon struggled to keep his long, narrow face impassive. 'That's what lawyer Wallace said its name was.'

'You've seen the will?' Sir John asked.

'Of course, Sir John. Widow Blanchard had little to give. She especially asked for Judas to be handed over to you.'

'I should have asked Wallace for a copy of the will.'

Simon again fished among the sheets of parchment on his desk.

'He brought one before you arrived, Sir John.'

The coroner snatched it out of his scrivener's hand, studied the clerk's writing, then threw it back. The parchment fell on the floor and, before he or Simon could do anything, the goat trotted forward; it seized the parchment and chewed it so quickly, the men could only stare in stupefaction.

'I think I know why it's called Judas.' Simon spoke up. 'It probably bites the hand that feeds it!'

Sir John fumbled for his miraculous wineskin where it hung on a special hook beneath the table. He opened the stopper and took a deep swig. The goat watched fascinated and took a step forward.

'Don't you dare!' Sir John warned. 'Don't you ever come near this!'

The goat, looking rather aggrieved, stopped but he continued eating the parchment.

'Lady Maude,' Cranston intoned, 'has a great horror of goats. The poppets.' He smiled at the thought of his twin sons, Stephen and Francis, they would like it. But his manservant Blaskett, now Lady Maude's firm ally in peace and war, would also object while those two imps of hell, the Irish wolfhounds, Gog and Magog, would tear it to pieces. Sir John took another swig of wine but kept one eye on the goat, which seemed fascinated. He was sure that the animal licked its lips.

'Well, come on, Simon, what do you propose? None of your impertinence!'

'Of course not, Sir John. But Brother Athelstan is your secretarius...'

Sir John's huge face broke into a grin.

'Of course!' He banged the table-top. 'Friars are supposed to love bloody animals, aren't they? He has a cemetery, he can keep it there. There's nothing in the will that says I can't give it away as a gift.' He narrowed his eyes. 'I could still give it to you.'

'Sir John, a wife and two children in a tenement in Pig's Barrow Lane?'

'Then the friar will have to have it.' He patted his stomach in delight.

'Remember, Sir John,' Simon declared sonorously. 'Athelstan is a Dominican. It's St Francis and his Order who have the reputation of caring for animals.'

'They are all the same to me,' Sir John muttered. 'Right!'

He eased himself out of his chair, put on his sword belt, sliding in the sword and dagger. As he threw the cloak round his shoulders he felt a nip on his thigh and glared down at the offending goat.

'You are bloody well named!' he growled.

'Oh, Sir John, look, it likes you!'

Judas was now nudging his new owner's tree-like thigh.

'Get a piece of bloody rope!' Sir John ordered. 'Tie it round the bastard's neck! It's off to Southwark to join the rest of the goats!'

Simon, who had secretly promised himself to watch Sir John's progress down Cheapside, hastened to obey. He fetched a piece of smooth hemp and expertly tied it round the goat's neck. Sir John snatched the other end, glaring balefully at his scrivener, then paused at a clattering on the stairs. A young man, dressed in a leather doublet displaying the colours of John of Gaunt, burst into the room. Judging by his sword belt the visitor was a knight. The young man's shirt was open at the neck and he wore a silver necklace with the 'S.S.' emblem of the House of Lancaster.

'What do you want?' Sir John snapped.

'I'm Sir Maurice Maltravers.'

Sir John glimpsed the piece of parchment in his hand.

'Congratulations! You work for my Lord of Gaunt?'

'I'm in his household, Sir John.'

'God have mercy on you.' Sir John pulled at the goat. 'Don't look surprised, young man. All manner of things end up in a coroner's court.'

'I have a message, Sir John. My Lord of Gaunt, he wishes to see you and Brother Athelstan on a matter of urgency at his palace at the Savoy.'

Sir John studied the young man from head to toe.

'Maltravers?'

'Yes, Sir John.'

Sir John chewed the corner of his lip.

'Oh, by the way, Simon.' He licked his fingers. 'Get it for me.'

The scrivener obeyed with alacrity. Sir John slipped the wineskin on to the hook of his belt, then tapped Sir Maurice on the chest.

'I knew your father. Yes,' he breathed. 'Same colour hair, same strong face, though his eyes were larger and his nose was straight.'

The young man coloured. He tightened his jaw.

'My nose was broken, Sir John, when I fought the French at sea.'

Sir John brought his great paw down on the knight's shoulder.

'By Mab's tits!' he roared. 'You are the Maltravers who took the *St Sulpice* and *St Denis*!' He pushed the wineskin into the man's hands. 'A brave feat, it will teach the bloody French to take to sea!'

Sir Maurice didn't know whether to be angry or pleased.

'Go on, have a drink!' Sir John urged. He gripped the knight's shoulder and stared across at Simon. 'You are in the presence of a hero, Simon! Just like his father. I was with him in France, you know? When the Black Prince went storming like the wind through Normandy. Like the dogs of war we were.'

Simon sighed and raised his eyes heavenwards. If Sir John started on the history of his exploits in France, they'd be here until Vespers. Thankfully the goat began to edge towards the parchment on the table. Sir Maurice, catching Simon's look, hastily pushed the wineskin back into Sir John's hand.

'My lord coroner, I must hasten back.'

'Aye.' Sir John sighed and stretched out a hand. 'I meant no offence, young man.'

Sir Maurice stared into the ice-blue eyes and recalled what the gossip said about this great coroner with his red face and bristling white moustache and beard. A man of integrity, a warrior, bluff and truthful, who didn't even spare the Regent his strictures. He grasped the older man's hand.

'None taken, Sir John. My Lord of Gaunt will tell you the reason for his summons.'

Sir John snatched the rope from Simon's hand and stood listening to the young knight go down the stairs.

'A veritable hero, Simon,' he repeated dreamily. 'Perhaps England still produces the like, its crops of heroes, brave men. Have you ever heard that line?'

The scrivener shook his head.

'I don't know who wrote it,' Sir John continued as if speaking to himself. 'Anyway, it goes something like this.' He threw his head back and put one leg forward, like a chanteur. 'Ah yes. That's it. "Since the beginning of time two things are constant: the greenness of the earth and the courage of man."' He wiped a tear from his eyes. 'Beautiful poetry! Oh, Satan's arse!'

Judas the goat had sidled up and was now nibbling at the wineskin. The coroner stared down at the goat which, as if he had taken a great liking to his new owner, stared innocently back.

'Haven't you read the Scriptures?' Sir John bawled. 'Judas went out and hanged himself. If you're not careful, my lad, the same bloody thing will happen to you! That's my wineskin.' He held the precious object up. 'You never, ever touch it!'

And, dragging the goat by the rope, Sir John left the chamber and went out into Cheapside.

If he had known what was going to happen, Sir John would never have done what he did that morning. The broad thoroughfare of Cheapside was thronged with people swirling like shoals of coloured fish among the many stalls. He was hardly out, pushing his way through the crowds, before people noticed.

'There goes Sir Jack and his goat!' someone shouted. 'A penny for the man who can tell the difference!'

Sir John gazed round, eyes popping.

'Tadpole!' he bawled at a scrawny beggar boy. 'Did you shout that?'

'Me, Sir John?' The dirty face was as innocent as an angel's, eyes rounded. 'Sir John, would I say such a thing?'

Muttering under his breath, he continued on his way. The sun was strong and the stall-owners were doing a roaring trade: leather goods, silks and tapestries, pots and pans, vegetables and fruits from the outlying farms and villages. The air was rich with the smell of horse dung mingling with the sweeter smells from the cookshops and bakeries. Young gallants from the court paraded in their long, gaudy jackets, tight hose and high-heeled leather riding boots, and protuberant codpieces: round slim waists hung brocaded war belts with sword and dagger pushed in. Their hair was prinked and crimped. The coroner looked away in disgust. He was sure some of the men even wore make-up.

'Pretty bum-boys!' he mumbled. 'No wonder the French have it all their own way.'

Everyone seemed to have thronged into Cheapside. Merchants in their costly robes, their wives in samite dresses, their ornate head-gear created out of wisps of veils which threatened to catch signs hanging over the shops behind the stalls. Apprentices scurried, seeking custom. A farmer was trying to get two bullocks up through the crowds to the slaughterers at Newgate. Outside the Peascod Tavern, men were wagering on a fight between a badger and a dog. In the open space before St Mary-Le-Bow, a blind bear danced while beggar children played a reedy tune on pipes. Felons from the Marshalsea and Fleet prisons, manacled together, clattered and clashed their chains as they were marched up to the courts, the tipstaffs keeping order with their white willow wands. Windows and doors were flung open, people were shouting and talking to passersby. A dung cart had turned over, spilling its messy contents out. Some of the ordure had landed on a fruit stall and bailiffs were desperately striving to prevent a fight breaking out between its owner and the dung-collector. Everyone fell silent as a funeral procession passed. The corpse was laid out on a stretcher covered by a sheet, carried by four friars who mumbled the prayers of the dead; an altar boy ran in front of them, holding a candle and ringing a bell.

Sir John kept his head down as he pulled at Judas who really needed no second bidding but trotted along as obediently as any trained dog. A group of whores came out of an alley, heads bald as pigeons' eggs, coloured wigs clutched in their hands. They espied Sir John and followed him, making up a lewd song about the coroner and his goat. Only when he turned round, his face like thunder, did the whores stop. One of them turned and lifted her ragged, dusty dress and they all fled laughing and joking among themselves. A few beggar boys then took up the game. Sir John sighed; by evening Lady Maude would know what he had done and he would have to explain.

'Oh Sir John, Sir John!'

He groaned and stopped. Leif the red-haired, one-legged beggar came hopping towards him as nimble as a cricket. Sir John had never met a more vexatious fellow but one look at poor Leif's scared face and the coroner's heart softened. Leif could wheedle a penny out of a miser.

'Sir John, have you heard me?'

The coroner used the opportunity to flail out at the urchins who scampered away.

'Why, Sir John, what a beautiful goat. Are you taking it home?'

Sir John gazed bleakly back.

'You've heard me, Sir John,' Leif gabbled, deciding it best to ignore Sir John's strange companion.

'In sweet heaven's name, Leif, what are you chattering about?'

'I've decided to become a singer, Sir John. A chanteur.'

And, without being invited, Leif threw his head back, one hand on his chest. 'My love,' he warbled, 'is like a flower, fresh and sweet.'

'Thank you, Leif,' Sir John bawled.

'I sang last night, Sir John, outside your chamber.'

'I thought it was cats fighting.'

Leif stared mournfully back. Sir John heaved a sigh and delved into his purse. He thrust a coin into the beggar man's hand.

'Look, Leif, there's a penny.'

'Oh, thank you, Sir John, is that for my singing?'

'No, Leif, it isn't. You are not to sing beneath my chamber. You will frighten the poppets. Secondly, you are not to follow me into the Holy Lamb of God. And, thirdly, you are not to tell Lady Maude I've been there.'

'Very good, Sir John.' Leif hopped away, warbling his head off.

'Come on, Judas!' Sir John urged. 'There's no problem in life which can't be resolved by a meat pie and a tankard of ale.'

And, like an arrow finding its mark, Sir John pushed his way across Cheapside into the tangy, warm welcome of the tavern.

The taverner's wife fussed over him. She brought a frothing tankard of ale and a meat pie. Sir John made the mistake of sitting back in his favourite seat near the garden window; when he glanced down, Judas was munching the greens round the pie and licking the pastry.

'Oh!' he groaned and called for a second dish. 'I just hope Brother Athelstan takes you.'

The taverner's wife, laughing and joking, brought across a second tray. Sir John held it on his lap and ate quickly, glaring suspiciously at Judas.

'I wonder what Athelstan will think about you?' he muttered.

But, there again, the coroner reflected, there were many questions he would like to ask his secretarius. He had been horrified by the stories, which had not been proved or denied, that Athelstan had been ordered out of London to Oxford. He had only been stopped at the last minute by the direct intervention of Prior Anselm. Cranston had made his own enquiries but could discover nothing. When he had summoned up the courage to question the little Dominican, Athelstan had just shaken his head and smiled.

'It's a possibility,' he confirmed. 'But I think, Sir John, I'll be in St Erconwald's for some time. Prior Anselm says there's no further need for me to be your secretarius. But I have begged him that I can continue and he has agreed.'

Sir John had to be comforted by that. Athelstan had first been sent to St Erconwald's and appointed his secretarius as a penance. Years earlier, Athelstan had fled his novitiate and, his mind full of glory, had joined his feckless younger brother in the armies in France. Stephen had been killed and Athelstan had returned, a changed and chastened man. Sir John, who had little time for prattling priests or mouldy monks, as he termed them, regarded Athelstan as a very special friend. If the Dominican ever left, some of the joy and warmth of his own life would be diminished.

The coroner licked his fingers, drained his tankard then put the dish on the floor so Judas could finish what was left of the vegetables. He slammed a coin on the table and walked back into Cheapside. The urchins were waiting. He groaned, gritted his teeth and walked along until he reached the corner of Poultry near the Tun on the corner of Lombard Street. This great open space was used by the beadles and bailiffs of the city to punish malefactors. A whore had been bent over a barrel; her grimy, fat buttocks were being lashed by a switch of canes. A counterfeit man was being branded on his left thumb. Another was getting his ears clipped. Sir John glanced away. He hated such sights. The stocks and pillories were also full. He recognised a cheeky, dirty face under a shock of white hair straining between the wooden slats placed round his neck.

'Why, if it isn't old Godbless!'

The man pulled up his head as far as he could, wincing with pain.

'God bless you, Sir John, it's kind of you to notice. You have a fine billy goat there. Cleaner and more obedient than a dog, Sir John.' He stretched his neck. 'Lord save us, I'm here to dusk and my neck's already aching.'

'What did you do?' Sir John asked, an idea forming in his mind.

'The watch found me with a piglet under my cloak. They claimed I was stealing it. I said I had found it wandering and was looking for its mother.'

Sir John laughed and called over one of the bailiffs.

'Free this man!' he ordered.

The bailiff wiped his dirty, sweaty face on a rag.

'But, Sir John, the law says...'

'I am the law. Now, sir, either you free him or I'll free him and make you take his place!'

Godbless was soon released. A small, sinewy man dressed in a motley collection of rags, he danced in glee at his liberation. The other malefactors in the stocks now began to shout.

'Sir John, over here!'

'Innocent as a lamb, I am, Sir Jack!'

'I didn't mean to hit the beadle!' another cried.

'I only drank four quarts of ale!' someone else bawled.

Sir John ignored them and seized the dancing Godbless. 'You've worked with animals, haven't you, Godbless?' The man stopped his dancing and nodded.

'Well, you've been freed to help the Crown.' Sir John passed the rope over. 'This is Judas and he's well named. I'm taking him to St Erconwald's. You will follow behind at least a good three yards.'

He passed across a coin. Godbless took it in the twinkling of an eye. The coroner leaned down and, grasping the beggar by the jerkin, picked him up till his face was level with his.

'Don't even think of it, Godbless!'

'What, Sir John?' Godbless's bright eyes gleamed.

'Running!' Sir John declared. 'Taking my goat and running.' He shook Godbless. 'Understood?'

'Every word, Sir John. I'll be your shadow.'

'Not too close,' Sir John warned.

He put the beggar man down and, with Godbless trailing behind him leading the little goat at a trot, Sir John Cranston, coroner of the city of London, swept down to London Bridge.

Chapter 3

Brother Athelstan leaned back in the sanctuary chair and gazed round at the members of his parish council. He drew a deep breath and glanced warningly at Watkin the dung-collector, leader of this council: one of the prime movers in everything which happened in St Erconwald's parish.

'Would you mind repeating that, Watkin?'

The dung-collector got up from his bench and walked into the middle of the circle of benches just inside the porch of the parish church.

'The cemetery is God's acre, yes, Brother?'

Athelstan nodded.

'And, according to Canon Law…' Watkin smiled round at the rest, eager to show his knowledge off.

Athelstan closed his eyes. He regretted, for the umpteenth time, ever telling his parishioners about Canon Law and their rights.

'According to Canon Law,' Watkin continued triumphantly, 'and the sayings of St Judas…'

'Peter,' Athelstan interrupted. 'Judas was the traitor. Peter was the chief of the apostles.'

'Same thing.' Hig the pigman, who prided himself on some knowledge of the gospels, spoke up.

'I beg your pardon! Have you been reading the same text as I?'

'Judas betrayed Jesus,' Hig the pigman insisted. 'And so did Peter.'

'Yes, but Peter asked for forgiveness. Judas didn't.'

Hig scratched his red, greasy hair. With his flaring nostrils and jutting lower lip, Hig looked like the beasts he cared for. Athelstan nipped his thigh; he should remember charity but he was becoming rather tired. He surveyed the people present. Pernell the Fleming woman was carefully examining the tendrils of her dyed orange hair. Cecily the courtesan kept leaning down to fasten a thong on her sandal. Every time she did so, her well-endowed bodice strained and all the menfolk immediately looked towards her. Ranulf the rat-catcher, however, was becoming impatient and he seemed more interested in his two pet ferrets which nestled on his lap, Audax and Ferrox, the scourge of all rats south of the river. Crim the altar boy was sticking his tongue out at Pike the ditcher's wife, a veritable virago of a woman; Athelstan wondered how long she would curb her temper. Huddle the painter was staring dreamily at the bare wall, lost in a reverie, desperate to do his painting of the Last Judgement. The rest, including Mugwort the bell-ringer and Amisias the fuller were staring owl-eyed at Watkin who was waiting for the sign to continue.

'Go on, Watkin,' Athelstan said wearily.

'It's quite simple,' Watkin said. 'God's acre, the cemetery, belongs to the parish. According to Canon Law and the sayings of Judas...'

Athelstan just glanced at Benedicta, laughing behind her hand as she raised her eyes heavenwards.

'All we intend to do, Father, is make sure the far wall of the cemetery is secure. We'll cause no hurt to anyone.

The sun sets late. Pike and I can dig the ditch and the next morning fill it in.'

'Why leave it overnight?' Athelstan asked.

'Oh, that's just to ensure that, ah…' Watkin looked at Pike for help.

'We do not want to do too much work, Brother. We'll also be able to judge if any water's trickling in from the brook on the other side. It's best to inspect such foundations in the full light of day.'

Athelstan was surprised but could see no real problem. He clapped his hands.

'Very good. Agreed.'

He paused as Bladdersniff the beadle burst through the door, his red, chapped face bloated with drink, his eyes bleary.

'That bloody sow's loose in your garden!'

Ursula the pig woman gave a screech and sprang to her feet. Despite her years, she fair ran out of the door.

'One of these days,' Pike muttered, 'I'm going to kill that sow. Cut it into collops!'

'You can't do that!' Manyer the hangman declared. 'That's theft. You could hang, Pike!'

'He'll hang anyway.' Watkin's wife spoke up.

'The next matter we must discuss,' Athelstan intervened quickly, 'is that the Guild of Rat-Catchers have asked to hold their Guild service here next week.'

Ranulf now stood up, cradling the two ferrets in his arms.

'I have agreed to that,' Athelstan continued. 'Rat-catchers from all over Southwark will attend. I will offer a Mass of thanksgiving, bless the cages, traps and ferrets…'

'And cats,' Ranulf added, glancing enviously at the great, one-eyed Bonaventure sitting so patiently by

Athelstan's feet. The rat-catcher licked his lips. He would pay gold for Bonaventure, a great assassin of mice and vermin, a superb hunter. Ranulf secretly worshipped the ground Bonaventure trod on and, unbeknown to the priest, had tried to inveigle the cat away with dishes of cream and salted herring. Bonaventure had taken the temptation but promptly returned to his master.

'You are all welcome to attend.'

Athelstan paused as the church door was thrown open and Sir John Cranston swaggered in, cloak over one arm, sword clanking against his leg. The coroner beamed round the parish council.

'With a number of notable exceptions,' he smiled at Benedicta, 'I have seen fairer faces in the stocks at Newgate.'

'You keep a civil tongue in your head!' Pike the ditcher's wife sprang to her feet. 'Just because you're coroner...!'

'Hush, woman, I'm only jesting. You are all my beloveds.' He tucked his thumbs into his sword belt. 'Brother Athelstan, a word?'

The parish council rose. If the truth be known they were slightly fearful of Sir John and his powers. A man, despite his girth and bluff ways, who had the eyes of an eagle and the hunting instincts of one of Ranulf's ferrets. Athelstan nodded at Benedicta.

'I suppose I'll be going soon,' he said. 'Make sure that Philomel's safe in the stables and leave some milk out for Bonaventura.'

The widow woman smiled and Athelstan's heart skipped a beat. He was glad he had not left Southwark and that beautiful, dark-haired, soft-eyed woman was one reason. Athelstan had examined his conscience: he did not 'lust after her in his mind's eye', as Scripture said, he just loved being near her, particularly when she teased him.

Once the church had emptied, Sir John closed the door. He pulled up one of the benches and sat opposite Athelstan. He flinched in distaste as Bonaventure, who seemed to adore the stout coroner, came to rub his body against his fat leg, arching his back in pleasure, tail high, eyes half-closed.

'I don't like cats.'

'He likes you, Sir John.' Athelstan got to his feet, put his hands in the small of his back and stretched. 'But I don't like parish councils.' He sighed. 'You're here on official business?'

'You can read my mind, Brother. His Grace the Duke of Lancaster, John of Gaunt, Regent of the kingdom, uncle to the King, requires our presence at the Savoy, immediately.'

'Why?'

'I don't know.'

'Ah well.'

Athelstan went to the door and then started back as a tousled Godbless trotted into the church, the little goat skipping behind him.

'What on earth?'

Godbless crouched down, putting one arm over the goat, which turned and nuzzled his unshaven cheek. Sir John quickly described what had happened.

'I can't keep it!' he wailed. 'The Lady Maude has a horror of goats.'

Athelstan caught the pleading look in his eyes.

'What's its name?'

'The four-legged goat's Judas. The two-legged one's Godbless.'

'Why Godbless?'

'Godbless is a pickpocket. He attends Mass just before the communion when the kiss of peace is exchanged. He grasps your hand, kisses you on your cheek and, as he whispers "God bless", tries to lift your purse.'

Athelstan crouched down beside the beggar man.

'Are you a thief, Godbless?'

'Not a very good one, Brother.'

Athelstan gently touched the goat. 'And this is Judas?'

'I likes him.' Godbless spoke up. 'And he likes me. I have no place to live either, Brother.'

'Friars are supposed to like animals,' Sir John offered.

'We are all supposed to like animals, Sir John, and this goat is a most handsome fellow. And so are you, Godbless.' Athelstan got to his feet. 'Godbless, I can't offer you a place in my house, there's barely enough room for one.' He thought of the overgrown cemetery, his constant pleas to Watkin and Pike to clean it up. 'But you can have the death house in the cemetery. When a corpse is put there for the night, you can sleep in my house. I'll leave a note for Benedicta the widow woman. She'll set up a bed and, perhaps, a stool. The place is clean, scrubbed and doesn't smell.'

Godbless's face creased in pleasure.

'In return you can look after the goat. It can graze in the cemetery. You can also keep an eye on what happens there.'

Athelstan felt a glow of triumph. He was always suspicious about how his parishioners used God's acre, be it Pike or Watkin in their drinking or the amours of Cecily the courtesan. He fished in his purse and brought out a coin.

'Take the goat. You'll find some rope in the death house. Let the animal graze but make sure that it's on a long lead, fasten it to one of the hooks in the wall.'

Godbless nodded and stared down at the coin.

'Then go down to the pie shop. It's at the end of the alleyway. Ask Merrylegs for one of his freshest pies and tell him that you have joined our parish.'

Godbless sprang to his feet but Athelstan grasped him by the arm.

'And we can't keep calling him Judas, can we? There was another apostle, one who didn't betray Christ; he had a name similar to Judas. Ah, that's it, Thaddeus!' Athelstan dipped his fingers into the holy water stoup and sprinkled both Godbless and the goat. 'I rename thee Thaddeus, goat of this parish!'

A short while later, after they had taken Moleskin's wherry along the Thames, Sir John and Athelstan disembarked at the quayside near the palace of the Savoy. They were greeted by retainers wearing the livery of John of Gaunt. They were let through the cordon and up the pebble-dashed path which led to the gates of the Savoy. More soldiers were on guard. Inside the vaulted gateway, which led into the gardens, knights and archers wearing the royal livery took Sir John's war belt and led them through the spacious, exquisitely laid-out gardens and into the perfumed coolness of the palace.

Athelstan gazed round in wonderment. The walls, floors and ceilings were of white stone and he thought it was pure marble. On either side of the galleries hung exquisite tapestries from Hainault and Flanders, brilliant flashes of colour depicting scenes from the Bible and antiquity. Such opulence grew more apparent as they went deeper into the palace. The floors were of shiny wood, which smelt richly of polish, and almost covered in great thick woollen rugs of different colours. Statues stood in niches, small portraits of former kings and princes hung in thick, black, wood-edged frames on the walls. Soldiers were everywhere. They guarded staircases, the entrances to chambers and thronged about them as they waited to be taken up to the first gallery where the Regent had his own chambers.

Athelstan recalled Sir John's monologue as Moleskin had rowed them along the Thames. How popular resentment against the Regent was growing, particularly in the shires and around the city: his tax-collectors, in particular, were being attacked, their demands refused. Even in the House of Commons, protests had been drawn up; the members demanded a reform of government and a thorough investigation into the war against France which had resulted in a recent truce due to the intervention of the papacy.

'We live in hard times, Brother Athelstan.' Sir John had shaken his head and looked out across the river at the ornate, high-pooped Venetian galleys, the war cogs of England and the great, fat-bellied merchant ships from Lübeck. Around these swarmed wherries, bum-boats, barges and fishing smacks.

'All this could end,' he had mournfully declared.

'What do you mean?' Athelstan had asked, just wishing Cranston would keep his voice down. Moleskin, although bent over the oars, always listened intently to the conversations of his customers. Cranston had taken a slurp from his wineskin.

'London's unprotected. We have a garrison in the Tower. Gaunt and the great lords have their retainers but, if a rebel army marched south, they could take London in a day.'

'Rebels?' Athelstan had asked.

'Peasants – the Great Community of the Realm. They are traitors.' Sir John had sighed. 'But many of their grievances are just. The peasants are taxed to the point of rebellion, they are tied to the soil. Their duties are fixed, their wages are paltry. If they can produce a leader, then God help us all.' He nudged Athelstan. 'And, if you read my treatise on the governance of the city, Southwark is our weakest point. The north is defended by walls but, once they sweep into Southwark and take the bridge, London will be at their mercy.'

Athelstan understood the coroner's disquiet. He knew some of his parishioners, particularly Pike, were members of the Great Community of the Realm and, although he had never said it, Athelstan believed Sir John was the only royal official able to walk unharmed through the narrow alleyways of Southwark. The coroner had a reputation for honesty while his friendship with the parish priest of St Erconwald's also afforded protection.

'Sir John Cranston, Brother Athelstan?'

The Dominican shook himself from his reverie.

The young knight on the stairs was not one of Gaunt's foppish retainers. Athelstan recognised a fighting man, in his dour, drab clothes, the buttoned sword belt clasped round his waist.

'Why bless me, if it isn't Sir Maurice.'

Sir John made the introductions. Athelstan shook the young knight's hand. He took an immediate liking to this knight with his blunt features and honest eyes. A

43

soldier, Athelstan concluded, a man direct in speech and action. As he followed Sir Maurice up the stairs, Athelstan reflected on how contrary John of Gaunt could be. A silken courtier, a man born to plot, Gaunt was still the son of Edward III, with the strength and the courage to attract warriors to him as well as the young fops and dilettantes. The latter constantly preened themselves, drenched their bodies in perfume, crimped their hair and dressed more fastidiously than high-class courtesans. Athelstan had seen them in their ornate, long-toed shoes and fantastic head-dresses and had observed the lisping way they talked. He tried not to judge but, often, he secretly agreed with Sir John that the warriors of England were no more than gelded palfreys, all show, with little mettle or fire.

Sir Maurice led them into the Regent's private chamber. A small, narrow room, it had wainscoting against the walls; the white plaster above was decorated with banners of Leon, Castile, France and England. Gaunt was sitting behind a great black desk. He sifted among the manuscripts as he talked in hushed tones to a clerk sitting on a writing stool beside him. Then he glanced up.

Athelstan couldn't decide whether Gaunt was angel or demon. He had the Plantagenets' striking good looks: blond hair, moustache and beard, high cheekbones and sapphire-blue eyes which could crinkle in merriment or become as hard as glass. He was dressed in an open-necked, pleated linen shirt, a silver Lancastrian 'S.S.' collar round his neck. His sleeves were pushed back, displaying gold gauntlets on each wrist, and the rings on his fingers caught the light and shimmered like fire. He dismissed the clerk and rose.

'Why, good Sir Jack.' He clasped the coroner's hand and turned to Athelstan. The Dominican caught the taunting look in his eyes. 'So, you are still at St Erconwald's, Brother?'

'Yes, my lord.'

Gaunt stretched his hand out and smiled dazzlingly.

'Like Sir Jack, Brother Athelstan, I have no time for priests but you are always welcome here.' He gripped Athelstan's hand firmly. 'Maltravers, close the door.' He waved his guests to the two chairs the clerk had pushed up before he'd scurried out. 'Do sit down.'

The wine Sir Maurice served was white, slightly bitter but ice-cold. Athelstan caught the tang and closed his eyes in pleasure, then he felt guilty and opened them. It was always the same with Gaunt, like walking into a spider's web, silken, soft but still very treacherous. Sir John, however, was enjoying the wine. He had already finished his goblet and was stretching out for Sir Maurice to refill it. The young knight did so, a lopsided smile on his face. Gaunt was slouched in his chair watching the coroner from under heavy-lidded eyes.

'You like your wine, Sir Jack?'

'Wine gladdens the heart,' the coroner quipped. 'Or so the psalmist says, and even the apostles drank deep.'

'It doesn't blur your wits?'

'No, my lord. Why, does it yours?'

Gaunt laughed and waved his hand. 'Enough of this jousting.' He waved airily at Maltravers. 'You know Sir Maurice?'

'By name and reputation, yes.'

'He's one of my captains,' Gaunt continued. 'He has waged war ruthlessly against the French by land and sea. Two months ago, off Calais, he commanded a small flotilla of ships which attacked two French men-of-war, the *St Sulpice* and the *St Denis*. The *St Denis* was sunk, the *St Sulpice* successfully brought back to Dover. Now the French soldiers and sailors were ransomed by the baker's dozen. However, five officers, men of quality, were captured. Pierre Vamier; Jean Gresnay; Eudes Maneil; Philippe Routier; and Guillaum Serriem. Being officers they were bound by the customs and usages of war to be ransomed, so they were taken to Hawkmere Manor.'

'A desolate place,' Sir John broke in. 'Near the priory at Clerkenwell.'

'A place of dread indeed.' Gaunt sifted through the manuscripts on his desk. 'I appointed as their captor, host, guest-master, whatever they wish, Sir Walter Limbright. He and his daughter Lucy have custody of the manor. Limbright is an old soldier. He hates the French, because they burnt his manor outside Winchelsea, killed his wife and two sons. He was at war while Lucy was visiting relatives at Hyde. Limbright would ensure the French were kept secure.'

'What has happened?' Athelstan asked.

'The French envoy to England,' Gaunt continued as if Athelstan hadn't interrupted, 'is Lord Charles de Fontanel. He's waiting downstairs.' Gaunt picked up the goblet and rolled it between his hands. 'I hoped the ransoms would be raised and these men released but, to answer your question bluntly, Brother, last night Guillaum Serriem was found poisoned in his chamber.'

'Last night?' Athelstan asked curiously.

'Well, to be perfectly honest, this morning, but his body was stiff and cold. The physician, Osmund Aspinall, he's a leech who owns chambers above an apothecary's in Cripplegate, reckoned the prisoner must have died shortly after he retired, nine o'clock in the evening.'

'He was definitely poisoned?'

Athelstan glanced fearfully at Sir John. The coroner had now drunk two goblets of wine very quickly and was slouched in his chair cradling his goblet, as a mother would a baby, eyes closed, the most beatific smile on his face.

'Oh yes.' Gaunt raised his voice as if to rouse Cranston. 'Discoloration of the mouth and tongue, a deadly pallor, marks on his belly and thighs.'

'And how was the poison administered?'

Gaunt scratched his chest and glanced testily at the coroner.

'If I knew that, Brother,' he snorted, 'you wouldn't be here. The chamber was locked from within. A guard stood at the end of the passageway. There's no window except a narrow aperture, no secret entrances, nothing. Serriem had drunk some wine before he retired but, when Limbright broke the door down, and there were others present, the cup was untainted. A thorough search was made of the room. Nothing suspicious was found.'

'And when did Sir Guillaum eat?' Athelstan asked.

'With the rest at about seven in the evening. He drank the same, ate the same, then played chess in the parlour.'

'Couldn't the poison have been administered then?'

'I doubt it. Again the same wine jug was shared. Nothing suspicious occurred.'

'And now the French are outraged?' Sir John opened his eyes and sat up, putting the cup down on the desk in front of him.

'Why, Sir Jack, I'm glad you've joined us!'

'My Lord Gaunt, I never left you.'

The Regent laughed softly. 'You are right, Jack. You can guess what has happened. According to the laws and usages of war, prisoners are held for ransom in our care. The French are demanding reparation and justice.'

'But there's more, isn't there?'

'Aye, Jack, there is. A week ago we made a truce with France, one very much in our interests. No war by land or sea.'

'But if the French believe,' Athelstan interrupted, 'that we are killing hostages, men of quality?'

'Exactly! They could declare it a *casus belli*, justification for war and the truce, so carefully arranged by the papal negotiators, would end.'

'And you believe this Serriem was murdered?' Athelstan persisted. 'It was no accident or suicide?'

Gaunt pulled a face and shook his head. 'Serriem had a wife and family in France, he was desperate to go home.' Gaunt turned and snapped his fingers. 'Maurice, if you will bring my Lord de Fontanel up here. Justice must not only be done,' he added wearily, 'it must also be seen to be done!'

Sir Maurice left. Gaunt sat staring moodily at the parchments on his table. He didn't even move when Sir John got up and filled his wine goblet. Athelstan looked round the chamber. How much, he wondered, was the truth? Gaunt was as slippery as a fish and Athelstan knew that they were about to begin the pursuit of a red-handed son of Cain, an assassin, a murderer. They would enter the domain of demons, seek out the truth to bring about justice, but it was never simple.

Athelstan was about to ask his own questions when he heard footfalls outside and Sir Maurice entered the room. The man who swept in behind him was dressed in a long houpelonde, a long, high-necked gown which fell beneath the knee, bound round the waist with a silver belt. On his feet he wore soft buskins ornamented with silver buckles, and a jewelled fleurdelys, on a golden chain, hung round his neck. He had bright red hair, a white puffy face and a hooked nose; the eyes were arrogant, narrow and close-set, the lips thin and bloodless. A man of fiery temper, Athelstan considered, sly and cunning as the weasel he looked. A man who also stood on ceremony. De Fontanel bowed at Gaunt and waited while Sir Maurice brought up a chair so he could sit next to the Regent. He lowered himself carefully, moving the silver dagger pouch so it didn't catch on the arm of the chair. Only then did he bother to notice Athelstan and Sir John. A quick, summary look then he stared above their heads while fiddling with the rings on his fingers.

'My Lord de Fontanel.' Gaunt moved sideways in the chair to face him. 'May I introduce Sir John Cranston, coroner of the city, and his secretarius Brother Athelstan, a Dominican?'

De Fontanel's eyes moved, snake-like. He looked quickly at Sir John and dismissed him with a flicker of contempt. He looked more intently at Athelstan as if he couldn't make up his mind who the Dominican was. He took the silver goblet Sir Maurice passed and handed it to Sir John.

'I do not wish to be poisoned,' he lisped. 'Not like poor Serriem! You, sir, will taste it!'

'Certainly!' Sir John grabbed the goblet, drained it in one gulp and thrust it back.

Anger spots glowed high in de Fontanel's cheeks. Gaunt lowered his head to hide his snigger. Sir Maurice hastened to fill the goblet again.

'My Lord de Fontanel,' Gaunt intervened. 'You are safe here.'

'You gave the same assurances to poor Serriem and now he's dead, poisoned.'

'That is not our fault.' Gaunt tapped the table and pointed at Athelstan and Sir John. 'These are my two officers. They will investigate Serriem's death. If it's murder, they will capture the felon and he will hang. You have my word.'

Gaunt emphasised the last four words and de Fontanel had no choice but to accept. He sipped from the refilled cup then, raising his head, studied the two officers.

'We are not what we appear to be,' the coroner said slowly. 'Monsieur, if you look into your battle rolls for the name of Cranston you will find it among the victors of many an affray against your country. There is a phrase: "A cowl does not make a monk and judge not a book by its cover".' His face creased into a smile. 'I beg you to do the same.'

'My lord,' Athelstan intervened. 'Do you ever visit Hawkmere Manor?'

The French envoy looked askance.

'You want us to find the truth,' Athelstan continued. 'That means, Monsieur, we must question everyone.'

'I go there,' de Fontanel snapped.

'And do you bring any food or drink?'

'I am not allowed to. Only a prayer book, some rosary beads.' De Fontanel put his cup down. 'My Lord Gaunt, you know my master's thoughts in this matter.' He tapped the Regent on the shoulder. 'We hold you personally responsible for the safe custody of our prisoners. So, let your officers investigate!'

He walked towards the door but paused until Sir Maurice hurried to open it for him. Gaunt waited till he had gone, his face mottled with fury.

'Now there goes a pretty peacock,' he said. 'I'd love to take his head in battle so he doesn't tap my shoulder again. Ah well.' He sighed. 'My clerk will have the commission ready for you. I would be grateful if you would go to Hawkmere Manor immediately. Maltravers will accompany you there.'

'You've had the place searched?'

'From cellar to garret,' Sir Maurice intervened. 'Nothing was found.'

'Could Limbright be poisoning his visitors out of spite?'

'Limbright has not got the imagination!' Gaunt scoffed. 'While his daughter is simple.'

'And there are no poisons in the manor?' Athelstan persisted.

'None whatsoever. Weapons are strictly controlled, as are the prisoners. They cannot leave its grounds, visitors are searched. De Fontanel can only visit them once a week.'

Athelstan made to leave. He could see that Sir John was beginning to feel uncomfortable and was genuinely concerned lest the coroner doze off again.

'One moment.' Gaunt got to his feet and went and put his hand on Sir Maurice's shoulder. 'Sir Jack, Brother Athelstan, I think you know Sir Maurice Maltravers: a warrior and my most loyal retainer.'

Athelstan narrowed his eyes. Now he studied him, the young knight looked white and peakish, his eyes red-rimmed as if he had been crying or slept poorly.

'Sir Maurice,' Gaunt continued, 'is a man deeply in love. He is much smitten by the Lady Angelica Parr.'

'Oh no!' Sir John groaned. 'Not the daughter of Sir Thomas? Parr is tight-fisted and avaricious. We attended the Inns of Court together years ago. He is so mean there are cobwebs in his purse. Now he controls everything, ships, wool and wine. They even say half the Commons, not to mention the court, are deeply in debt to him.'

'Sir John, as usual, you are succinct and truthful,' Gaunt replied. 'I am deeply indebted to Sir Thomas and he has great aspirations for his daughter. The hand of an earl, perhaps, even one of my own kinsmen, a member of the royal family?'

Gaunt turned and stared at Sir Maurice and, for the first time ever, Athelstan caught a genuine look of compassion in the Regent's eyes.

'Sir Maurice,' Gaunt sighed, 'is the younger son of a younger son of a younger son.' He waved his hand. 'He made the terrible mistake of courting the Lady Angelica, even trying to elope with her.'

'Oh dear!' Sir John breathed.

'Oh dear, yes. He has been forbidden near the house and Lady Angelica is safely ensconced with the venerable sisters, the nuns of Syon on the Thames.'

'Oh, heaven's tits!' Sir John groaned.

'Precisely. A house ruled by the very venerable Mother Monica! A woman who strikes more terror in some of my court than the massed armies of the French. Sir Thomas has petitioned me,' Gaunt continued, 'to keep Maltravers away and to send to the convent a venerable father, a man of sanctity, to instruct his daughter in obedience and love for her father. You, Brother Athelstan, are the chosen one.' He lowered his voice. 'And that's the problem. You are also to use all your powers to advance the cause of Sir Maurice.'

Chapter 4

Cranston and Athelstan, with a woebegone Sir Maurice in tow, left the Savoy Palace. They took a barge further along the Thames to Fish Wharf and threaded their way along the narrow runnels which wound through houses and shops towards St Paul's. At first they had been too nonplussed to speak. They were accustomed to accepting the Regent's commissions to investigate this or that, but the prospect of becoming heralds for this knight of the doleful countenance sitting opposite them in the barge truly confounded them. Athelstan's mind teemed. How could he do anything? His knowledge of women, and he smiled to himself, well, the least said the better! Sir John broke the silence and leaned over and grasped the young man's knee.

'I know what it's like, lad,' he growled. 'Years ago, when I pursued the Lady Maude, I wasn't like this; sleek as a greyhound I was, fast as a swooping hawk, my heart and soul on fire. It was just poor old Jack Cranston then but courage and tenacity will achieve the desires of your heart.'

Sir Maurice thanked him. Athelstan could see the mirth in the young man's eyes at the picture of a sleek and swooping Sir John.

'Ah yes, those were the days,' Sir John repeated as they made their way through the alleyways. 'What a siege of love, and I tried every stratagem.'

Athelstan had to hang behind them because he'd begun to laugh so much his shoulders were shaking. He couldn't really think of Lady Maude as a castle while the prospect of Sir John deeply in love was a thing of wonder.

Sir John, one hand on Sir Maurice's shoulder, steered him through the crowds. Athelstan, trailing behind, realised that he had been sheltering in St Erconwald's so long the crowds, the smell, the press made him feel uneasy. The sun was strong and the heat made his rough serge gown cling to his sweat-soaked skin. Sir John loved the city but Athelstan always found it strange, filled with images, pictures, which reminded him of scenes on a painted wall.

Two men on a corner of Old Bowyers Row were teaching their pet weasels how to kill a rat. Further along two beadles were making a whore fumigate herself by standing over a dish of burning coals, her dirty skirts pulled up under her breasts. Apprentices came out from behind stalls to catch Sir John's arm. He shook them off as he did the greasy fingers of the owners of the cookshops who always regarded Sir John as a generous patron. The dung carts had not yet reached this part of the city and the lanes and alleyways were still full of rubbish from the previous day. The sewers down the streets brimmed with dirt. Cats, dogs, pigs and even a few chickens scrambled among the muck looking for tidbits. Street signs creaked in the light breeze which had sprung up. Above them, windows of the lean-to houses had been thrown open. People talked and shouted to each other. Now and again, if the street scavengers weren't looking, they tossed out refuse on to the growing piles.

At Paternoster Row they had to stop. Sir John even paused in his advice to Sir Maurice as a strange procession of men and women, dressed in bright yellow, made their way up Newgate. These wore their hair long and untended and walked in unison; every so often a bell would ring. They would stop, clap their hands and leap into the air shouting 'Hosanna!'

'The Joyeurs.' Sir John spoke over his shoulder at Athelstan. 'Just look at the silly buggers!'

The Dominican did, fascinated. He had heard of these men and women who believed that the Second Coming was near and patrolled the city in feverish expectation. According to them, Jesus would appear at Blackheath and found the new Jerusalem.

'There must be sixty of them!' Sir John muttered.

The Joyeurs heightened Athelstan's sense of unreality with their strange uniform walk, abrupt stops, the clapping of hands and raucous shouts.

Once they had passed, the three continued. They entered the Shambles, the beaten paving-stones awash with blood and gore from the butchers' stalls and slaughterhouses. Outside Newgate, the stocks had been set up and the beadles were inviting citizens to throw rotten vegetables at the unfortunates fastened there, hands and heads clasped tightly between the wooden slats. Further up another crowd was waiting to visit relatives in the city prison. Turnkeys in their shabby leather aprons were moving among them taking bribes, choosing who should go in first.

At last they were free of the press, making their way up through the city gates and across Smithfield. Athelstan sighed with relief. The stench and the heat were not so intense and the great open expanse was deserted, although stall-holders were getting ready for the great horse fair the following day. They crossed some waste ground. Sir John paused to take a few gulps from his wineskin. Sir Maurice refused but Athelstan was only too grateful to wash the dust from his throat. They continued along dusty track-ways which wound between the hedgerows, the noise and bustle of the city giving way to the chirping of birds and the hum of crickets. At last they reached Hawkmere Manor. The grey, forbidding curtain wall was dominated by a high timbered gate-house. Archers stood there, men-at-arms along the ramparts. Athelstan pulled at the great bell.

'Piss off!' one of the archers shouted down.

'I'm Sir John Cranston!' the coroner bellowed. 'And, if you don't open this bloody gate, I'll hang you from the gatehouse!'

There were muttered curses followed by the sound of footsteps. A small postern door in the great iron-studded gate swung open and a shamefaced archer ushered them in. Sir John poked him in the chest.

'Don't ever tell me to piss off, lad!' He pulled back the archer's hood, revealing a mangled left ear. 'Who did that?'

The narrow-faced archer forced a grin, revealing his black and bleeding gums.

'The French caught me outside Calais.'

'You are a bloody liar! The French would have taken two of your fingers off, not your ear!'

The archer looked crestfallen. 'I stole a goose outside Calais,' he muttered.

'That's better.' The coroner glanced across the cobbled yard which stretched up to the main door of the manor.

'Now, lad, run ahead and tell Sir Walter Limbright that Sir Jack Cranston is here.'

Athelstan opened his pouch and gave the archer the commission they had collected from one of John of Gaunt's clerks. The archer hurried off. Athelstan looked up at the manor.

'A gloomy place to live in,' he commented. 'And a gloomy place to die!'

Hawkmere was built out of grey ragstone, four stories high. Chimneys had been added on at each end of the sloping, red-slated roof. The front door was black and forbidding. The steps leading to it were choked with weeds and crumbling. The windows were either arrow slits or small squares of wood, not filled with glass but protected by shutters from within and iron bars on the outside. It reminded Athelstan of the great block houses in France, built by the English to control crossroads, bridges and fords over rivers.

The archer had disappeared round the back. Athelstan could see now why Hawkmere had been chosen as a prison. On the other three sides of the house ran a great curtain wall which probably defended the outhouses and buildings behind it. He glanced at his companions; Sir John was standing, legs apart, eyes half-closed. Sir Maurice looked as if he were a thousand miles away and, once again, Athelstan wondered how they could possibly help this young man's futile pursuit of his beloved. Sir John knew Sir Thomas and so did Athelstan. Sir Thomas had a reputation for being hard-fisted and stony-hearted. A man who lent monies to everyone and always demanded a good profit in return.

'Come on, Athelstan,' Sir John growled. 'I'm not standing here baking in the sun.'

He marched across and up the steps, the other two close behind, and hammered on the great oaken door. It swung open and a servant ushered them in.

The inside of Hawkmere Manor was as gloomy as its exterior. The hallway was so dark, cresset torches spluttered in their iron holders. They were taken down a shabby passageway, their boots ringing hollow on the hard grey paving-stones. Sir Walter Limbnght was waiting for them in his chamber just near the Great Hall. A small, surly-looking knight, he had thinning grey hair, eyes close-set, a cynical cast to his mouth. He was unshaven and his dark-brown doublet was stained. He rose to greet them.

'I was told of your arrival, Sir John. I was coming...'

'We decided not to wait,' Sir John snapped. 'It's hot outside.'

'Would you like something to drink?' Sir Walter became nervous as he realised he had been caught out in his bad manners.

'Perhaps later,' Athelstan intervened quickly.

Sir Walter handed the commission back.

'It's not my fault,' he wailed. He picked at a stain on his tunic. 'I've kept the prisoners safely housed and protected. No one comes in here apart from that arrogant fop de Fontanel and, when he does, I watch him like a hawk. My Lord of Gaunt can't...'

'Where's the corpse?' Sir John demanded.

Sir Walter blinked. 'Yes, yes, quite, you'd best come with me!'

He led them out of his chamber along a passageway which smelt of stale vegetables. He reached the foot of a wooden spiral staircase. A pale young woman with light brown hair was sitting on the bottom step. She was picking at the floor and didn't look up as they approached.

'Lucy! Lucy!' Sir Walter glanced at Sir John. 'This is my daughter.'

The young woman glanced up; her face was vacuous, her eyes empty, her lower lip hung loose and a trail of saliva ran down her chin. A pretty-looking girl but her soul was gone, her wits fuddled.

'I'm going to press some flowers, Father.' She became aware of the visitors and squinted up at them. 'They are not supposed to be here.'

'Hush now, Lucy! They are from my Lord of Gaunt.'

'Have they brought some money?' she asked.

'It's Sir John Cranston,' Sir Walter replied. 'He's coroner of the city, come to view the corpse.'

'All Frenchmen are corpses,' she replied. 'And one's up there, stiffening and cold, smelling like a fish.'

'God have mercy on her!' Sir Walter said. 'Her wits wander. Sir John, she has no great love of the French.'

They reached the second gallery. The passageway was narrow and dark, the floor boards unpolished, the white plaster battered and peeling. Nevertheless, the doors to the chambers they passed hung straight and secure. Sir Walter stopped at one of these and pushed it open. The room was large but poorly lit. The shutters on the windows were thrown back but the little sunlight which poured through did nothing to lift the gloom or the summer breezes soften the stench of death and decay. A crucifix hung on the far wall, a few sticks of furniture and two battered leather coffers stood scattered around. On the narrow cot bed lay the corpse. Athelstan glimpsed a protuberant nose, greying skin; the dirty sheet meant to cover it had slipped to one side. Although he had given the last rites to many people, Athelstan was always struck by how pathetic a corpse looked. This was no different.

Athelstan crossed to the bed. He was not a physician but one glance told him that Guillaum Serriem had died in agony. The eyes were open, the pupils rolled back, the mouth hung slack. The skin of the face was puffy and discoloured. Athelstan pulled up the shift, noting the dark purple blotches which discoloured the chest and the muscular stomach. He opened the small writing-bag he always carried and took out a thin-stemmed horn spoon. He forced this into the mouth; the cadaver was stiff though the jaw was still slightly slack. The pink skin inside the mouth had turned a dark purplish hue, the gums and tongue were swollen. Athelstan sniffed. There was an odour, slightly sweetish. Athelstan knew and recognised a number of poisons but not this, which had the sugary smell of marzipan. He inspected the corpse for any recent wound or mark. Serriem's body was lean and muscular; it bore the high, pink, furrowed cuts where old wounds had healed but nothing out of the ordinary. Athelstan whispered the Requiem, made the sign of the cross over the corpse and pulled the sheet over that ghastly face. Sir John was sitting on a stool mopping his brow. Sir Maurice was playing with the wrist guard, Sir Walter was going round the room touching things as if he might find something significant. The door was pushed open. A young man entered, tall, thin and stooped, long brown hair falling to his shoulders. He was sharp-eyed and clean-shaven with a kindly face.

'Osmund Aspinall,' Sir Walter introduced him. 'He's our leech and apothecary.'

The physician hitched his fur gown and pulled up the belt which hung loose round his thin waist. He shook Sir

John's hand and then Athelstan's, peering at them closely as if short-sighted.

'I'm a physician,' he joked. 'Most people call me a leech. I have chambers in Cripplegate and Sir Walter here pays me to keep an eye on the prisoners.' He sat on the edge of the bed and patted the corpse. 'Poisoned, yes?'

'How do you know?' Athelstan asked, going to sit on the small bench under the window.

Aspinall shrugged. 'Brother, there are as many poisons on the market as there are pigeons round St Paul's. Belladonna, henbane and at least three types of arsenic.'

'But this one?' Sir John asked.

'I can't recognise it but, as I have said, there are so many.'

'How was it administered?' Athelstan asked.

'Oh, by mouth. There's no cut on the corpse.'

'Could it have been an accident?'

'Possibly.' Aspinall gestured at the window. 'There's a herb garden down there, with berries and plants which might kill a man.'

'How long does it take such a poison to work?' Sir Maurice asked.

'It depends. I knew of an old woman in Guttersnipe Alley who was poisoned by her son over a period of days but this was one which acted quickly. It would disturb the humours, clog the blood and, by the look on the corpse's face, he probably choked.'

'Well, well, well.' Sir John tapped his boot on the floor. 'And where would they get poisons from?'

'There's none here,' Sir Walter insisted. 'None whatsoever.'

'And you, Master Aspinall?'

The physician spread his long fingers and played with the gem-encrusted ring on one of them.

'My lord coroner, I have heard of you and Brother Athelstan.' He laughed drily. 'Sharp of eye and keen of wit. I assure you that I brought no poison into here, left no potion, gave no medicines. The prisoners are soldiers, seamen, hard and sturdy. The food could have been improved and their humours were disturbed by being confined but nothing else.'

'And you know nothing of the prisoners or this man's death?'

Aspinall got to his feet. 'I know nothing, Sir John.'

'Why are you here today?'

'I came to ensure all was well. I inspected the corpse this morning but thought I should return, just in case.'

'In case of what?' Athelstan asked, getting to his feet.

Aspinall turned at the door and leaned against it, hands behind his back. He stared up at the ceiling.

'Brother, you are the coroner's secretarius. I am a physician, not a master of logic. We have a man poisoned. Now it could have been an accident. He may have found something in this house and eaten it but, God knows, that's not the truth.'

'So?'

'In my experience, Brother, when such deaths occur they are not isolated events.'

'You mean others will be poisoned?'

'I know they will be. Oh, I thought about it this morning. Why should anyone kill Serriem? Hawkmere Manor is close and securely guarded; the murderer must know that he stands a good chance of being caught. So Serriem's death was meticulously planned. It was no crime of passion and it may be one of many.'

Athelstan scrutinised the physician. Aspinall spoke sense. Was there conflict between the prisoners? He glanced sideways at Sir Walter. Or a paying-off of old scores?

'I've also checked the stores and the wine cellar.'

'You had no right,' Sir Walter protested.

'I have every right, Sir Walter. I am physician to the prisoners. My Lord of Gaunt has paid me good silver. However, do not trouble yourself. The meat and cheese could be fresher, the wine sweeter but the food stores are not tainted.'

'Are there vermin here?' Athelstan asked, remembering Ranulf the rat-catcher.

'Of course.'

'You put down no poison?'

'We have three great cats.' Sir Walter smiled sourly. 'We do not feed them and they are half-wild, they take care of the vermin.'

'When did Serriem retire to bed?'

'With the rest at nine o'clock. They supped at seven, walked in the garden. Serriem played checkers with one of the prisoners. Pierre Vamier.'

'And the relationships?' Sir John asked. 'Between the prisoners?'

'They are cordial enough.' Aspinall spoke up. 'Sir Walter will confirm this. They keep to themselves. They are homesick for their families in France, eager for their ransoms to be raised. Yet.'

Sir John undid the stopper of the wine and took two great gulps. He offered it to his companions but they shook their heads.

'Well, go on.'

'In the last week to ten days,' Sir Walter said, 'something has changed, they do seem wary of each other.'

'How were they captured?' Athelstan asked.

'I did that.' Sir Maurice spoke up. 'There are five of them, or there were. Vamier, Gresnay, Routier, Maneil and Serriem. They were captains, lieutenants and masters of the two great French cogs of war: the *St Sulpice* and the *St Denis*. Our wine fleet from Bordeaux had sailed up into the Channel. Now, it is customary for the ships to disembark some of their cargo at Calais and make a dash across the Straits into Dover. The *St Sulpice* and *St Denis* were waiting for them.'

'And what happened?' Athelstan asked.

'I was in Dover at the time,' the young knight continued. 'Commanding a large force of knights, hobelars, men-at-arms and archers. We had four craft at our disposal led by a cog of war, *The Great Edward*. The Constable of Dover Castle received information that the *St Sulpice* and *St Denis* would be waiting for our ships so we took to sea. It was a long and bloody fight: the *St Denis* was sunk, the *St Sulpice* captured.'

Athelstan picked up his writing-bag, tying the cord at the top.

'That's almost miraculous,' he observed. 'From where did the Constable of Dover Castle get his orders?'

'By courier from London. The message was general. It simply said that our wine fleet would be leaving Calais and French privateers were busy in the Channel.'

'A remarkable coincidence.' Sir John, wheezing and puffing, got to his feet.

'What are you implying?' Athelstan asked.

'Something I've suspected.' Sir Maurice spoke up. 'The *St Sulpice* and *St Denis* came out of a French port. They had to be prepared and provisioned for sea.' He shrugged. 'It was common gossip that the Regent had a spy in the French camp who sent him news about this.'

'And now the French captains themselves suspect this?' Athelstan asked.

'Possibly.'

Sir Walter rubbed his hands together, pleased that suspicion had been diverted from him.

'It could well cause animosity amongst the prisoners,' he declared, bright-eyed, 'if they thought someone was the traitor, perhaps Serriem?'

Sir John clapped him on the shoulder. 'And you, Sir Walter?'

'I know what you are thinking.' The knight gaoler shrugged Sir John's hand off. 'Don't worry, Sir John, I thought the same as soon as I knew Serriem was dead. Here's old Limbright, a man who hates the French, who killed his wife, sons and drove his daughter witless. What a marvellous opportunity for revenge!' He drummed his fingers against his dagger. 'But I didn't want them dead, Sir John. I just wanted them prisoners. I wanted them to experience the hurt that I felt. To pine for their families as I did. To walk round and round a room and feel the grief of separation.' He faced the coroner squarely. Athelstan noticed the spots of anger high in his cheeks. 'And if I wanted to kill them, Sir John, I'd do it honourably. I may be the knight of the dirty jerkin, ageing and bitter, but it would be sword against sword, or lance against lance, not poison in the dead of night.'

'Well said! Well said!' Athelstan commented.

'And the corpse?'

'It will be interred in some churchyard!' Sir Walter snapped. 'If the French want it home they'll have to pay for it!'

'I'd best be leaving,' the physician interrupted.

Aspinall bid farewell, and quietly left.

Sir Walter waited until the footfalls faded.

'Now there goes a man,' he muttered sarcastically, 'who believes that blunt, honest speech covers a multitude of sins.'

'What do you mean?' Athelstan asked.

'Our good physician is what he claims to be but he likes visiting Hawkmere Manor.'

'Stop talking in bloody riddles!' Sir John snapped.

'Aspinall is a bachelor; he's taken a liking to young Gresnay.'

'You mean he's a lover of men?'

'I didn't say that, Sir John. Serriem did. Aspinall is recently arrived in London. I know little of him. Anyway, Gresnay had a fall downstairs. Aspinall came to examine him. Nothing more than bruised ribs. Serriem cracked a joke about our physician being as tender as a woman. Gresnay and the physician became rather flustered, very embarrassed. A fight might have ensued but Vamier intervened.'

'Is there anything else we should know?' Sir John asked.

'Very little! The French seem a close-knit group of sailors and soldiers who've fought against the Goddamns since their youth. They give little away.'

'And how long will they remain here?' Athelstan asked.

'They are all from fairly wealthy families. But the ransom is steep, ten pounds in gold each.'

'Why so high?'

'Talk to any ship owner along the Thames,' Sir Maurice answered. 'The *St Sulpice* and *St Denis* were hated and feared. Those two warships did terrible damage to English shipping. They are only receiving what they served up to others.'

'Wait! Wait!' Sir John held his hand up as Sir Walter went to open the door. 'They commanded warships?'

'I've told you.'

'Sir Maurice, when the *St Sulpice* was taken, what was its cargo?'

The young knight scratched his chin. 'Most of it was armaments, some chests and coffers which were immediately sealed with the Regent's insignia. The cargo always goes to the Crown,' he added wryly.

'And the ship?' Sir John persisted.

'Oh, it now flies under English colours, it's been renamed the *Carisbrooke*.'

Athelstan cradled his writing-bag. Something was very wrong here. Why should a man be murdered in such close confined quarters? Was it a coincidence that the sly and subtle John of Gaunt had asked him and Sir John to help, in the affairs of the heart, the knight who had commanded the ships which had brought these Frenchmen to such a poor pass? We are in the dark again, Athelstan reflected; shown bits and pieces but denied the whole picture. He glanced quickly at the coroner, who was now showing obvious signs of the generous swigs from the wineskin. He had a fixed smile on his face, and was licking his lips and patting his stomach.

'Come on, Sir John,' he urged. 'And you, Sir Maurice, let's visit our French guests.'

The prisoners were assembled in the long, dingy hall below stairs. A narrow, gloomy room with rafters like a barn, its plaster walls had turned a dingy yellow from the countless fires in the crumbling, canopied hearth. Trestle tables stood about, badly scrubbed. Two thin-ribbed wolf hounds were busy licking the table-tops for morsels.

The French were seated on a dais sharing a jug of wine and a platter of roast chicken. Athelstan suspected that Sir Walter provided this to placate his prisoners and restrain them from launching into a litany of protests about their conditions. They were a taciturn, hard-bitten crew; younger than Serriem. Their hair was cropped, their faces weatherbeaten. They were dressed in dingy clothes, shabby jerkins with frayed, faded shirts beneath. The only exception was a girlish-faced young man with thick, red lips and eyelashes any girl would envy. He had allowed his blond hair to grow and his skin was so white Athelstan wondered if he rubbed paste into it.

They hardly bothered to acknowledge their visitors but kept talking among themselves until Sir Walter struck the table with his hand.

'Ah, good morning, Sir Walter,' one of them said. 'We have visitors?'

Their gaoler made the introductions. Routier, with his close face, was the first to greet them. Maneil, surly, his left eyelid drooping, constantly fingered the deep scar on his cheek. Vamier was pleasant-faced, or at least he smiled with his eyes. Athelstan took an immediate dislike to the blond-haired Gresnay who simpered in silent mockery at them. Their command of English was very good. They ignored Sir Maurice, just acknowledging his presence with nods of their heads. Athelstan was surprised but he whispered that, unlike the knights of chivalry, sea captains nursed animosities and jealousies: they regarded him as the cause of their misfortune. Sir Walter rearranged more chairs round the circular table. He offered some wine but Athelstan quickly refused.

'I suppose you've heard about Serriem? Poor Guillaum?' Routier glared at Sir Walter. 'It's all a sham,' he railed. 'We are prisoners, kept against our will, exorbitant ransoms are demanded. Now we are to be poisoned!'

Sir John got up and leaned across the table.

'I am no sham, sir! If murder is committed, justice must be done!'

Routier blinked and sat back.

'In which case,' Gresnay lisped, flicking his blond hair, 'you are going to have to perform a miracle.'

'Now, why is that, sir?' Athelstan asked.

'Why, Brother,' Gresnay replied, 'all of us took an oath that we would not eat or drink anything someone else didn't also taste.'

Chapter 5

Gresnay's words created a pool of silence.

'I am sorry?' Athelstan stammered.

'Don't you understand your own tongue, Brother?' Vamier snapped. He tapped Gresnay on the arm. 'Jean has spoken the truth.'

'What is the truth?' Sir John asked.

'We are officers of the King of France,' Vamier declared. 'We are prisoners here but we fear for our lives. Sir Walter's hatred for our nation is well known.'

'And good reason for it!' Sir Walter burst out.

'Hush now!' Athelstan held his hands up.

'But it's true,' Vamier continued. 'Why!' He caught the look of puzzlement in Athelstan's eyes. 'Hasn't he told you? It was the *St Denis* which attacked Winchelsea when his wife and sons died.' The Frenchman lifted his shoulders and spread his hands placatingly. 'Of course, it was a different crew, different men. No man here would agree to the wanton slaying of a woman and her sons. But, Sir John, you have fought in France?'

Sir John nodded; Athelstan recalled himself and his brother Francis entering a French town which had been sacked by English archers. Women lay dead in the streets, their throats cut, their dresses pushed back and, beside them, young children. The glory of war had died at such sights. Athelstan glanced at Sir Walter. The knight's face had grown pale, his lips were moving soundlessly, beads of sweat ran down his cheeks.

'I'm no assassin,' he said hoarsely. 'Aye, I hate you. If I had my way, I'd see you all hang on the gallows for the pirates you are!'

A fight would have broken out but Sir John banged the table with his fists.

'When did you take this oath?' he asked. 'What did it signify?'

'When we came here,' Routier said, 'and we realised we were in the charge of Sir Walter.' He gestured at the platter. 'Sir Walter himself will tell you: we only eat from the same dish and drink from the same jug.'

'And last night?' Athelstan asked.

'The same. We dined here on what was supposed to be some fish, drank the same putrid wine and ate the same mouldy bread.'

His companions lowered their heads to hide their amusement. Sir Walter would have retorted angrily but Athelstan caught his wrist.

'They are only baiting you,' he whispered.

'If we met him on the field of battle,' Gresnay declared, 'we'd do more than that, Brother!'

'One day you might!' Sir Walter shouted, his lips flecked with spittle.

'But there's another reason, isn't there?' Athelstan asked.

The change in the French knights was remarkable. They dropped their lazy, insulting demeanour. Vamier shuffled back on his chair, Routier pulled across the wine jug and refilled his cup.

'Come! Come!' Athelstan insisted. 'You are hardly a band of brothers, are you? After all, once you were cocks of the walk, masters of the Narrow Seas, and then one day your two ships are trapped between English men-of-war and the port of Calais.'

'Taken in a fair fight!' Routier protested. 'Fortune's fickle wheel and fortune is blind. Perhaps next time we meet, Sir Maurice will know what it's like to be taken prisoner?'

'Oh, answer the question!' Sir John snapped. 'Two French ships taken in one day! That smacks of treachery! You were expecting fat-bellied cargo ships full of wine from Bordeaux. Aye. The best claret, rich and red, the only good thing that comes out of France.' The coroner grinned. 'That's not true, but we can sit here all day like little boys in a street insulting each other.'

'We were betrayed.' Vamier rapped the table-top with his fingers.

'And the traitor could be among you now?' Athelstan asked.

'Possibly.'

'It could have been anyone.' Gresnay waved his hands.

Sir John smiled beatifically across at him.

'Young man, I'm in London yet I know that, in French ports, men-of-war are being prepared. I know that. The seagulls know that, the rats on board ship know that.' His face straightened. 'But how many men know what's contained in sealed orders? Come on, how many?' He pointed at Routier. 'I ask you a question, sir, how many people on the *St Sulpice* and the *St Denis* knew where you were to sail, when, and what your destination was?'

'There were six of us,' Routier admitted. 'We four, Serriem and Dumanier. He was killed in the fight.'

'So, if there was a traitor,' Sir John continued sweetly, 'it could have been Dumanier, although the Judas kind usually ensure that they are safe, it might have been Serriem or, gentlemen, one of you.'

The consequent silence was abruptly shattered by two of the great house cats which had trapped a rat further down the hall and were busy in its noisy destruction. Sir Walter drew his sword and went down. One of the cats, the rat dangling from his mouth, hurried off hotly pursued by his companion.

'Death is all around us,' Maneil observed.

'And it may strike again,' Athelstan replied. 'We are not here, sirs, to play a part and walk away. The Regent himself has intervened. If there is a traitor among you, he may want you all dead. Or, there again, you may know who the traitor is? Was it Serriem? Did you carry out lawful execution of him? After all, you have just assured us that none of you eat or drink anything one of your companions does not partake of. Nevertheless, Serriem was poisoned.'

'Are you saying we forced something between Serriem's lips?' Maneil asked.

'It's possible.'

'But we dined together last night, Sir Walter's guards all about us. We talked, we played chess, there was no feeling of resentment. Serriem was a good companion, a born sailor. If there is a traitor it certainly wasn't him.'

Athelstan took out his ink horn, a sharpened quill and a square of parchment. He used a pumice stone to ensure it was smooth then he quickly wrote down their names and a short description and what he had learned. When he glanced up, the coroner was now sitting slouched in his chair, head back, mouth open, sleeping peacefully. Athelstan could tell the French were not impressed.

'Sir John does not regard Serriem's death as important,' Gresnay quipped.

'My lord coroner,' Athelstan replied, putting his quill down, 'is a hard working, very tired man who should be back in his own court, not listening to a pack of lies.'

'Lies!' Routier yelled.

'Yes, sir, lies! Someone is lying here.'

'Then why not ask him?' Routier pointed at Sir Walter. 'Brother Athelstan, we have no poisons. Our noble gaoler has already searched our possessions.'

'Is that true?' Athelstan asked.

Sir Walter nodded. 'I found nothing,' he confirmed. 'Nothing at all.'

'What about the garden?' Sir John opened his eyes, smacking his lips.

Routier gasped, open-mouthed. Athelstan hid his amusement. Sir John seemed to have the ability to sleep and listen at the same time.

'What about the garden?' The coroner rubbed his face. 'There are plants growing there.'

'Why not test us?' Routier retorted. 'We are sailors, my lord coroner, not gardeners. I speak for the rest: unless someone told us to the contrary, I wouldn't know one herb from another.'

This drew murmurs of agreement from his companions. Athelstan stared down at the square of parchment. Nothing, he thought, we are learning nothing here.

'One last question. Serriem was with you all the time?'

'I've told you that,' Routier replied wearily. 'We supped here. We walked in the garden. We played chess, dice, other games. Nobody saw Guillaum drink or eat anything after he had left the table.'

'You are sure of that?'

'When the guards came to take us to our chambers, Serriem was alive and well. He took his wine cup up but it contained nothing we, too, hadn't drunk.'

—

A short while later Sir John, Sir Maurice and Athelstan left Hawkmere Manor.

'I'm glad we are out of there!' Sir John exclaimed as soon as they were out of earshot. 'A godforsaken place!' He paused for a drink from his wineskin.

'What do you make of it?' Sir Maurice asked.

Athelstan stared back at the high, grey curtain wall and repressed a shiver. Many of the deaths he and the coroner had to deal with were the results of accidents or sudden fights. Now and again, as today, they would enter a different world, what Athelstan privately called the 'Devil's Domain'. Hawkmere was one of these. A place seething with malice, resentment, lies and bloody-handed murder.

'I feel angry,' he muttered then regretted his words.

'What do you mean?'

'Nothing.'

Athelstan waved his hand. He didn't wait for the rest but left the pathway and walked across the wasteland. It dipped; at the bottom was a small mere or lake. The sun had begun to dry it up, the water receding, leaving a round, muddy circle where plants and under-growth died through lack of nourishment. A desolate place. Athelstan sat down under the cool shade of a tree. Above him a thrush sang its little heart out. Sir John came and stood over him.

'What's the matter, Brother?'

'I don't know, Sir John. It's just a feeling, a premonition of danger.'

'For yourself?'

Athelstan shook his head. 'For all their effrontery, Sir John, those Frenchmen are frightened and so is Limbright.'

'You mean none of them is the murderer?'

'I'm not saying that. There may well be more deaths at Hawk-mere but, at this moment in time, there's very little we can do.'

Athelstan watched a pedlar leading his donkey up the trackway. The fellow was dressed in leggings and boots and a woollen jerkin with the hood pulled over his head against the sun. He turned and waved at them. Athelstan sketched a blessing in his direction.

'Now there goes a happy man,' he said. 'Very few possessions and never long in one place.'

'What's that got to do with Hawkmere?'

'Those men shouldn't be there. Sir John, how could Serriem have been murdered? Limbright knows the finger of suspicion points at him and those Frenchmen were wary of him from the start. They even took an oath to be careful what they ate or drank. We know Serriem touched nothing to create suspicion: there's no mark on his body and his room was locked and secured.'

'We didn't ask them about that,' Sir John remarked.

'We'll leave that for the time being. Though it's inconceivable, Sir John, that someone forced themselves into Serriem's chamber and made him drink poison.'

'It could have been a trick. Someone pretending to be a friend.'

'In which case, Serriem was very stupid for it must have been Limbright. From what I gather he keeps the keys of those chambers on his person.'

He looked over the coroner's shoulder. Sir Maurice was crouched down, plucking at some flowers.

'Ah, the lovelorn knight,' Athelstan said. 'But he'll have to wait. Now, Sir John, if I wished to buy a poison, something out of the ordinary, where would I go in London?'

'If you went to an apothecary or leech like Aspinall, those who have been granted a licence by the City Council, they would make an entry in their ledgers.'

'So, an assassin wouldn't go there?'

'No, he or she wouldn't. They'd go along to Whitechapel or even Southwark to those children of the night who deal in philtres and potions, magical powers, the crushed skin of toads or mushrooms plucked at midnight.'

'And they are numerous?'

'Well, to quote the Gospels, their name is Legion for they are many. Most of them are quacks, cunning men. They'd sell you a powder but it would be nothing more harmful than chalk. The real assassins are very few.'

Sir John closed his eyes and concentrated, sifting through names he knew, those men and women who lived in the shadow of the law, whose collars he would love to finger but never had the evidence.

'Vulpina is the one. Well, that's what she's calling herself now. Years ago she was known as "Hotpot Meg", a lecherous woman, a famous whore.'

'What happened?' Athelstan asked curiously.

'Someone marked her face and slit her nose. No one knows the reason why. Anyway, "Hotpot Meg" became Vulpina, a dealer in magic potions. Queen of the Poisoners is our Vulpina. You could start with her. However, first, let's deal with our lovelorn knight.'

They returned to the trackway and explained that they were going into the city.

'And what about me?' Sir Maurice spread his hands. 'I don't mean to sound plaintive.'

Athelstan grasped his hand. He felt sorry for the pain in this young man's eyes.

'Tell my Lord Regent that we have matters in hand. Don't worry,' Athelstan offered. 'Love always wins through.'

The young knight seemed unconvinced but he thanked them and walked away.

'A grand fellow,' Sir John said, taking another swig from his wineskin. 'Reminds me of myself in my youth, bold of eye, lean of body...'

'Yes, yes, Sir John. Oh, Sir Maurice!' Athelstan called out.

The knight turned.

'Who buys supplies for Hawkmere Manor?'

Sir Maurice looked down at the trackway, scuffing at it with the toe of his boot.

'It's one of my duties,' he shouted back and, turning on his heel, walked away.

'What on earth was that about?' Sir John asked.

'Just a thought, my lord coroner.'

'But the physician said he had checked the foodstuffs!'

'What puzzles me,' Athelstan replied, 'is that here we have five men who have taken every protection against poison. We are not too sure whether they are terrified of Limbright or frightened of the traitor in their midst. Now I don't think the poison,' he continued, 'was collected from the manor garden. We are not even sure whether anything poisonous grows there. And, even if it does, such poisons have to be prepared. You don't just pluck a little foxglove and give it to someone to eat. Now, the prisoners were searched, probably many times after their capture: a powder, poisons would have been noticed.'

'So?'

'So, Sir John, logic dictates that either the poison was brought into the manor and given to one of those Frenchmen to poison Serriem, and perhaps others, though God knows the reason why...'

'Or,' Sir John finished for him, 'the poison was obtained by someone who can enter and leave that manor at will.'

'Exactly! Which brings us to Limbright. Perhaps his daughter, fey though she be, our good and glorious physician Aspinall or, perhaps, even Sir Maurice.'

'I don't think Maltravers is a poisoner. He's a soldier and a warrior.'

'No, no, Sir John, he's a servant of the Regent. Maltravers in war may be a different person: caparisoned for the fight he will go out and smite his enemies. At home, however, he's like a restless war horse, sent hither and thither on this menial task or that.'

'And?' Sir John asked angrily. 'Speak your mind, Brother.'

'We have a powerful merchant in London, Thomas Parr. John of Gaunt could bribe him by offering him the hand of a prince in marriage but he does not. Instead, he advances the claim of this brave but penniless knight.'

'In return for which Maltravers will agree to do whatever Gaunt wants?'

'Perhaps.'

'But why, my good monk?'

'Friar, Sir John.'

'Same bloody thing! Why should Gaunt want these Frenchmen dead? He's going to gain a great deal of money from their ransoms, as well as keep them off the sea, well away from English shipping.'

'That would be reason enough,' Athelstan countered, but he could tell that the coroner didn't believe him.

'Come along, my good friar, let's visit Sir Thomas Parr.'

They walked across the wasteland, leaving the trackway as a group of courtiers thundered by on their horses, laughing and joking, their gaily decorated clothes bright in the sunlight. They chattered among themselves, hardly sparing a second glance for the fat coroner or the little friar. They held hawks and peregrines on their wrists; the birds were hooded, their jesses clinking like fairy bells. Behind them padded dogs, lurchers and mastiffs under their whippers-in. Sir John narrowed his eyes and watched them go.

'They are going down to the marshes,' he said. 'I feel sorry for the poor herons. That's what wrong with this city, Athelstan: the rich don't give a fig while the poor, they sit in their hovels and watch narrow-eyed and think about the weapons they have hidden beneath their mud-packed floors.'

Athelstan looked in alarm. 'Sir John, you sound fearful?'

'You would as well, Brother, if you've read what I have.'

As if to match the coroner's words, the sun slipped behind a cloud and a racing shadow sped across the fields.

'You believe the great revolt is coming, don't you?' Athelstan asked.

'I know it is, Brother, but Gaunt and his cronies won't listen. You remember France.' He led Athelstan back on to the trackway. 'The English, Athelstan, do not put their trust in knights but in the yeomen, the farmers and the peasants with their long bows. Now we are driven out of France, except for Calais, all these soldiers have returned home to eat hard crusts and drink brackish water. The shadow men, those who spy for the Regent, claim that weapons and arms are being brought into the city. Worse still, the peasant leaders have allies here, men who should know better: these believe they can win the race by dividing their wager and placing equal amounts on each horse.'

'Meaning?'

'If the revolt fails they will support Gaunt. However, if the rebels seize the city, capture the Tower and march on Westminster, there are those who will come out of their hiding holes, ready to support the "Great Community".'

Athelstan stopped walking. He watched the riders retreat into the distance. He always feared this. He was a priest in Southwark and tended to his parish. Along the narrow, filthy alleyways, he'd heard the rumours, the whispered talk beneath the gaiety and bustle of life; a sense of deep grievance and, time and again, that slogan, that chorus of the working man: 'When Adam delved and Eve span, who was then the gentleman?'

'Come on, Brother. Let's visit Sir Thomas Parr. While we walk I'll tell you a story about the nun, the friar and the lecherous goat.'

They entered the city, taking the path through Martins Lane down to Cheapside. It was now early afternoon. Some of the stalls had closed so their owners could take refreshment in nearby taverns and cookshops. Sir John gazed hungrily at these but Athelstan urged him on.

'Sir Thomas might offer us good wine,' he coaxed. 'We must have our wits about us, Sir John.'

On the corner of Westchepe a crowd had gathered. A man dressed in gaily coloured rags, his hair white as snow, eyes gleaming in his sunburned face, was declaiming to the crowd: 'Woe to the rich! To those who feed upon soft meats! Fill their bellies with sweetened wines! The day of reckoning is about to come! Circles of fire will fall upon the city! The highways will swarm with the worms of the earth! In their thousands and their tens of thousands!' He paused to draw breath.

Athelstan recognised this wandering preacher as one who supported the Great Community of the Realm. The 'worms of the earth' was a common term for the peasants, the oppressed serfs, the landless labourers.

'They will be led by angels!' the preacher continued. 'And they will ring the bell of doom!' He started to clang the handbell he carried.

The crowds of shopkeepers, apprentices, chapmen and tinkers, the pedlars, the beggars and cripples from the alleyways gathered round, heads nodding, eyes gleaming. A group of market beadles stood on the fringe, nervously plucking at the daggers in their belts, tapping their staffs of office against the ground.

'And what have we to fear?' the preacher continued. 'Death? We live a living death!'

A growl of approval rose from the crowd.

'Hey there, Pig's Arse!' Sir John grabbed a scruffy little man running through the crowd, a long thin dagger jutting out from the sleeve of his jerkin.

'Ah, Sir John, good day.' The beggar looked fearfully up at the coroner.

'Now, Pig's Arse,' Sir John breathed quietly. 'I would not start cutting purses here. This merry lot will turn ugly in a while and they'd hang you out of hand!'

Pig's Arse scuttled off. Sir John looked over the heads of the crowd. A group of soldiers were coming up Westchepe, wearing the livery of John of Gaunt and Fitzalan, Earl of Arundel.

'Here they are!' The preacher had also glimpsed them. 'Come to silence the Voice of Truth!'

The crowd turned as a man. Daggers were drawn and, as if from nowhere, a group of men dressed in dark-brown leather jerkins appeared. They carried bows with quivers full of arrows slung over their backs.

'Lord have mercy!' Athelstan said. 'Sir John, this will turn ugly.'

Sir John drew his sword and advanced, waving it as if he were Hector of Troy.

'Hey there, my beauties! Lovely lads all! This is Cheapside, not Poitiers!'

'Bugger off, Sir Jack!' someone shouted.

Cranston's hand went behind his back as he drew his dagger. The preacher had vanished like a wisp of smoke. Sir John advanced threateningly upon the archers.

'We've no quarrel with you, Jack Cranston!' one of them shouted, face hidden deep in a hood.

'If you don't piss off, you will have!'

The archers slung their bows and disappeared among the stalls. The rest of the crowd began hastily to disperse. Sir John resheathed his sword and dagger.

'Come on, Athelstan, time we moved on.'

They continued up Cheapside just as the soldiers arrived. Athelstan glimpsed Pig's Arse running like one of Ranulf's ferrets towards the mouth of an alleyway, a small purse clutched in his hand.

'You were very brave, Sir John!'

'Like a hawk swooping for the kill,' he replied. 'Now, for real trouble!'

They turned into a lane leading up to Goldsmith's Hall. The thoroughfare was broad and swept, the sewer had been cleaned and filled with fresh water from a conduit. The houses on either side were large and spacious with red-bricked bases and black and white timber upper tiers. The gables were ornate and gilt-edged, the doors squarely hung. Pots of flowers hung from the walls and the air was sweet with the fragrance from the gardens laid out in front of the houses. The sun glinted and shimmered in the mullioned window glass: some of these were even coloured and decorated with heraldic devices.

Sir Thomas Parr's was the stateliest of these mansions. It stood in its own grounds, two small apple trees on either side of the path leading up to the smartly painted door. This was decorated with shining iron studs, its large brass knocker formed in the shape of a knight tilting in a tourney. On either side stood huge pots of herbs on a charcoal base, the fragrant smoke curling up in billows like incense in a church. Men-at-arms lounged along each side of the house: city bullies, hired by this great merchant, they were dressed in his livery, white surcoats displaying a mailed fist holding a sword. They kept well away from Sir John's threatening look.

'I don't like these buggers!' the coroner muttered. 'Small, private armies. Look at them, Brother, they can't keep their hands away from their swords and daggers. Too much red meat and too little work, always eager for a fight.'

Athelstan quickly inspected the men. They were city boys in their tight fitting hose and high-heeled boots. They were well armed; some even carried crossbows with small pots of bolts attached to their leather war belts.

Sir John lifted the knocker and brought it down with a crash.

'I enjoyed that,' he muttered.

He did it again. The door swung open.

'What's your business?'

'What's your name?' Sir John barked.

'Ralph Hersham, man-at-arms to Sir Thomas Parr.'

'I'm Cranston the King's coroner. Now, sod off, and let me in!'

Chapter 6

They were ushered into the most luxurious parlour whose walls were decorated with oak panelling. The paving-stones were scrubbed white and covered with thick, woollen rugs. A chandelier of candles hung from the pure white ceiling. Pots of flowers stood on the elegant furniture arranged round the room. Chairs and stools were placed in a semicircle round the mantelled hearth. No fire was burning, but the grate was clean and polished. On shelves above the mantelpiece gold, silver and pewter pots gleamed. Carefully carved heraldic devices covered the windows, the shutters held back by scarlet ribbons. Hersham gestured at them to sit in the quilted window seat which overlooked the lawn and small flower beds along the side of the house.

'Can I ask your business?'

Hersham's thin, sallow face was still mottled with fury. He couldn't keep his fingers away from his dagger hilt. A true bully boy, Athelstan thought: a man who liked to swagger the alleyways.

'You are Sir Thomas' henchman?' Sir John asked, rubbing his hands then turning away to look at a small rose bush in the middle of the garden. I'd like one of those, he thought. I wonder how Parr grows them? He turned back to Hersham. 'Well?'

'I am Sir Thomas' bodyguard and steward,' Hersham replied.

'You are not a Londoner, are you?'

'From the south coast, Sir John.'

'Well, we can't wait here all day. Run along and get your master.'

If looks could kill, the coroner would have dropped dead on the spot. Hersham left the chamber, slamming the door behind him.

'I cannot tolerate such men!' Sir John whispered through clenched teeth. 'In my treatise on the governance of London...'

Athelstan leaned back against the head-rest. He closed his eyes, enjoying the cool breeze from the garden.

'Sir John, I beg you, keep your voice down and your opinions to yourself until we get out! Remember, Parr has not committed a crime! We are here to ask a favour.'

The door swung open and Sir Thomas came into the room, Hersham behind him. The merchant prince was dressed in a coloured cote-hardie with fur tippets hanging down from the elbows. His hose were shiny as if pure silk. He wore no shoes but the soles of the hose were covered in soft brown leather. An embroidered belt round his waist carried a gilt-edged purse and a small poignard.

Athelstan's heart sank when he studied Sir Thomas' face, which possessed hard, harsh features, narrow eyes, a bulbous nose and lips. The man looked as if he constantly sat in judgement on everything and everyone. He glanced at Athelstan, who raised his hand in salutation. Sir John made no movement but just stared back. Athelstan recalled that these two men knew each other. Parr was the first to break the silence. He came forward, hand extended.

'Well, well, Jack. I've seen you from afar. You've grown over the years.'

'In heart as well as body,' Sir John replied, grasping Parr's hand. 'It's been a long time, Thomas.'

Parr clasped Athelstan's hand then snapped his fingers and Hersham moved one of the chairs closer so he could sit down.

'They say you like claret, Jack.'

'The same people also say you love wealth, Thomas.'

Parr laughed, a thin, nasal snigger while his eyes remained watchful.

'And the Lady Maude? She is well and happy?'

Sir John nodded.

'Isabella died.' Parr glanced over their heads, his eyes softened. 'It's terrible watching someone you love die, isn't it, Jack? A summer fever. She was out in the garden tending that rose bush. She came in, the sweats upon her. By the following evening she was dead.'

'I'm sorry.' Athelstan spoke before he thought.

'So am I, Brother.' Parr now studied him from head to toe. 'I've also heard of you, Athelstan. They say you are a good priest.' His eyes moved back to Sir John. 'Despite the company you keep! But, come, we'll have some wine.'

Hersham served three gold-chased goblets. Sir John sipped and closed his eyes.

'Pure nectar,' he breathed.

'The best of Bordeaux, Sir Jack. I've had it ready for you. I wondered when the Regent would send someone.'

'Did you know we were coming?' Athelstan asked.

'There's not much which goes on at the Savoy Palace, Brother, that I don't know about. A silver piece here, a few groats there, and servants sing like birds in the trees. So, before you ask, the answer is no. Sir Maurice is a goodly knight, a brave man, a warrior, but he's poor, virtually landless and brings nothing but his sword.'

'And his heart,' Sir John riposted. 'A good, strong heart, Thomas. Like yours, years ago, when you and I ran ragged-arsed round the Inns of Court.'

'And what about Angelica?' Athelstan asked. 'Doesn't she love Sir Maurice? Are you going to marry her off as you would take a mare down to some stallion? A cold, loveless match?'

'Angelica knows her duty.' Parr put his wine cup down and played with the ring on his finger, his face softened. 'She is my only child and I love her dearly. However, she must see the error of her ways in betrothing her heart to some poor knight errant.'

'She loves him,' Athelstan declared. 'And he loves her, Sir Thomas. And I tell you this…'

'You'll tell me what?' Parr interrupted. 'You'll tell me what, Brother? What do you know about love, about women, about lust?'

His face was pale. Athelstan sensed this man's troubled spirit, at war with himself and, therefore, at war with everyone around him.

'I know nothing about maids or the songs of troubadours,' Athelstan answered. 'But I know a great deal about love, Sir Thomas, and it never dies.'

'In which case you may visit my daughter Angelica at the nuns of Syon and tell her about love for her father as well as duty, obedience and fealty!' He got to his feet.

Athelstan didn't like the smirk on Hersham's face. The man was leaning against the door, arms folded, gently clicking his tongue. Athelstan had to breathe in deeply to control his own anger. Sir Thomas was being nasty for the sake of it.

'Weren't you poor once?' he asked.

'Aye and Sir John was once slim. Life changes, Brother Athelstan, and what is yesterday but a pile of dust?' He walked towards the door. 'You have my permission to visit Angelica, but I will not talk to you again on this matter.'

Athelstan placed his cup on a table. He noticed a carving of a wooden ship and, painted in small, gilded letters, its name, *The Great Edward*.

'Do you own that cog, Sir Thomas?'

Parr shrugged. 'I contribute to its maintenance and have a share in whatever it captures. Nevertheless, Brother, before you speak, no, it does not soften my heart towards Maltravers! Now, Sir John…'

The coroner and Athelstan soon found themselves back out in the thoroughfare. Behind them Ralph Hersham said something to the henchmen lounging about; there were guffaws of laughter. Sir John turned to confront them but Athelstan plucked him by the sleeve.

'Leave them, Sir John, there'll always be another day.'

They walked back into Cheapside. It was now late afternoon, some of the stall-holders had already finished their trading, and the crowds were beginning to disperse. Sir John smacked his lips. Athelstan also felt hungry but he wanted to go back to St Erconwald's, to ponder the day's happenings. Yet, he ruefully reflected, they still had further business.

'Sir John, I know you'd like a blackjack of ale and a pie but the day goes on, and we have a lady to visit. Vulpina.'

Sir John reluctantly agreed and they walked up Westchepe, down Ivy Lane, passing the great soaring mass of St Paul's Cathedral. Along its cemetery wall sat the rogues and vagabonds who sought sanctuary in St Paul's graveyard beyond the jurisdiction of the city officers. They recognised Sir John and hailed him with raucous raillery. Athelstan pulled his hood close up over his head as Sir John, still angry at Hersham's mocking laughter, hurled good-natured abuse back.

'One day, my lovelies!' he shouted before they turned a corner, 'I'll see you all on the gallows ladder!'

Invigorated by this exchange, he walked a little quicker, almost dragging Athelstan with him, out along Fleet Street and through a warren of mean alleyways into Whitefriars.

Whitefriars was not a wholesome place. The houses and tenements were shabby, ill-painted, the plaster decaying, the paint-work flaking. The streets seemed like needles pushed between the overhanging houses which blocked out the sun and hid the sky. Dark, cavernous passageways abounded, where beggars thronged at alley mouths and whores stood brazenly in the doorways soliciting custom. All around them swirled the rogues and rifflers of London.

Sir John was never checked. Apart from the occasional hurled obscenity, the coroner was a respected and feared figure. If provoked, it was not unknown for the coroner to enter one of the alehouses and arrest a whole gaggle of rogues by the scruff of their necks. At the end of one alleyway he stopped, fingers to his lips.

'The streets of hell, Brother,' he breathed. 'In daylight it's safe but, once darkness falls, the demons appear.'

As if in answer a group of dwarfs and mannikins, just over a yard high, came hurtling out of a doorway and ringed the coroner, jumping up and down like noisy children. They were dressed in a motley collection of rags and scraps of armour. One had a small helmet on his head. Another carried a shield. They greeted Sir John like scholars would a favourite master. Athelstan recognised the 'scrimperers' who lived in Rats Castle; dwarfs who lived together for self-protection. They were known to hire their services out to night-walkers and housebreakers as there wasn't a window they couldn't slip through or passageway too small.

'Sir John! Sir John!'

Sir John clapped his hands and offered their leader, who rejoiced in the name of Sir Galahad, a draught from his wineskin. The diminutive, seamy-faced dwarf took it, almost falling flat on his back as he tilted his head to drink.

'Lovely boys!' Sir John remarked. 'And what news do you have for Sir Jack?'

The scrimperers replied in a volley of high-pitched voices, talking the patois of the London slums. He listened, nodding benevolently, then crouched down as Sir Galahad beckoned him close to speak in his ear.

'Well I never! Well I never!'

The coroner dropped some coins into the little man's hand.

'They want you to bless them, Brother.'

Athelstan lifted his hand in benediction. He could hardly believe this, it was just like a scene from some dream. But, as soon as he began the benediction, they all went down on one knee, heads bowed.

'Give them a special blessing!' Sir John urged.

'I give you the blessing of St Francis,' Athelstan intoned, keeping his face solemn. 'It can only be given once a month and you are to receive it.'

They now went down on both knees. Athelstan felt a pang of compassion at the way they folded their little hands before them.

'May the Christ Jesus show His face to you,' he said. 'May He smile at you. May He keep you safe all the days of your life.' He sketched the sign of the cross in the air.

Sir John caught his wrist.

'They also want an invitation,' he said hoarsely.

'Where to?' Athelstan asked.

'To St Erconwald's.'

Athelstan's heart sank but he kept his face creased in a smile.

'They are moving house,' Sir John continued. 'They say they are unsafe here.'

'Oh, don't tell me, Sir John, they have chosen Southwark?'

'Apparently, yes. They know one of your parishioners, Ranulf the rat-catcher. They have heard about his Guild.'

Athelstan knew what was coming next and his heart sank even further.

'They like you, Athelstan. You see, they have formed their own Guild.'

'And they want to make St Erconwald's their church?'

'Don't refuse. They are very valuable, Brother, to me.'

'You will be most welcome,' Athelstan said.

Sir Galahad spoke again, fast. Athelstan knew a little of this patois: he recognised the words 'house' and 'rat-catcher'.

'Apparently,' Sir John translated, 'Brother Ranulf has used these in attics and cellars as well as tunnels to discover where the rats have their nests. He has found them a house not far from St Erconwald's, on the corner of Cat Stall Alley.'

Athelstan smiled. 'Oh, God help us, Sir John,' he whispered as the scrimperers, chattering with excitement, disappeared up an alleyway. 'St Erconwald's is going to become...'

'Are you going to say the refuge of all that is strange and wonderful?'

'Precisely, Sir John, more like Noah's Ark. Filled with all types of God's creatures.' He pushed back his cowl. 'But what did the scrimperers want with you?'

'Oh, they were telling me the gossip of the area: that little affray we saw in Cheapside this morning? Evidently agents of the Great Community of the Realm are now swarming in the city; their only difficulty is they have no arms.'

'They seemed well equipped this morning.'

'Oh, a few arrows, yes. I tell you, Brother. If the storm bursts, this city will see savage fighting. The Tower and the other fortresses along the Thames will be fortified. Many of the merchants like Thomas Parr will turn their houses into castles. The peasants may march on the city with their hoes and rakes, mattocks and old long bows but they'll need more serious weapons.'

'Couldn't they transport them into the city before-hand?'

'Every cart coming into the city is inspected by the market bailiffs and beadles, not to mention Gaunt's legion of spies. The scrimperers also informed us,' Sir John continued, walking slowly on, 'that an unknown priest has been seen in the area.'

'Is that strange?'

'Priests do not come here. Whitefriars is dangerous even for those who live in it. Their leader, Sir Galahad,' he went on, standing outside an old tavern and looking up at the fly-blown windows, 'said he was in an alleyway about ten days ago. He was jostled, the man sketched a blessing and whispered his apologies in what Galahad recognised as Latin.'

'What are you looking at, Sir John?'

'I used to visit this ale-house when I was a lad. It was called the Mulberry Tree. Oh, it's seen better days.' He opened the door.

'Sir John, if you need refreshment...'

'No, Brother, just your company!'

They walked into the evil-smelling taproom, a dank, musty place. The windows were boarded and shuttered, a few oil lamps were lit, filling the room with a greasy smell. In their flickering light the customers who sat on over-turned casks looked even more like shapes and shadows from a nightmare.

'Good day everyone!' Sir John bellowed. 'And God bless you!'

Athelstan narrowed his eyes. He could make out the wine tuns on the counter, the small glow of the oven, a few beer barrels.

'Piss off, Jack!'

'Now that's no way to talk to an old friend is it? Who's that? My goodness, it's one-eyed Isaiah! There are warrants out for you, my lad. An unsolved burglary in the Poultry?'

'I am as innocent as an angel,' the voice croaked back.

'What do you want, Cranston?'

A figure came out of the shadows. Athelstan first thought it was a man but, in the light of one of the oil lamps, he realised that, despite the leather jacket, leggings and boots, it was a woman. Her stained cambric shirt, slightly too small, emphasised her swelling breasts and thick, fat neck. The face was grotesque: the nose split, a long red ugly gash from top to tip while dagger marks criss-crossed her face. A large pearl dangled on a silver chain from one ear lobe.

'Now, now, Jack, you haven't come to arrest old Isaiah, have you?'

He took one step back and bowed mockingly.

'No, Mistress Vulpina, I have not. I wish a few words with you.'

'Then you'd best come.'

She led them into a far corner of the taproom and up some narrow, rickety stairs. The chamber above was a stark contrast to the evil drinking den below. The windows on one side boasted coloured glass. The walls were painted white and hung with coloured cloths.

The floor was red-tiled, scrubbed clean, and the furniture looked as if it had been bought from a guild carpenter in Cheapside. Flowers grew in small containers and sachets, filled with perfume, were fixed to the wooden beams along the ceiling. Vulpina led them across to a far corner where chairs were neatly arranged round a polished, oval table. A silver salt cellar stood in the centre, shaped in the form of a castle. She offered them wine but Sir John, surprisingly, refused. Vulpina laughed throatily. In the full light Athelstan could see how, in former days, she must have been a beautiful woman. Her eyes were dark brown, large and lustrous even though they shifted restlessly from one place to another. She was unable to meet their gaze but moved about, touching the salt cellar, staring out of the window or pretending to listen to sounds from the taproom below.

'You haven't come for one-eyed Isaiah.' She peered at Athelstan. 'You are the Dominican?' Her lips curled in a sneer. 'I have few priests among my customers.'

'For ale and beer?' Athelstan asked.

The sneer on Vulpina's face faded.

'What do you sell?' Athelstan persisted.

Vulpina tugged nervously at a tuft of her cropped dark hair.

'Everything.'

'Including poisons?' Cranston asked.

Vulpina sat back in her chair, hands cradled in her lap, and batted her eyelids.

'Oh, Sir John,' she cooed.

'Don't play "Hotpot Meg" with me! There's not a herb that grows, not a potion which can be distilled, unknown to you.' He gazed up at the ceiling. 'I wonder where you keep them, eh?'

Cranston got up and walked round the chamber. He stopped to inspect the wooden panelling placed against the far wall.

'A veritable warren!' he exclaimed. 'Eh, Vulpina? When I was a lad, the Mulberry Tree was known for its secret passageways and hideouts. People could come and go in the dead of night and not be noticed. I don't think it's changed. Who has visited you recently, Vulpina?'

'If I told you, Sir John, you'd only blush. Come and sit down. You have no warrant or licence to enter here.'

'I could get one.' He came back and lowered himself into the chair. 'Now that would be a good day's work, eh, Vulpina? Me and a dozen burly lads from the city. I wonder what we'd find here?' He pulled across the silver salt cellar. 'I am sure this once graced a house in Cheapside.'

Vulpina snatched it back.

'What do you want, Cranston?'

'I want you to tell me about poisons.'

'Do you wish to buy one?'

'Yes.' Athelstan spoke up. 'I want you to sell me a poison.' He paused. 'Which I can take but will do no harm. However, if I poured it into Sir John's ale he would be dead within an hour.'

'Impossible!' she snorted.

'You are sure?'

'Brother, there's nothing grown under the sun, of a noxious nature, which won't harm everyone who takes it.' She shrugged. 'To be sure, some will affect you more than others: just like ale or wine will render one man sotted before another.'

'And you know of no such poison?' Athelstan persisted.

'If I did, Brother, I would be very interested. Why do you ask?'

'Hawkmere Manor,' Sir John said.

The coroner had hit the mark; Vulpina tried to school her features but a shift to her eyes, a flicker of her tongue betrayed her.

'I've heard its name, an old, gloomy place.'

'It houses French prisoners,' Sir John explained. 'One of them was poisoned.'

'Ah!' Vulpina smiled, clicking her tongue noisily. 'So you put the blame on old Vulpina? Sir John, I tell you the truth. I sell potions and philtres to lovelorn ladies, to men who may wish to get rid of a rival. I do not ask them who they are or where they come from. I am an apothecary.'

'You are a killer! A red-handed assassin!' He got to his feet and leaned over the table. 'One day, when I have time and the necessary warrants, I'll come back here.' He went to the door. 'We are going to leave this lovely place.' He waited until Athelstan joined him. 'And I don't want to be followed. No fracas or sudden affray in the streets below. You've been no help, Vulpina, and I'll remember that!'

'Sir John!'

He walked back into the room.

'You are here on Gaunt's orders, aren't you? You're his messenger boy.'

'I'm no one's boy!'

Vulpina sneered, her head going back. She studied Sir John under half-closed lids. Athelstan repressed a shiver. He did not like this place: the more he stayed, the more certain he became that he was in the presence of real malevolence, that this woman was steeped in evil. He was used to the rapscallions and rogues of Southwark, people like Pig's Arse and Godbless who stole and thieved because they had to. Vulpina, however, enjoyed the evil she distilled, revelling in the chaos and the sorrow it caused.

'I'm waiting, Hotpot!'

'You are Gaunt's man.' She clicked her tongue again and lifted her hand. Athelstan noticed that she wore a skin-tight leather gauntlet on her right hand. 'I can give you a list of customers, Cranston!' she hissed. 'They'd include the so called mighty and good who would have little time for your nose-poking and querulous questions and that includes my Lord of Gaunt! Or rather his lovesick knight. What's his name? Maltravers? I understand he's the laughing-stock of the city. He's taken a couple of French ships so he thinks he can slip between the sheets with Lady Angelica Parr, does he?'

'What are you saying?' Sir John took a step threateningly forward.

Vulpina lifted a whistle which hung on a silver cord round her neck.

'Come on, Fat Jack!' she taunted. 'One blast from this and we'll see how you and your priestly friend can cope with my legion of rats from below!'

He drew sword and dagger. Vulpina's face lost some of its arrogance.

'Go on!' he said. 'Let's go at it, Vulpina. Heaven or hell, but you will be dead.'

The Queen of Poisons took a deep breath and let it out noisily.

'Fine, fine, Sir John. I want you out of here and I don't want your enmity.' She let the whistle fall. 'Gaunt's man has been here.'

'Maltravers?'

'The same.'

'What did he want?'

'A love philtre.'

'For what?'

'I didn't ask him. He also bought some poison. I asked him why. It was nothing exceptional, some henbane, a little belladonna.'

'And did he give the reason for that?'

'He said it was rats. In his own chamber. He asked for it as an afterthought.' Vulpina smiled. 'But I saw your quick-eyed Dominican friend, when you mentioned Hawkmere Manor. I've had visitors from there. Limbright for one, Sir Walter constantly comes here, takes a little digitalis he does, and a few other potions, St John's wort for a start.'

Athelstan studied this woman and wondered how many secrets she held.

'Oh, and the list goes on. The good physician Aspinall? He, too, is in my book.' She realised what she had said and quickly tapped the side of her head. 'My ledger is between my ears, Sir John. And, Sir John, that's all I can tell you.' Vulpina waggled her fingers in mock farewell.

'Thank God we are out of there!' Athelstan breathed as they walked back up the main alleyway out of Whitefriars. 'Sir John, what a tangle of weeds we've got here.'

'It's a tangle all right.' The coroner stopped and scratched his head. 'We really should visit the Lady Angelica, but Brother...'

'No need to apologise. My legs are tired and my belly's empty. I want to go back and talk to Bonaventura.'

'Not to mention Judas the goat!'

'Thaddeus,' Athelstan corrected him. 'It's Thaddeus now, Sir John. But, what about this?'

'We frightened Vulpina. And so she threw us morsels. Don't forget, my good friar: Lady Maude visits an apothecary up Cheapside and buys poisons for the rats in our cellars, but that doesn't make her a murderess.'

'Yes, but she doesn't hide it, Sir John. Limbright, Maltravers and Aspinall have questions to answer.'

Sir John chewed on the corner of his lip then abruptly turned and stared down the alleyway.

'What's the matter, Sir John?'

'Vulpina's a murdering bitch, Athelstan, but she's no fool.' The coroner scratched his whiskers. 'Earlier, when we stopped to talk to the scrimperers, I had the feeling of being followed. Now I am certain of it. A shadow down the lane moved a little too slowly.'

He took a step forward but Athelstan caught at his arm.

'Sir John, let us go home.'

Athelstan stared about at the dingy houses, the lean, pinched faces which peered out from behind shabby doors, the clusters of beggars in alleyways. He saw one of them move and caught the glint of steel.

'Let's go home, Sir John,' he repeated. 'This is all a tangled web and we have truly entered the Devil's Domain!'

Chapter 7

Athelstan sat at his table and moved the candle a little closer. The evening had turned surprisingly chill so he had lit a fire which now crackled merrily in the hearth. Bonaventure, not yet ready for his nightly hunt, sat on the table delicately lapping a dish of milk. Every so often he would lift his head, his one good eye fixed curiously on his strange, eccentric master. Athelstan tickled the cat's nose with the tip of his quill. Bonaventure didn't flinch. He blinked and turned, staring into the far corner.

'I know what you are after,' Athelstan said.

The friar had seen a mouse scuttle across the floor of the hearth.

'But it's only a small mouse, Bonaventure. A harvest one. He's probably wandered in and will certainly wander out.'

Bonaventure purred deep in his throat.

'Soft as a shadow,' Athelstan went on. 'Sleek and fast. What do you think of Thaddeus?'

Bonaventure, of course, had gone out to inspect both the goat and Godbless. He had brushed the beggar man's leg with his body and sniffed at the goat. Athelstan, who had been present, knew that this lord of the alleyways regarded Thaddeus as beneath his attention.

Godbless had certainly made himself at home. Benedicta had kindly provided a straw-filled mattress, a bolster, two blankets, a dish and a pewter cup. Godbless now acted like a lord of the manor while Thaddeus was busy cropping the grass. Athelstan had taken him out a dish of stew from the pot Benedicta had brought together with some bread wrapped in a cloth and a jug of watered wine, a gift from Joscelyn at the Piebald Tavern.

Athelstan lifted his head and listened to the sounds of the night. Sometimes he would go out and wander the alleyways, stopping to talk to the beggars and night-walkers, the whores and drabs, the flotsam and jetsam of this decayed quarter of the city. Other times, when his mind was teeming, he would climb to the top of the church tower and stare up at the sky. Athelstan felt guilty at such indulgence but, the more he stared at the stars, the more he became aware of the power of God and the sheer beauty of this Creation. If only he could discover more. If he could only test the theories. Did the planets sing while they turned? Why did some stars gleam brighter than others? What held them in their place? They moved but, like the moon, kept their courses. What stopped them from falling to earth? And the meteors, particularly those bright ones which seared the heavens with their fiery tails, did they govern the affairs of men? Athelstan picked up his cup and sipped at it. He really must raise that matter with Prior Anselm. The Church condemned astrology but hadn't Christ's birth been heralded by a new star? And when the Saviour died hadn't the skies been blotted with darkness? Or was Aquinas the great writer correct? Was Creation the reflection of God, nothing to do with the affairs of Man?

Athelstan stared down at the parchment. 'From the sublime to the ridiculous,' he observed. He looked at the

heading, 'Hawkmere Manor', and the questions he had
listed.

> *Item – Five Frenchmen were imprisoned in that*
> *solitary place waiting to be ransomed. Was one of*
> *them a traitor? Had he revealed to the English*
> *Crown the movements of the St Sulpice and the*
> *St Denis? If that was the case, why wasn't one*
> *prisoner favoured more than the rest? It could be*
> *arranged. More comfortable quarters in the Tower.*
> *Or would that expose him? Show the truth and*
> *so make it impossible for him to return to France?*
>
> *Item – How did Serriem die? He was definitely*
> *poisoned. But how, if he only ate and drank*
> *what the others did? Or had he been inveigled*
> *into eating something, a delicacy which, to such*
> *an imprisoned man, might prove irresistible? But*
> *surely that would put him on his guard? Moreover,*
> *in that atmosphere of suspicion, surely no prisoner*
> *would want to be seen favoured above the rest?*
>
> *Item – Who was the murderer? One of his*
> *companions? But where would they get the poison*
> *from? And how would they administer it without*
> *provoking suspicion?*
>
> *Item – Sir Walter Limbright was a bitter, resentful*
> *man who hated the French. He claimed there were*
> *no poisons in the manor. However, if Vulpina was*
> *to be believed, he had been one of her customers;*
> *the same could be said of Sir Maurice Maltravers*
> *and Master Aspinall. Was the good physician*
> *embroiled in the affairs of Hawkmere? Had he*

taken offence because of a possible liaison with the girl-faced Gresnay?

Item – What happened the night Serriem died? Who had locked the door? Had anyone checked on the prisoners? What was the state of the room when it was opened?

Item – Did the French know there was a traitor in their midst? Had all these men been condemned to die? Was the poisoner Gaunt? Had he instructed this traitor, if he was at Hawkmere Manor, to poison the rest? But wouldn't that expose his agent? And what would happen to him? A simulated death, before being secretly pensioned off to some lonely manor on the Welsh marches?

Item – An unknown priest had been seen at Whitefriars. A possible customer of Vulpina? But who would that be?

Athelstan glanced up. I wonder what Sir John's doing, he thought. He smiled to himself as he recalled the two poppets. Never had he seen two sturdy sons so resemble their father: balding heads, fat, red faces, little paunches and sturdy legs. The poppets spent most of their day telling each other off or chasing Gog and Magog around the house. Athelstan returned to the parchment.

'There's something wrong here, Bonaventure,' he said. Something intangible he couldn't grasp. He recalled Gaunt slouched in his chair. 'That's it!' Athelstan stroked Bonaventure. 'My Lord Regent is like a cat who has taken the best of the cream and intends to go back for more.'

What was he so pleased about? Gaunt had a lot to gain, Athelstan reflected. The Commons would be pleased that notorious French privateers were now in prison. He had the ransoms to look forward to while Maltravers was one of his henchmen so the Regent could bask in his reflected glory. And Vulpina? Despite the wine he had drunk, old Jack Cranston had really shaken that woman's wickedness. She was nervous, eager to give tidbits of information so she could hide the rest. Athelstan put his face in his hands. There were links: Maltravers had taken the two French ships; Gaunt was now furthering Sir Maurice's cause with the divine Lady Angelica. Sir Thomas Parr partly owned *The Great Edward*, the ship Sir Maurice had used in his fight against the French privateers. Sir Maurice had bought poisons. He also supplied Hawkmere Manor with food. Why should a knight banneret be engaged in such petty details? True, in a great lord's household, even a retainer like Maltravers would have a wide range of tasks: some petty, others matters of life and death. But where was all this leading to?

Athelstan got to his feet and stretched. Bonaventure copied him and leapt down from the table. The cat padded over to the door. Athelstan opened it.

'Good hunting!' he said.

He was about to close the door again when a voice called, 'Brother Athelstan!'

'Who is it? Ah, Godbless, you gave me a start!'

The beggar man, Thaddeus trotting behind him, walked into the dim pool of light.

'What's the matter, Godbless? Can't you sleep? Are you hungry?'

The beggar man looked up, his eyes heavy with sleep.

'There be ghosts in God's acre.'

'Ghosts! Godbless, go back to bed! The only ghosts in that graveyard are Cecily the courtesan or Watkin and Pike. You have not met these, have you?'

Godbless shook his head.

'There are no ghosts. Go back to bed. Lock your door.'

'Brother, I be really a-feared and so be Thaddeus.' Godbless looked longingly past Athelstan.

'All right!' The Dominican stepped back.

Godbless sped like an arrow through the door, Thaddeus scampering after him. The beggar man sat down in front of the hearth.

'I always likes a fire,' he sighed. 'My wife used to light one.'

Athelstan, curious, put the latch on the door and drew the bolts. Thaddeus, he noticed with some amusement, was crouched next to Godbless.

'Were you married, Godbless?'

'Aye, Brother, came from Dorset. A yeoman farmer like the other mad buggers who took the King's penny and went to war. When I came back my wife and child were dead, sick of the plague. The manor lord had knocked down the fences, turning plough land to pasture, grazing it with sheep. I hate sheep. Fond of goats but can't stand sheep.'

'In the Gospel it's the other way round,' Athelstan joked.

'Don't be angry, Brother, but I don't believe in the Gospels. I'm not a Christian.'

'In which case,' Athelstan commented, 'you are in good company. Very few people are, Godbless.'

The beggar man squinted up at him. 'One day, Brother, I'll repay you for your kindness.'

Athelstan patted him on the shoulder. 'I'll get you some blankets.'

He made Godbless comfortable, told him there was food in the buttery and climbed the steps to his bed loft. There he washed his hands and face in the water bowl, took off his gown and slipped into his narrow cot bed. He prayed for a while. From below he heard Godbless snoring.

'Strange,' the Dominican mused. Godbless was a solitary man. He probably wandered the lanes of England and was used to sleeping in the most godforsaken spots but, tonight, he had been frightened. What had Godbless seen in the graveyard to wake him up, to make him so a-feared? Athelstan drifted off to sleep.

—

Vulpina sat in her chamber and regarded the cowled, masked stranger.

'Are you French?' she asked. 'Are you a priest?'

'Don't ask questions, Mistress.'

Vulpina was assured; his voice was low, cultured. She noticed his hands, for he had removed one of his gauntlets, showing that they were soft and white, not those of a man who dug the earth and grubbed for a living.

'You have come for some more of the poison?'

'And I cannot tarry long.'

Vulpina nodded and rose to her feet. She went across to the wooden panelling and pressed a secret place so it opened. From here she took out a large, wicker basket and a leather-bound ledger and brought them across. The stranger undid his purse. Vulpina's eyes glistened at the silver coins shaken out in a twinkling pile. She glanced sideways at the two bully boys who stood on either side of the door.

'A good night's profit,' she exclaimed, clapping her hands.

'Aye and more,' the stranger replied. 'I'll be a constant customer.'

'Then let's celebrate this alliance.'

Vulpina clapped her hands again and nodded at one of her bully boys. He brought across two goblets brimming with wine. Vulpina raised hers.

'To silver and gold and all it brings.'

The man raised his goblet but didn't sip it. He got to his feet. Vulpina looked up in alarm but the man was moving quickly. The throwing knife he drew from beneath his cloak caught the bully boy's back as the fellow returned to his position. The other one was so startled, his hand had barely touched the hilt of his dagger when the stranger moved swiftly, bringing the small arbalest hooked on his belt out and up. A click, and the whirling bolt struck Vulpina's bully boy straight in the face. The poisoner sprang to her feet. She tried to brush by this murderous stranger but he caught her by the shoulder and when she turned, lashing out at his face, this only helped him loop the garrotte more securely round her throat. She struggled and fought like a cat but the garrotte was now like a piece of steel choking off her breath. Vulpina crumpled to the floor. The assassin, bending over her, kept the garrotte string tight until her death tremors ceased. He picked up the wine goblets and poured the contents over her corpse. The bully boy who had taken a dagger in the back was moaning, so the stranger moved quickly to slash the unfortunate's throat. He picked up the book of poisons, sat down and went through it carefully, turning the pages over. When he was satisfied, he took the basket of poisons and the ledger and pushed them into the hearth. He then went to the saddlebags he had left just inside the door and pulled out the wineskin which he had filled with oil and poured this over the carpets. The fire had already caught at the baskets, the pots exploding, the chamber filling with an acrid smell. The assassin took a fire brand out. He went and opened the shutters and stared down: the crumbling wall provided enough footholds. He threw the firebrand into a pool of oil and eased himself out. Even as he climbed down, the flame caught the oil. Vulpina, her bully boys, her potions and poisons and all the contents of her secret chamber, were caught up in a sheet of raging fire.

—

Murder also made itself felt in another part of the city, as if it were some loathsome shadow which could scurry as swiftly as the wind along its alleyways and runnels. The Golden Cresset Tavern which stood opposite the hospital of St Anthony was a merry, spacious ale-house with a broad taproom and luxurious chambers for wealthy merchants and others who visited the city. Margaret, the chamber-maid, was however puzzled about two of her customers.

First, a young knight, Sir Maurice Maltravers, had come to the tavern saying someone wished to meet him there. Margaret remembered him because he looked handsome yet rather sad and lonely. He'd sat for an hour in the corner cradling a blackjack of ale, absentmind-edly watching a juggler who had come to pleasure the customers in return for a hot meal and a goblet of wine, but then he had gone. Secondly, the young woman who had arrived late in the afternoon and hired a chamber above stairs had hardly shown her face. Tobias the tap boy had tried the latch but the door was secure and, when he rapped, no answer was made. Margaret went across to where her father the taverner stood beside the butts.

'What is it, girl?'

'Our lady guest,' she replied. 'It's been some hours now, Father.'

The taverner wiped his greasy fingers on his apron. It was late Saturday evening and the taproom was beginning to fill. Young fops with their doxies, travellers staying over till Monday.

'We'll be busy soon.' He sighed. 'Oh, very well, come on.'

He followed her upstairs and rapped on the door.

'What name did she give?' he asked.

'Mistress Triveter.'

'Mistress Triveter!' he called, feeling slightly ridiculous. 'Mistress Triveter, are you well?'

No answer. He knocked again.

'Mistress Triveter, I beg you, I must open this door!'

He jangled the keys which swung on a cord from his belt. He fingered through them looking for the master, but when he slipped this into the lock he groaned: the chamber key was still inside.

'Father,' Margaret appealed. 'I think there's something very wrong.'

'We can't force the door.'

They went downstairs out into the cobbled yard. Tobias the tap boy brought across a ladder and, at his master's bidding, gingerly climbed up.

'Go on!' the taverner urged. 'Open the window!'

Tobias drew back the shutter; the casement window beyond was slightly open and he climbed into the gloomy room. At first he didn't believe it. The bed looked as if it had been slept in, at least the blankets had been disturbed. Later, he told customers in hushed tones, he first thought Mistress Triveter was standing on a stool but then he gave a low cry. The stool had been kicked away and the young woman, her lustrous red hair falling round her face, was swinging by a rope lashed to one of the rafters above.

–

Athelstan took off his robes, placed them on the table in his small sacristy and bowed to the crucifix. He then knelt on the prie-dieu and recited a short prayer of thanksgiving.

'Brother Athelstan!'

He turned. Crim the altar boy was dancing from foot to foot.

'Go outside if you want a pee, boy. I've told you not to drink from the water butts before Mass. It's cold and it'll go straight through you.'

'It's not that, Brother.' Crim crinkled his face. He'd washed it but the dirt was simply pushed up around his ears. 'Is it a sin to belch in church?'

'Why, Grim?'

'Because I was doing it during Mass. Mother made a stew last night…'

'It's no sin.' Athelstan patted him on the head. 'Always remember, Crim, sin comes from the will. You must mean evil or disrespect and God has mercy on a rumbling stomach. Are you well now?'

'I will be soon, Brother.'

And the boy dashed out of the side door, heading for the enclosed privy on the outside of the church.

Athelstan walked back into the sanctuary. He ensured all was well and went down the nave; most of his parishioners were thronging in the porch. Watkin's and Pike's wives had put up a trestle table and were busy selling church ales drawn from small kegs and barrels placed on stools. Athelstan wondered how much of the money would eventually find its way into parish coffers. Yet he was resigned to such losses. His parishioners weren't thieves, just very poor and, as he'd remarked to Sir John, it's easy to be virtuous when you are not tempted.

'Morning, Brother.' They all raised their battered, leather black-jacks of ale.

'It's a beautiful day, Brother.' Pernell the Fleming woman spoke up.

Athelstan agreed; he had been out for a walk before Mass. He'd left Godbless and Thaddeus in the cemetery and checked on Philomel. The old war horse never seemed to age and ate as if his life depended on it. Athelstan walked to the door of the church. Parishioners sat on steps enjoying the sunlight. Children ran around, dogs yapped. Ursula the pig woman's huge sow came rumbling up, heading straight for Ranulf the rat-catcher who had a stack of apples between his feet. He was snapping them with his hands, sharing them out to his brood of a family, all dressed the same in their little black jackets with hoods and cowls like their father's. Athelstan went back into the church where a small crowd now thronged round Godbless.

'There's ghosts in the cemetery,' Watkin declared sonorously.

'Ah yes.' Athelstan looked waraingly at Cecily who was combing her long, blonde hair with her fingers: the minx stared innocently back. 'Who was in the cemetery last night?'

A chorus of: 'Not me, Brother!' greeted his question.

'Well, someone was. Godbless here definitely heard something.' He looked questioningly at the beggar man, Thaddeus standing proudly beside him. 'What exactly did you see, Godbless?'

'Shapes and shadows in the moonlight,' Godbless replied mournfully. His eyes looked troubled. 'I do not mean to cause any trouble but I know what I saw.'

Athelstan excused himself and went outside. The cemetery was quiet except for the buzzing bees and a host of butterflies which swarmed like miniature angels over the green grass. A peaceful, serene place with its crumbling headstones and decaying wooden crosses.

Athelstan followed the path to the death house and looked in. Godbless had certainly made himself at home. In fact, Athelstan had never seen the place look so clean and homely. He closed the door and glimpsed the pile of earth on the rim of the ditch Watkin and Pike were digging along the cemetery wall. He walked across. The earth was dry and powdery, baking under the summer sun. Athelstan stared down at the ditch: it must be three to four feet deep but he could see nothing untoward. He walked round the cemetery but discovered only a faded pink ribbon. He smiled and picked it up.

'Brother, are you hiding?'

Athelstan jumped. Sir John was standing near the church, Sir Maurice Maltravers beside him.

'Lord save us!' Athelstan whispered. 'It must be trouble.'

Sir John never bothered him on a Sunday. Indeed, it was becoming customary for Moleskin to row Athelstan across the river so he could spend the afternoon with Jack and his family, especially on a day like this. They would sit in an arbour in Sir John's garden. The coroner would sup his ale and pontificate upon everything and everyone, Athelstan listening quietly beside him. The poppets would stagger around, the two great mastiffs doze in the shade.

'What's wrong, Sir John?'

Athelstan walked towards them. Sir Maurice looked pale, even sickly, his face haggard, his eyes red-rimmed from lack of sleep. Sir John, on the other hand, looked the picture of health. He was dressed in his Sunday best, a purple doublet over a cream satin shirt, tied at the neck with a silver collar. He opened the wallet on the shiny belt round his great girth, took out a small scroll and thrust it into Athelstan's hand.

The Dominican sat down on a gravestone and studied it. The writing was small, the letters imperfectly formed.

> *To my beloved, I have journeyed up from Dover. I have begged to see you but you have refused. So, what is life without love? You have used me. You have forsaken me so I have forsaken life. Signed: Anna Triveter.*

'What is this?' Athelstan asked.

'You'd best come with us,' Sir John said. 'Our young knight here has a great deal of explaining to do.'

Athelstan returned to the church where Benedicta was sitting on a stool talking to Bladdersniff the bailiff. The young widow woman looked up.

'Lock the church,' Athelstan told her. 'Keep an eye on the house and Godbless. Oh, by the way.' He thrust the piece of faded pink ribbon into her hand. 'Tell Cecily the graveyard is for the dead to lie in, not the living!'

Sir John and Sir Maurice were waiting impatiently at the corner of the alleyway. Sir John marched as if he were advancing towards an enemy, his whole body bristling with anger. Athelstan looked across at Sir Maurice but the young knight was like some tired dog lost in his own sea of troubles.

They didn't take a wherry. Sir John was too impatient. Instead they strode across London Bridge. Athelstan quietly murmured a prayer of thanks that Master Burdon, the diminutive keeper of the bridge gate, did not espy them, for he always loved to chat to Sir John. Athelstan averted his eyes from the poles jutting out over the bridge bearing the severed, rotting heads of traitors. The alleyways between the shops and houses built on either side were quiet. They passed the chapel of St Thomas. From inside Athelstan heard singing as the community of the bridge attended their Sunday Mass, then they were across, going up through the quiet streets.

'What is the matter, Sir John?'

Cranston stopped and wiped the sweat from his brow.

'We are going to the Golden Cresset. It stands opposite St Anthony's hospital in Bishopsgate. Last night,' he tapped his wallet where he had returned the scroll, 'or yesterday evening, a young woman, Anna Triveter, hired a chamber. She locked and bolted the door, closed the shutters and promptly hanged herself.'

Athelstan closed his eyes.

'She must be twenty summers old,' Sir John continued. 'She had apparently come from Dover. Her palfrey is still in the stable. Apparently a young woman of some repute.'

'And what is she to do with you, Sir Maurice?'

'Well, our young Hector here, when he was in Dover, formed a relationship with a Mistress Triveter.'

'What sort of relationship?'

'You saw the scroll.' Sir John pulled it out.

Athelstan read the line on the reverse side.

'Oh heaven protect us!' he whispered. 'I didn't see this: "To my husband Sir Maurice Maltravers".'

'She is not my wife!' Sir Maurice retorted.

'Did you know Mistress Triveter?'

'I have never met her in my life.'

'Have you seen the corpse?'

He shook his head.

'Have you ever been married before?'

Again the shake of the head.

'Was there a woman in Dover?'

Sir Maurice looked away.

'Well?' Sir John asked sharply. 'Answer the question, Sir Maurice!'

'There was a woman,' he replied. 'A young wench. One of the many who hung around our camp near the port. She was comely enough.'

'And her name?'

'Anna, that's all I remember.'

Athelstan breathed in and closed his eyes.

'Yet,' he said slowly, 'we now have a woman who has committed suicide and left this letter for you.'

'Hell's teeth!' Sir John cursed. 'Sir Maurice, I trusted you.'

'And you still can!' the knight retorted. 'I am a soldier, Sir John. Like other young men, I drink ale and ogle the wenches but that was before Angelica!'

'So why should a young girl commit suicide in a London tavern?'

'I don't know, Sir John! I really don't!'

They continued up into Cheapside, crossing Carfax. Here the streets were not so empty now. The cage on top of the great water conduit was full of all the rabble apprehended the previous evening by the city watch. Some lay in the great wooden stockade still suffering from drinking too much. Others shouted greetings to friends, a few cursed as Athelstan and Sir John passed.

At last they reached the Golden Cresset. The taverner was waiting for them in the taproom surrounded by his scullions and servants, white-faced and anxious.

'Where's the corpse?' Sir John demanded.

Athelstan could see that the coroner was very, very angry. He didn't even bother to seek any refreshment.

'You haven't touched anything, have you?' he asked as the taverner stepped forward.

The man, dressed in his church attire, shook his head. He looked awkward and ill at ease in his rather large polished boots.

'Have you been to Mass?' Athelstan asked kindly.

'Oh yes, Brother. I don't know your name?'

'Brother Athelstan. I am parish priest at St Erconwald's. I'm also secretarius to my lord coroner here.'

'We've been to Mass but I left Tobias the tap boy. He guarded the chamber. I didn't want those piddling beadles in...'

'Take us up!' Sir John ordered.

They climbed the stairs to the gallery. The young boy seated with his back to the door pressed down the latch and swung the door open.

'Oh, sweet Lord!' Sir Maurice gasped.

'I know you.'

Athelstan turned. A young woman stood in the doorway pointing at Sir Maurice.

'You were here yesterday evening, in the taproom!'

He just slumped down on the stool and put his face in his hands.

Chapter 8

'Come on!' Sir John urged. 'Help us cut the poor woman down!'

While Sir Maurice held the corpse, Sir John sawed through the rope. The body was laid on the bed. Athelstan leaned down, noting that the face was swollen and purple, the tongue protruding, the eyes darkening, all beauty and grace spoilt by her violent death throes. Athelstan, heavy-hearted, whispered into the poor girl's ears the Act of Contrition followed by the words of absolution. He heard a squeaking in the corner and, without thinking, picked up a pot which lay on the table and flung it angrily at the rat scurrying there. As he loosened the noose knot, the body, now stiffening, trembled a little. He brushed back the hair and tried to close the eyes but they remained half-open, gazing sightlessly upwards. He took a rag from the wash bowl, carefully wiped the woman's mouth and chin then glanced round. The taverner and his daughter, goodly folks, stood in the doorway.

'It's not your fault,' Athelstan said. 'Where's the woman's baggage?'

The taverner opened a coffer at the foot of the bed and brought out a pair of saddlebags. The contents comprised nothing but a change of clothing, shoes and a small purse containing a few silver coins. Athelstan handed two of these to the taverner.

'For your trouble,' he offered. 'Sir John, where will the corpse go?'

'Once we have viewed it, since it is summer,' the coroner replied lugubriously, 'she must be buried quickly. Send your tap boy,' he told the taverner, 'to the Harrower of the Dead. You know who he is?'

The taverner swallowed hard and nodded.

'Before you go,' Athelstan said. 'A few questions. When did this young woman come here?'

'Yesterday afternoon.'

Athelstan gestured at the corpse. 'And she was dressed like this, a blue taffeta dress?'

'No,' his daughter replied. 'She was wearing travel garb, a brown smock tied at the neck and a kirtle beneath. She gave me these to wash, they are in the laundry house now.'

'Then what?' Athelstan asked. He smiled. 'Oh, your name?'

'Margaret. I came up here. She was a young gentle-woman. She said she had travelled from Dover.'

'And?'

'By the time I came up she had changed. She gave me the clothes and said to have them washed and dried; the cost was to be put on the final reckoning. I asked if she wanted something to eat or drink. She refused so I left.'

'And her horse?'

'A brown-berried palfrey,' the taverner said. 'Still in the stable below, saddled and harnessed.'

'Continue.' Athelstan sat on the bed at the side of the corpse.

The taverner shuffled his feet.

'Well, the hours passed. My daughter became concerned but the door was locked and bolted from the inside. So Tobias the tap boy climbed up from the stable yard.' He spread his hands. 'I then sent for the coroner. I was going to cut her down but I know the city regulations: the corpse must be left as you'd find it.'

'Good man.' Sir John took a sip from his wineskin.

'I assure you, sir, we have touched nothing nor have we taken anything from this poor girl. I know nothing of her death.'

'And no one visited her?'

'Not even this young man here?' Athelstan pointed at Sir Maurice.

'He was in the taproom,' Margaret replied. 'Cradling a blackjack of ale and looking very woebegone but, to my knowledge, he never came up here.'

'Nor asked to see Anna Triveter?' Athelstan asked.

Margaret shook her head.

'Very well.' Sir John drew himself up. 'Master Taverner, this is the corpse of the young woman who came here?'

'It is, my lord coroner.'

'And you have taken nothing from the corpse or her belongings?'

'No!'

'Very well.' Sir John turned to Sir Maurice. 'Sir Maurice Maltravers, knight banneret of His Grace the Duke of Lancaster, do you recognise this corpse?'

'No, sir, I do not.'

'Have you, or did you, have dealings with her?'

'I did not.'

'On your oath?'

'On my oath, Sir John, I had nothing to do with her in life and I certainly had nothing to do with her in death.'

'Then this is my verdict,' the coroner declared. 'Anna Triveter, supposed inhabitant of Dover, did feloniously kill herself on Saturday evening, 29th August in the year of Our Lord 1380. Right!' He clapped his hands. 'Now we've got that over. Master Taverner, you may keep all the woman's possessions, including her clothing, her horse and silver. When the Harrower of the Dead collects her corpse, you must arrange for honourable burial in the paupers' graveyard at St Mary-Le-Bow and pay for a chantry priest to sing five Masses before the Feast of the Epiphany next. On your oath do you accept?'

'I do, my lord coroner. But...'

'What's the matter, sir?'

Athelstan trusted the taverner, who had a broad, honest face, a family man who'd acted honourably. Many an innkeeper would have filched the silver and claimed the horse had been stolen. The taverner wet his lips.

'Well, Brother. I now recognise you. You are Athelstan, aren't you, from St Erconwald's in Southwark? Watkin the dung-collector sometimes comes here!'

'I am sure he does,' Athelstan replied dryly. 'He's well known in many of the taverns in the city.'

'As I am,' Sir John added warningly. 'But what's the matter, fellow?'

'She's a suicide,' the taverner blurted out. 'She should be buried at midnight at a crossroads outside the city!'

'She's a poor girl,' Athelstan replied. 'Who probably killed herself while her wits were fuddled.' He picked up the corpse's hand and looked at the fingernails carefully. 'And we don't know whether it's suicide or not, do we?'

'The coroner has pronounced his verdict.'

'The coroner has pronounced his verdict on what is obvious. However, the more I stand here, the greater a niggling doubt grows.'

He moved to the bed and began to study the young woman's hair most carefully, parting it, letting the strands run through his fingers. He reminded Sir John of Lady Maude examining the two poppets' heads for lice.

'Can I go?' the taverner asked.

'Yes, but stay downstairs until the Harrower of the Dead arrives and we are finished.'

Cranston leaned against the wall, mopping his brow while Sir Maurice stood, arms folded. Athelstan continued his examination of the woman's corpse: the hair, the nails, then he lifted the skirt and began to examine her torso.

'Should you do that?' Sir Maurice asked.

'A corpse is a corpse. The soul has gone, all beauty of the body is dead.'

He examined the woman's belly carefully. The skin of the thighs was covered in pimples and blotches. He shifted the corpse to look along the back.

'What are you searching for, Athelstan?'

The Dominican made the body decent.

'Are you going to say she was hanged?'

'Here we have a young woman,' Athelstan said. He clicked his tongue against his lower lip. 'She calls herself Anna Triveter and travels from Dover to London. Her one desire is to see her beloved Sir Maurice Maltravers. Young man! You can lean against that wall and sulk or you can co-operate with us.'

'I am not sulking,' Maltravers retorted. 'Brother, I am furious! I did not know this woman. And until Sir John here sent a message to the Savoy Palace, I didn't know...'

'Of course you didn't,' Athelstan interrupted cheerfully.

'What's that?' Sir John lowered the half-raised wine-skin.

'It's a matter of logic,' said Athelstan. 'Anna here arrives at the Golden Cresset.' He pointed to her boots which lay just within the doorway. 'Pick those up, Sir John.'

Cranston did so; they were small, rather fashionable, made of leather with silver buckles.

'Look at the heels and soles.'

The coroner did so.

'They are clean, aren't they?'

'She could have done that herself.'

'Oh, she did.'

Athelstan walked over to the wooden lavarium which bore a bowl, a jug and, on the floor beneath, a pile of rags. He picked one up. It was dirty and wet.

'Brother.' Sir John glowered at the Dominican. 'Don't let's dance round the mulberry bush. It stands to reason the woman was tired and exhausted after her journey. She cleaned her boots as many a traveller would. She changed her garb and sent it to the wash-house.'

'And then she'd just commit suicide.' Athelstan pointed to the rope. 'Where did she get that from?'

'There's a coil left in every room.' Sir Maurice spoke up. 'In case of fire.' He pointed to what was left of the rope still lying in a corner. He went over and picked up the knife still lying there. 'She cut some of this, put one end round the beam, formed a noose and put that round her neck.'

'But,' Athelstan objected, 'why should a young woman who is desirous of seeing you, Sir Maurice, come into this chamber, change her clothing, wash her boots, bolt and lock the door and then hang herself? Above all, where did she get the writing material?' Athelstan asked. 'For that last lovelorn letter?'

'I see what you mean,' Sir John breathed.

'I don't think she committed suicide. I doubt if her name's Anna Triveter and I don't think she came from Dover.' Athelstan smiled apologetically at Cranston. 'I am sorry to upset your verdict so soon, but it's best if these matters are kept secret!'

'Continue!' the coroner barked.

'Anna Triveter is probably a whore. If you examine her finger-nails, Sir John, down near the rim around the skin, you'll see the traces of paint. If you examine her hair it is beautiful, lustrous and red, but among the roots you will find the traces of dye. Her body is marked, small cuts on her back. Welts which healed some time ago. I suspect she has been whipped or received the end of a birch, whether in punishment or pleasure,' Athelstan continued dryly, 'I do not know. Suffice to say, Sir John, Sir Maurice, this is not some young gentlewoman.'

'But why?' Sir John asked. 'What did happen?'

'She's a whore. And brought here to act the part. She's given a change of clothing, a set of saddlebags and some silver. She arrived at the Golden Cresset and, following instructions, has her clothes taken down to the wash-house while she wipes her boots.'

'But why?' Sir John again asked.

'Oh, Sir John, you've travelled many a day between Dover and Canterbury.'

'Of course. In summer the Pilgrims' Way is white chalk. It clings to your cloak. I've seen the travellers look so dusty you'd think they were covered in snow.'

'Precisely, Sir John. She has her clothes washed and her boots cleaned.'

He glanced at Sir Maurice. The young knight was just staring, open-mouthed; now and again his gaze would shift to the corpse stiffening on the bed.

'Now this is a busy tavern,' Athelstan continued. 'People coming and going, particularly on a Saturday. Poor Anna, who thinks she's never earned so much money so easily, lies down on the bed. She has done what she has been ordered to and waits for further instructions. The assassin enters. He locks and bolts the door behind him and crosses to the bed. Poor Anna is asleep, she struggles awake but the assassin's hand or probably a garrotte string is round her throat. She is dead before she can really gather her wits. The assassin's clever. He doesn't steal any of the silver but takes the knife she carried and cuts some of the rope. One part goes round the rafters, the other round the poor dead girl's neck. She's left hanging there. The rope is thick, harsh: the bruising and discoloration of death hides the real cause of death, strangulation by the garrotte string.'

'And the assassin?' Sir Maurice asked.

'Oh, he'd be cowled in some disguise. He'd wait for the tavern yard below to be empty. He then went to the window.'

'But the shutters were closed!'

Athelstan walked over. 'I know from Sir John that this is one of the easiest tricks of the guild of housebreakers. The assassin closed one side of the shutter, climbed out on to the sill, pulling the other behind him, then dropped to the ground.'

'But he could have been seen, even seized?'

'Sir John, it would only take a few seconds to flee and be lost in some city side street. Anyway, who'd be brave enough to challenge him?'

'And the letter?'

'Oh, before the murderer left, the love note was placed near the corpse. One final thing. Sir Maurice, you know a great deal about horses. Go down to the stables, carefully check the palfrey this young woman is supposed to have ridden all the way from Dover, then come back and tell us what you have found.'

The knight hurried off.

'It's the first time I've seen any life in him,' Sir John remarked, closing the door. 'Do you really believe, Athelstan, this poor woman was murdered?'

'See for yourself, Sir John. Look at the hair, the nails, the neck.'

'Yes, I see it,' he said, holding the fingers. 'Just near the quick of the thumb, traces of paint.'

He examined the woman's hair and then looked carefully at the neck, scarred horribly by the rope. He'd barely finished when Sir Maurice reentered the room. It was the first time Athelstan had really seen him smile.

'Brother, I tell you this.' The knight rubbed his hands. 'The palfrey's a sturdy little cob but it has no more travelled from Dover than I have. The hooves are freshly shod.'

'That could have been done when they reached London,' Sir John said.

'I don't think so, Sir John,' Athelstan replied. 'I suspect poor Anna Triveter travelled no more than a mile.'

'Parr!' Sir Maurice cried. 'This is the work of Sir Thomas Parr!'

'But it's clumsy.' Sir John spoke up. 'Sir Thomas is a man who can call on an army of retainers and indulge in the most subtle stratagems.'

'It is clumsy,' Athelstan said. 'Young man.' He walked towards the knight. 'We have questions for you and a lot depends on your answers. This was an evil and cunning trick. True, Sir John and I can prove that Anna Triveter no more travelled from Dover, than we have journeyed from Jerusalem. But that's because both of us are trained in the art of observation, logic and deduction. We are skilled hunters,' Athelstan continued, 'of the sons of Cain: those who kill in the darkness and then step out into the light, wipe their lips and say they've done no wrong.' He pointed to the corpse. 'However, to the untrained eye, here is a young woman who claims to be handfast to you. She has travelled from Dover and, because of your rejection, took her own life. So, a few questions and some are repetitious. Have you ever met this woman before?'

'No, Brother, on my soul!'

'But you consorted with a girl called Anna in Dover?'

'Yes, Brother, a whore. I've been shriven of my sin and done penance.' Sir Maurice licked his lips. 'I beg you to keep that as a matter for the confessional. It was before I met the Lady Angelica. Since then I have had eyes for no other woman. My life has been chaste, my mind and soul pure.'

He spoke so passionately, Athelstan accepted the knight was telling the truth.

'Very well.' Athelstan tightened the cord round his waist, fingering the three knots there, each a reminder of his vows of poverty, chastity and obedience. 'We now have Anna Triveter who walks into this play unannounced. We know she is a whore. However, she comes here and pretends to be your common-law wife who has travelled all the way from Dover. She cleans her boots and has her travelling smock washed because she wishes to hide the fact that she has probably travelled no further than from one of the wards in the city. She has been hired by someone who kills her, hoists her corpse up on the end of that rope and leaves a letter for the world to read. The assassin then slips out of the window. Agreed?'

Sir Maurice nodded.

'So, why did you come to this tavern yesterday?' The Dominican held up a hand. 'No, let me tell you: a messenger came to the Savoy Palace and asked for you?'

'One of the oldest tricks in the book,' Sir John observed.

'It was a beggar boy,' Sir Maurice replied. 'He arrived at the Savoy about two hours after I left you. The guards stopped him but he said he had an important message. I came down, and the boy, a little street urchin, said that, at the Golden Cresset, there was a messenger waiting for me from the Lady Angelica.'

'Ah!' Athelstan exclaimed. 'That would confirm my suspicions. Go on!'

'I didn't think twice. I came here, bought a blackjack of ale and stayed for over an hour.'

'Didn't you bother to ask anyone?' Sir John asked.

'By the time I reached the Golden Cresset, my ardour had cooled. I wondered if I had been deceived. Was it a trap? I told the tavern wench my name and said I expected someone. Time passed. I finished the ale and I left, angry at such trickery.' He scratched his head. 'I didn't know whom to blame. Such pettiness was beneath Sir Thomas Parr. I thought it might be one of my companions in the Lord Regent's household inventing a jest, a jape to while away the time.'

Sir John came across and, moving the blankets, began to cover up the corpse.

'But you can see I'm innocent!' Sir Maurice cried.

'Oh, I'll change my verdict. But don't you understand, Sir Maurice? Brother Athelstan and I know the truth but what will the world think? A woman lies here dead! The letter! The gossip will seep out like wine from a cracked vat. Sir Thomas Parr will hear about it.' The coroner gazed sadly at him. 'Worse still, the Lady Angelica too.'

'Sir John has the truth of it,' Athelstan agreed. 'Even if we change the verdict, they'll accuse us of covering up a crime of one of Gaunt's henchmen. Can't you see, Sir Maurice, the assassin probably knew we'd discover the truth but the damage is done. If you throw enough mud, some always sticks!'

Sir Maurice's hand went to his dagger, his face white with fury. 'I'll kill any man who accuses me! I'll call him out!'

'Oh, for the love of God!' Sir John cried. 'What are you going to do, Sir Maurice, fight every man in London?'

'Sir Thomas Parr knows the truth,' Sir Maurice spat back. 'He arranged all this.'

'Sir Maurice! Sir Maurice!' Athelstan grabbed his hand. 'I could prove in a court of law that this young woman was murdered and did not commit suicide but we still don't know who she is or where she came from.' Athelstan paused. 'We have no proof that Parr or anyone else is guilty of her death. The finger of suspicion still points at you. It blemishes your reputation and tarnishes your honour.'

'It creates a doubt,' Sir John said. 'And that was the whole purpose of this terrible crime. Is Sir Maurice Maltravers who he claims to be? It could take months to comb the records of Dover, and even longer to find out where this young woman actually comes from. And in the end the gossip will be through the city. Sir Maurice seduced some young gentlewoman, secured her body, after marriage celebrated by some hedge-priest, then he rejected her so the young woman took her own life.'

Sir Maurice's face was now white as a sheet, beads of sweat coursed down his cheeks.

'I'm a fighting man,' he whispered. 'I see my enemy and I meet him honourably on the field of battle: shield against shield, sword against sword. I cannot deal with this.'

'Oh yes you can.' Athelstan pushed him towards a stool and made him sit down. He then stood over him, one hand on his shoulder. 'We have other questions.' He paused.

Footsteps sounded up the stairs and along the gallery followed by a knock on the door.

Athelstan had met the Harrower of the Dead before but he still flinched as the man came into the chamber. A tall, black cowl was pulled over his head, his face covered by a death mask. He came into the room, black leather leggings creaking. In one hand he carried a canvas sheet neatly folded, in the other a length of rope.

'My lord coroner, we meet again.' The Harrower's voice was low, soft, well modulated.

'Aye, sir, death is always busy. And his leavings are scattered throughout the city.'

The Harrower moved across to the bed. In a businesslike manner he moved the corpse, gently wrapping the canvas sheet round it, tying it secure with his piece of rope. The taverner stood in the doorway, his face ashen.

'Will this take long?' he moaned. 'There are customers, my trade will suffer.'

'It will do nothing of the sort,' the Harrower replied, his voice muffled. 'People will flock to you to ask what happened. You'll sell more ale than you would on a Holy Day or May Day.' He secured the corpse and lifted the sheeted body gently like a mother would a child. 'It should be buried soon, my lord coroner.'

'Today. The innkeeper will pay you all dues. A pauper's grave in St Mary's but not in the common ditch: by herself with a wooden cross bearing her name. The taverner will provide it. God rest her!' The coroner turned away, waving his hand.

The Harrower left. The taverner crossed himself and closed the door behind him. Athelstan waited until the sound of footsteps faded.

Sir Maurice sat on the stool, arms folded, ankles locked, tense and watchful. Athelstan felt a pang of compassion.

'Right, Sir Maurice!' he began. 'You claim you are innocent and I believe you, though later I will ask you to swear to that. However, first, you must not blame Sir Thomas Parr. Your betrothal to the Lady Angelica must have provoked resentment and jealousy, even hatred, from many others at daring to aspire so high. You are also a hero responsible for the capture and destruction of two marauding French privateers. You yourself said that you thought your visit here yesterday was some joke, a trick arranged by people in Lord Gaunt's household. Moreover, there are others in the city, such as Monsieur Charles de Fontanel the French envoy. He, too, will have taken an active interest in your doings. So, I beg you, keep a quiet tongue; do not lash out and make accusations which cannot be resolved.'

'In the meantime.' Sir John came over and thrust the miraculous wineskin at him. 'Go on, take some!'

He did, a generous swig which Sir John copied. He offered it to Athelstan but the Dominican shook his head.

'I have not eaten yet, Sir John.'

'Oh, well, please yourself. In the meantime we have other questions. Why did you go to the Lady Vulpina and buy a love philtre and some poisons?'

Sir Maurice coughed and put his face in his hands.

'You did go there, didn't you?' Athelstan asked quietly.

The young man sighed noisily. 'Vulpina is well known among the courtiers. I'll be honest, when Sir Thomas drove me away, I thought I would die. I went to her for a potion. I was stupid enough to think it would soothe the passions boiling within me. I hated the woman, sly, cunning and evil. Laughing at me behind her eyes, smirking at the bully boys who guarded her while I traded. I felt so embarrassed. I also asked for some poison.'

'To kill the rats in your chamber?' Athelstan intervened.

'Brother, please don't try to trap me. My Lord of Gaunt has his own rat-catchers. I bought it because,' he sighed, 'I felt mortified to be there.'

'I think you are two things,' Athelstan smiled. 'You are a brave warrior, Sir Maurice, and you are a hopeless liar. What you've told me is so fumbling, so ill prepared, it has to be the truth though God knows where we go from here.'

'I must see Angelica.' Sir Maurice grasped Athelstan's hand. 'Please, Brother, you must!'

Athelstan glanced at Sir John but the coroner looked mournful and shook his head.

'If I were a Dominican…' Sir Maurice said.

Athelstan let go of his hand and walked to the window. In the yard below the ostlers were beginning the day's work, leading out horses and, with huge rakes, dragging the dirty straw from the stables. An idea occurred to him but the time was not yet.

'We've examined the corpse,' Athelstan said slowly. 'We know the truth and there's not much more we can do. Sir Maurice, did you buy provisions for the prisoners at Hawkmere?'

'I've told you that, Brother. I go to Cheapside with one of the Regent's stewards. I simply buy what has to be bought and then it's taken by cart to Hawkmere.'

'And you have nothing to do with the prisoners themselves?'

'You've met them, Brother, they have as little time for me as I for them.'

'What do you mean?'

'My Lord Regent has held them for ransom but, in my eyes, they were pirates. They may have carried letters from their King in Paris but they attacked English cobs and killed their sailors. I'd have hanged all five out of hand.'

'Sir John Cranston! Sir John Cranston!'

Athelstan looked down into the yard.

A tipstaff carrying his white wand of office stood under the window.

'What is it?' Athelstan asked.

'My lord coroner is needed in Whitefriars. A message from the Guildhall: a woman's house, Vulpina's, was burned to the ground and her remains have been found.'

Chapter 9

Sir John Cranston mournfully surveyed the charred, reeking remains of what had once been his favourite tavern. Beadles and bailiffs kept back the crowd of beggars and alley people who thronged to gape at the site and look for any pickings. The three corpses pulled from the burned building now lay under a soiled canvas sheet.

'What I've eaten will stay,' he said. 'Pull it back!'

The bailiff, a black vizard across his face, his eyes watering, grasped the sheet.

'It's not a pleasant sight, Sir John.'

'She wasn't when she was alive, so what's the difference?'

The man pulled the sheet off. Athelstan turned away, his hand covering his mouth. The corpses were nothing but charred, mutilated flesh, black from head to toe. The eyes had watered, the skin round the face had shrivelled, making them look like grotesque gargoyles.

'Were they dead?' Sir John asked. 'When the fire broke out?'

'Dead or drunk. God knows what happened.'

The beadle turned one of the corpses over. The wooden bolt had burned but Athelstan could see the steel tip embedded deep in the charred flesh. Sir John walked away. Athelstan and Sir Maurice followed him, their boots crunching on the blackened ash. Sparks still floated up and the air was thick with acrid smoke.

'And everything was burned with her?' Athelstan sighed. 'Any records of potions and philtres all turned to ash.' He walked back on to the cobbles.

'What do you think, Sir John?' the beadle asked.

'Probably murder,' he replied. 'Brother?'

Athelstan gazed at the devastation.

'Someone probably visited Mistress Vulpina last night but it's pointless asking these what they know.'

The gallows men and wolfs-heads were watching them with narrow eyes, mournful that Vulpina, once the queen and patroness of these mean and foul alleyways, was now no more.

'Somebody came and killed Vulpina and two of her henchmen.' Athelstan shrugged. 'Some oil, a firebrand; as you say, Sir John, these buildings are old and dry. They burn like stubble under the sun.'

'My lord coroner.'

Sir John turned to see who spoke. The man standing behind him was small and pink-cheeked, with light blue eyes. With a shaven face and fluffy, white hair he reminded Athelstan of an ancient cherub. A short distance away three men-at-arms, wearing the royal livery, stood, hands on the hilts of their swords, their conical steel helmets gleaming in the sun, the broad nose-guards almost concealing their faces.

'Well I never!' Sir John stretched out his hand. 'Brother Athelstan, may I introduce to you Gervase Talbot, a man who is not as innocent as he appears. A lover of fine claret, subtle and cunning as a fox. Once chief clerk in the chancery of Edward the Black Prince, God bless his memory.'

Talbot stood on tiptoe and exchanged the kiss of peace with the fat coroner. He then did the same with Athelstan. The Dominican caught a fragrance of Castilian soap as well as a woman's perfume, light and sweet. Talbot's hand was soft but his grip was firm.

'Brother Athelstan, I've heard of you.' Gervase spoke just above a whisper, as his eyes wandered to the destruction behind him.

'So, Mistress Vulpina's gone to meet her maker, has she? Then God assoil her, she'll need all the mercy she can. A wicked woman…'

'Gervase, it's Sunday, you should be in your garden, tending your roses or singing one of your songs. A fine voice has Gervase,' Sir John explained.

'I'm still choir master in the church of St Oswald.' Gervase's hands disappeared up his sleeves. 'But move away, Sir John, the smoke here sours my mouth and spoils my throat.'

Sir John and Athelstan followed him across to the mouth of an alleyway. One of the soldiers immediately wandered up the runnel to ensure all was safe. The other two stood between their master and the crowd of curiosity-seekers.

'Gervase is Master of the King's Secrets,' Sir John explained.

Athelstan nodded. He'd heard of such an office, staffed by chancery clerks with a house just off Fleet Street. These clerks governed the spies and agents of the English court both at home and abroad. They listened to sailors and merchants, piecing together scraps and tidbits of information.

'You've to come with me, Sir John, and you, Brother Athelstan. My Lord of Gaunt is waiting for you at the House of Secrets.'

Sir John groaned. 'No rest for the wicked.'

'No, I am afraid not, Sir John. My lord Regent will tell you all. Sir Maurice!' he called out. 'You too!' His cherub face creased into a smile. 'I've heard about the death at the Golden Cresset,' he whispered. 'Is Maltravers involved?'

'A farrago of lies,' Athelstan retorted. He was curious about this little man and what the Regent should want with him and the coroner on a Sunday morning.

Gervase took off in a quick walk, almost a trot, his bodyguards all around him.

'What's this, Sir John?' Athelstan asked, plucking at the coroner's sleeve.

'I don't know. But something has happened. Gervase loves his roses and very rarely misses an opportunity to sing in the choir on a Sunday morning. Therefore it must be serious, indeed. My Lord of Gaunt should be out with his hounds hunting the deer.'

They left Whitefriars, entering the more salubrious areas around Fleet Street. The lanes here sloped towards the sewers in the middle. Athelstan quietly thanked God that it hadn't rained for the slope was quite precarious and the sewers brimmed with dirt. At the same time Athelstan kept an eye on the signs which hung out over the shops and could deal the unwary a nasty rap on the head. The 'Cupid and Torch' of the glazier, the 'Cradle' of the basket-maker, a naked 'Adam and Eve' for those who sold apples and 'Jack in the Green' for the brewers. On the corner of Bride Lane the collectors of dog turds, armed with small shovels, were filling their baskets for sale to the tanners and curers of skins.

'For some people,' Sir John observed, 'there is no Sunday or day of rest.'

He stopped a water tippler and paid for a ladleful from his bucket but he threw the ladle back and spat noisily.

'Your water's brackish!' he shouted at the small, mean-faced man. 'Empty it in the sewer and obtain some fresh or I'll have you whipped at the cart's arse!'

The man hurried off, the bucket bouncing across his shoulders, its water slopping out.

'In my treatise on the governance of the city...'

'Come on, Sir John!' Gervase Talbot stood on a corner of an alleyway.

'Yes, quite!' The coroner hurried on after him.

The House of Secrets stood in Rolls Passage which ran off Chancery Lane. It was a tall, narrow house with a red-bricked base, black beams and plaster on the upper stories. The windows were glazed with iron bars protecting the outside. The door was narrow but reinforced with great iron-studded nails. Gervase pulled at the bell. The door swung open and a clerk ushered them in. Inside the passageway was paved and clean swept. The walls were covered with polished panel work, above which coloured cloths and painted canvas sheets hung. The air smelled sweet with the smell of parchment, candles, sealing-wax and ink. On the ground floor were small chambers, most of them closed; but one was open and Athelstan espied the high stools and desks of the clerks, the latter covered in green baize cloth.

John of Gaunt was lounging in a room at the back of the house. He was sitting on a stool, sifting among the manuscripts on the floor. He smiled as they came in.

'My lord coroner, my apologies, and you, Brother Athelstan. However, as you can see,' Gaunt indicated his hunting jacket, leggings and boots, his spurs clinking at his every move, 'I, too, was preparing for other business but Gervase here said that he had matters to share with me.' He looked across at the hour candle beneath its glass. 'Come then, let's not waste time.'

Gervase called a clerk, more stools were brought in, their seats covered in quilted cushions. White wine was served, with fruits and nuts in small silver dishes. While Gervase was making his preparations Athelstan looked at his surroundings: there was a small mantelled hearth but virtually every wall in the room was covered in shelves and on these leather pouches, neatly tagged, were arranged in tidy piles. The large window at one end provided light. The candles in bronze brackets on the wall had hooded caps, protection against any spark.

'This is my second home,' Gervase remarked, following Athelstan's gaze and sitting down. 'Here, Brother, we have the gossip of the courts. Who's in favour at Avignon? Which cardinal will take bribes? Who's been elected to the Council of Ten in Venice? Which courtier is in the ascendant in Paris?' He lifted his goblet. 'I give you secrets.'

'Before we begin,' Gaunt interrupted, 'Sir Maurice, I heard about the business at the Golden Cresset.' He smiled. 'Or rather, Master Gervase told me. Sir Jack, you've been there?'

'I have, my lord, and Sir Maurice is as innocent as a newborn babe. A subtle, nasty trick to bring him into ill favour with his beloved.'

'That is not the style of Sir Thomas Parr.' Gervase spoke up. 'I have heard of your troubles, Sir Maurice.' He smiled sympathetically.

'It may have something to do with this,' Gaunt said. The Regent wagged a finger playfully at Sir Maurice, his handsome face crinkled into a smile, eyes narrowed. 'You are not in favour with the French, Sir Maurice. The *St Sulpice* and *St Denis* were two of their finest ships.'

'Do you think the French could have arranged the business at the Golden Cresset out of spite?' Sir Maurice asked hopefully.

'Perhaps, perhaps. But let's listen to what Master Gervase has learned.'

'I was disturbed early this morning,' Gervase began. 'Pompfrey was so excited. My spaniel,' he explained. 'A merchant had arrived from France, his name and status do not concern you but he's a good limner, a sniffer out of secrets. He often drinks in the taverns in the Ile de France and brushes shoulders with the clerks from the French chancery.'

'He's also well paid,' Gaunt interrupted harshly.

Gervase forced a smile which never reached his eyes.

'Of course, my lord. However, the man does risk life and limb. Silver and gold do not make up for legs and arms broken on the wheel at Montfaucon or bring you back from the gallows when your neck has been wrung.'

Athelstan lowered his head to hide his own smile. He rather liked this soft, gentle-spoken man who seemed as wary of the Regent as himself.

'Now, my friend from Paris was all excited. He'd left that city some days ago and travelled to Boulogne then on to Calais. We have a truce with France but he had to make sure that he wasn't being followed. Now the French have a master spy. We know something of him. He calls himself Mercurius, after the Greek god. He's well named. Secretive, sly, able to change his appearance. He's not only a spy but a very good assassin. We have heard of his exploits in the north Italian cities, Pisa, Genoa, Venice. Last year he was in Germany performing certain tasks for his masters back in Paris.'

'Such as?' Athelstan asked.

'Spying, trading in secrets and, above all, murder. A clerk from the French chancery ostensibly went on pilgrimage to the shrine of the Three Wise Men at Cologne. What he didn't tell his masters in Paris was that he took certain secrets with him and sold them to the burghers of Cologne. These were trade secrets: information which could allow someone to control the market in wines. Great rivalry exists between the vineyards of France and those of Germany. The clerk was well rewarded. Of course, he couldn't return to Paris but, on the receipt of his ill-gotten gains, he set himself up in some estate, a pleasant house overlooking Cologne Cathedral. One afternoon he was found swimming in his own carp pond, a garrotte string round his neck. The city council had no proof, but the whisper in the merchant community was that Mercurius had paid this French traitor a house visit.' Gervase sipped at his wine. 'Now, Sir Maurice here caused a great stir when he took the *St Sulpice* and *St Denis*. The French believed that we had a spy high in their councils. No, no.' He held out his hand. 'I must be more precise. They believed that one of the senior officers on board ship was in the pay of the English court.'

'And is that true?' Sir John barked.

'Jack, Jack.' Gervase shifted his head. 'You may ask but you know I won't answer. Suffice to say the French believed that.'

'And they have sent Mercurius to London?'

'Precisely: that's the news our merchant brought.'

'But there are always French spies in London.' Cranston's face showed his annoyance at these subtle, silken treacheries. 'And a Frenchman is a Frenchman wherever he goes.'

'I didn't say he was French,' Gervase replied. 'We know a great deal about Mercurius. He's not French or Gascon but English. A clerk in the Bishop of Norwich's household, he joined a free company and went to France. He was captured. Now the French have a way with freebooters, they just hang them out of hand. Mercurius, whose real name was Richard Stillingbourne, entered into a deal with his new masters: in return for his life and a bag of silver he was released. He led the French back to where his free company was quartered and organised their slaughter. Mercurius has a passion and skill for killing as other men do for riding a horse or singing a song. Now, my belief is that the French have sent him into England and that he is responsible for the death of Serriem at Hawkmere.'

'And so he could be anyone?' Athelstan asked.

'He could be one of the parishioners. He might even be Aspinall, the physician. One of the servants, a chapman, a tinker, a guard. He's a master of disguise. He can appear stooped and aged, the beggar on the corner, or haughty and arrogant.' Gervase grinned at Sir Maurice. 'Even the young knight with a falcon on his wrist.' He spread his hands in mock innocence. 'Even a humble clerk.'

'Would de Fontanel know of this?' Athelstan asked.

Gaunt shook his head. 'The French envoy has taken a house in Adel Lane; it's watched day and night. No stranger has approached it.'

'And de Fontanel?'

'He never goes out.' Gaunt smirked. 'He might be frightened. My guard dogs know him, the foppish way he dresses, the ridiculous hat!'

'He's only a minor envoy,' Gervase added. 'Sent to vex and irritate. Mercurius will answer only to the Chancellor in Paris.'

'If the French believe,' Gaunt continued, 'that there is a traitor among those men at Hawkmere, Mercurius will kill him.' Gaunt leaned forward, his face drawn with excitement.

For a moment he reminded Athelstan of a wolf he had seen in the Tower, the sharp, pointed face, the hooded, unblinking eyes, the hunched shoulders.

'I have prayed,' Gaunt said, 'that one day, Mercurius will enter our web. The French have whistled up a dance and dance we must but, Sir Jack, Brother Athelstan, and you Master Gervase, I want Mercurius' head. He is more important than all the ships the French can muster in the Narrow Seas.'

'But he's not only here for that, is he?' Athelstan pointed across at Sir Maurice. 'They also hold you responsible for the loss of their ships. I am not threatening you,' Athelstan continued, Gervase now nodding his head. 'Mercurius could also be in England to kill you.'

'I agree,' Gaunt said. 'But these men at Hawkmere are his real prey.'

'Why not move the prisoners?' Sir John asked. 'Take them out of Hawkmere, up river to the Tower?'

'It's tempting,' Gaunt replied, 'but I don't think we'll achieve much. The capture of Mercurius is important. We have a better opportunity if they are kept in the more, how can I put it, open surroundings of Hawkmere? Moreover, if Mercurius is one of them, it will make little difference. At this point of the dance, the French have it all their own way. If the prisoners die, they'll appeal to the Pope in Avignon, depict us as breakers of the truth, violaters of the Papal peace. Of course, the murders will continue but the French don't really care. They hope to kill the traitor. Perhaps make an example of him and, for all I know, slay one of my principal household knights.' Gaunt sniffed. 'Mercurius may have slain Vulpina to close her mouth.' He slapped his leather gauntlets against his thigh. 'You, Sir Maurice, should be very careful. This business at the Golden Cresset may well be the work of Mercurius. Well, Gervase, now we have Brother Athelstan here, there is one other matter.'

The Master of Secrets looked away and cleared his throat.

'Ah yes, yes, there is. You know, Brother, the doings of the Great Community of the Realm?'

'All London does.'

The Master of Secrets undid his white shirt. Athelstan noticed with amusement the hare's-foot slung on a chain round his throat. Gervase caught his gaze.

'It's to ward off the colic,' he explained, rubbing his stomach.

'Continue!' Gaunt ordered harshly. 'My falcons and dogs await, the day draws on.'

'I have it on good authority,' the Master of Secrets went on, 'that the Great Community of the Realm is very active in Southwark and may well have agents who are members of your parish.'

'I know nothing of that,' Athelstan replied quickly.

'There are many priests, hedge-parsons among its leaders,' Gaunt intervened silkily. 'They lard their talk with quotations from the Scriptures on the equality of man.'

'Then, my lord, they quote most accurately.'

'In reality,' Gaunt retorted, 'they are as devoid of Christ as they are of grace.'

'In which case, my lord, they have a great deal in common with the people against whom they plot.'

Sir Maurice's head went down. Sir John's hand covered his eyes while Gervase looked up at the ceiling as if searching for cobwebs. Gaunt held Athelstan's gaze.

'One day, Brother.' He got to his feet. 'One day, all of this nonsense will come to a head. I'll hang every man jack of them!'

'They are only hungry,' Athelstan said. 'They eat hard bread. They give rags, soaked in wine, for their babies to suck. Sometimes in winter the only meal they have is the snot they swallow.'

'Brother!' Sir John intervened warningly.

Gaunt's expression abruptly changed. He smiled and brought his hand down on the little Dominican's shoulders.

'Only an honest man speaks the truth, Brother.' He opened his purse, shook out some silver coins and thrust them into Athelstan's hand. 'Buy your poor some bread. Tell them to pray for John of Gaunt.' He put on his gauntlets. 'But tell them, if they are caught in arms plotting against the Crown, they'll hang.' He walked to the door and turned, his hand on the latch. 'I set you a hard task, Brother,' he said quietly. 'I want you to help Sir Maurice here for he is a man I'd like my own son to grow into. I want these murders stopped. I want to see Mercurius' head on a pole over London Bridge. Do that and, I swear, the streets of Southwark will run with wine. Now, as I have said, my dogs wait. I bid you adieu.'

He closed the door and sauntered down the passageway. Gervase put his face in his hands and sighed.

'Brother, you go too far.'

'It's the only time I've been frightened.' Sir Maurice spoke up, grabbing his cup and drinking greedily from it.

Cranston had finished his and was now helping himself to a generous swig from his wineskin.

'What on earth possessed you, Brother?'

'I don't know,' Athelstan replied. He sat down because his legs were now shaking and a sweat had broken out all over his body. He looked at the silver coins in his hands. 'I suppose I get tired of seeing the poor starve. You've met my parishioners, Sir John, Watkin and Pike. Lord save us, plot against the Crown! They can hardly piss straight! Master Gervase, do you have names of those involved in Southwark?'

The Master of Secrets shook his head. 'Only tittle-tattle,' he replied. 'Gossip from the market place. Shadows and shapes glimpsed at the dead of night!'

'And Mercurius?' Sir John asked. 'Is there anything else we should know? A description?'

Gervase shook his head. 'What I know you now do.' He grasped the wrist of the young knight. 'But, Sir Maurice, you should walk carefully. I know you are not frightened, a man of war, bold and brave. However, this is no fight on board a ship, the clash of arms on some battlefield. Mercurius will come like a thief in the night and ye know not the day nor the hour. More importantly, he may not even come himself but send others. Be on your guard!'

They left the House of Secrets and walked up through Newgate into Cheapside. The broad thoroughfare was empty apart from Leif the beggar and others of his ilk. The red-haired bane of Sir John's life was standing on the stocks. He balanced himself precariously, holding the great wooden post, the other hand on his chest, head thrown back, eyes closed, entertaining his companions with a song.

'As God lives!' Sir John exclaimed, staring across at the motley crew. 'Just listen to that, Brother.'

Athelstan had to agree that Leif as a singer left a great deal to be desired. As if in answer to a prayer, a window of a shop above Leif was thrown open.

'For the love of heaven!' a voice bawled and the contents of a chamber pot splashed out, but Leif was quicker, hopping like a squirrel from the stocks. He turned and shook his fist.

'I must be home,' Sir John said. 'Brother Athelstan, Sir Maurice, will you join us to eat?'

'Sir John, I thank you,' Athelstan replied. 'But today I must have words with Sir Maurice here. Perhaps it might be safer at St Erconwald's than elsewhere. Sir John, I will ask for your assistance tomorrow.'

'Tomorrow is tomorrow. But, today is Sunday. My poppets await and I want to be home before they miss their daddy too much.'

He stomped off, gathering speed as Leif suddenly caught sight of his great fat friend. The beggar gave a screech of welcome and staggered towards him.

'Poor Sir John,' Athelstan said. 'Come.'

They made their way down Cheapside and across London Bridge. Southwark was empty, sleeping under the hot summer sun. Athelstan found the church quiet, the front door locked, Godbless and Thaddeus dozing on the steps. Benedicta had seen to Philomel and left a pot of stewed meat and some fresh rolls. So Athelstan, Sir Maurice, Godbless and Thaddeus, not to mention Bonaventure, dined like kings that afternoon. Afterwards

Godbless returned to the cemetery taking Thaddeus and the mercenary Bonaventure with him. Athelstan opened the great chest beneath the small window and took out the garb of a Dominican monk.

'My brothers at Blackfriars always send me fresh robes at Easter and Christmas. Some are longer than others.'

Sir Maurice's jaw dropped. He looked even more concerned when Athelstan dipped again into the chest and brought out a pair of long, sharp shears.

'Brother?'

'Yes, Brother,' Athelstan replied. 'You are no longer Sir Maurice Maltravers but Brother Norbert of the Dominican Order. You are going to let me crop your hair, form a small tonsure, teach you how to walk and talk like a Dominican, if that's possible.'

The grin spread across the young knight's face.

'Tomorrow, we are going to visit that child of God, Lady Angelica Parr, at the convent of the nuns of Syon.'

Sir Maurice jumped to his feet like a boy who's been promised a much-prized reward.

'Is that possible, Brother?'

'Provided you keep your wits about you and Lady Angelica doesn't betray us, who will know?'

'What happens if Sir Thomas has a guard there?'

'Fighting men are not allowed in convents and the nuns of Syon are a law unto themselves, as you will find out.'

'But, Brother, won't you get into trouble?'

Athelstan closed the lid of the chest. 'Sir Maurice, I am always in trouble. And, for the love of God, what is wrong with what we are doing? It's all for love! That will be my defence!' He gripped the shears more securely. 'But, for everything under the sun, there's a price. Brother Norbert, loosen your jerkin.'

An hour later Sir Maurice Maltravers quietly confessed that he had been transformed. His dark hair was cropped, a small tonsure at the back. He was now garbed in the black and white habit, a knotted cord round his middle. He practised walking up and down the kitchen, hands up his sleeves, eyes downcast. Bonaventure had returned and curiously watched this strange transformation. Athelstan laughed and clapped his hands.

'And they will allow us in the door?' Sir Maurice asked anxiously.

'Oh, not us,' Athelstan replied. 'But there's not a door in London Sir Jack Cranston can't get through.'

'And what will happen inside?'

'Well, I don't expect you to go down on one knee and make a confession of love,' Athelstan said, stroking Bonaventure, who had jumped on to his lap. 'But you can talk.' He pulled a face. 'About love in general, spiritual terms. However, you must observe the disguise and the secrecy I have given you. If you break that I will leave and give no further help.'

'And what will come of this?' Sir Maurice asked anxiously.

'Sir Maurice, I am a Dominican and this is St Erconwald's. I am not a miracle-worker, so we'll take each day as it comes. Stay there!'

Athelstan went into his bed loft and brought down a gilt-edged tome bound in calfskin.

'These are the writings of St Bonaventure.' He handed the book over. 'No, not the cat. A great Franciscan, a doctor of theology. His writings on love, particularly that which should exist between a man and his wife, make refreshing reading. There's a favourite passage of mine where he says that the best friendship which exists must be that between husband and wife. You sit there and read it.' Athelstan moved towards the door. 'I am going to pray in church, for a little guidance and some protection. Afterwards, we'll visit Godbless and make sure he is the only living person lying down in our cemetery!'

Athelstan left the house. He checked on Philomel who was standing up, leaning against the side of his stall fast asleep. The Dominican crossed to the church. Engrossed in his thoughts, he failed to see the shadow at the bottom of the alleyway watching him intently, a malignant, dark presence. Once the priest had gone inside, the watcher crouched down again to continue his close study of the church and the little house beside it.

Chapter 10

Dusk was falling, cloaking Whitefriars in darkness. At this time its main streets and offal-filled alleyways came to life. Cunning men and beggars swarmed like rats over a midden-heap looking for plunder, for the unwary, for the vulnerable, ready to turn on each other at the slightest hint of weakness. A place of mean houses, narrow lanes and even meaner hearts. Mercurius knew it all.

He had been here years ago skulking from the law and the way he walked, the swagger, dagger and knife pushed into his belt, were sufficient warning for those who lurked in doorways or peeped from behind broken shutters. He entered the Ragged Standard, a large, evil-smelling tavern only a stone's throw from the Carmelite monastery from which the quarter took its name. The taproom was lit by thin, weak tapers which gave off an acrid stench.

Mercurius pulled his vizard closer around his face and ensured the cowl was full across his head. He sat by the window and looked out at the gathering dusk. The taverner had made a pathetic attempt at laying out a garden, a patch of sun-scorched weeds fenced off from the dusty, tawdry herb plots by sheepshank bones and the skulls of different animals. A slattern came over. Mercurius pulled out a silver piece.

'Ale,' he ordered. 'Properly drawn and the blackjack had better be clean!'

He removed a small arbalest from the hook of his belt and placed it on the table. The slattern hurried off. Outside in the stable yard, two stallions jigged at the ostler and reared neighing, lashing out. Some of the customers went across to watch the fun. One rogue shouted that he was prepared to accept wagers that the ostler would be hurt. The taverner, a greasy barrel of a man, shoved them aside and walked out, a flaming brand in his hand, to separate the two stallions.

Mercurius eased himself in the corner. In the middle of the floor sprawled a member of a troupe of travelling actors, drunk as a sot. The man lay spread on his back, the devil's mask still clasped to the top half of his face. A little boy crouched next to him wiping away the pool of spittle filling his slack mouth. Across the taproom other members fought for the takings. They hushed for a while as the flame man came down the street, ringing his bell and shouting at householders to be careful; fires were to be doused and candles made safe. Someone else bawled raucously that he had a fresh maid for sale.

The clamour in the stable yard now being stilled, the customers swirled back. Cunning men divided their takings, professional beggars, armed with wet rags, wiped off the paint and saltpetre which they used to display fictitious wounds. Mercurius waited, his eyes constantly moving, vigilant for any sheriff's man or one of Gaunt's spies. He did not know whether the English knew he was in London but he could take no chances. The business at Hawkmere was going well, yet he was not responsible.

He saw two shadows come to the door – his guests had arrived. They swaggered across, glimpsed the crossbow and recognised the sign. As they pulled across stools and sat down, Mercurius sipped from his tankard and studied them. Like two peas from the same rotten pod; they wore leggings and boots, their chests were naked except for leather jackets, the sleeves cut off, copper bands round their muscular arms. Their heads were completely shaven, their faces sharp and narrow-eyed. One of them fingered the copper ring in his ear lobe.

'You are the one?'

'I am.'

'And what do you want?'

The assassin clicked his fingers and the slattern hurried across. Two more blackjacks of ale were ordered. One of the shaven-heads leaned forward, arms on the table.

'We cannot sit here all night. What do you want? Our horses are outside. We can take what we want and go!'

'If you talk to me like that again, I'll kill both of you now.'

'How?' the taller shaven-head sneered.

'Look under the table.'

The man did so and glimpsed the other arbalest the assassin had placed on his thigh. It was loaded, the barb pulled back, the finger on the clasp. The shaven-head swallowed hard and looked at his companion.

'We meant no offence.'

'Of course not.'

The slattern returned with the blackjacks. The cowled stranger put the arbalest down and tossed a small purse on to the table.

'Six silver pieces, Venetians freshly coined. Three for you now, three more when the task is done.'

'Who is it?'

'Sir Maurice Maltravers, henchman in the household of my Lord of Gaunt.'

The leading shaven-head coughed over his beer.

'One of Gaunt's men?'

'I've heard that name.' The other spoke up. 'He took a ship in the Channel. A fighting man.'

'In his mail and armour, yes,' the assassin replied. 'But not in the garb of a monk. You'll find him in the priest's house at St Erconwald's in Southwark, you know the place, I'll wager.'

The shaven-heads nodded in unison.

'He'll be there whenever you wish. A knife in the back, an arrow in the throat...'

'We don't kill priests,' the leading shaven-head protested. 'The friar who is also there, Athelstan. He's well known and liked.'

The assassin dug into his purse and brought out four silver coins which he placed on top of the small purse. The shaven-heads smiled.

'On second thoughts, every dog has his day!'

The leader went to pick up the silver but the assassin seized his wrist.

'You don't live here, do you? You live in St Mary Axe Street. You have a sister there, or they say she's your sister. One thing, sir, don't take that silver unless you intend to carry out the task.'

'It will be done.'

'Good!' The assassin sat back. 'And, if the priest dies, the more the merrier.'

He drained his tankard and got to his feet. He slipped one arbalest on to the hook of his belt, keeping the other in his hand.

'How do we tell you that your task is done?'

'Oh, you don't,' the assassin replied softly, patting the man on the shoulder. 'I'll know and, don't worry, I'll come visiting you. Now, sit for a while and finish your ale.'

Then he was gone.

—

Athelstan celebrated an early morning Mass. Sir Maurice Maltravers, not yet changed into his robes, served as an altar boy. They were joined by Godbless and Thaddeus, who made an attempt to nibble the altar cloth. Bonaventure, of course, also arrived. The cat always stared at the chalice, his little pink tongue coming out as if he suspected it contained milk. Pernell the old Fleming woman, her hair now dyed a garish yellow, also attended, kneeling beside Ranulf the rat-catcher. Once Mass was over Ranulf came shambling into the sacristy. He waited patiently until Athelstan had divested.

'Brother, we are all ready.'

Athelstan remembered just in time. 'Oh, of course, the Mass for your Guild.'

'Can it be Wednesday morning, Brother? About ten o'clock?'

Athelstan swallowed hard but Ranulf looked beseechingly at him, a gaze which reminded Athelstan that he had promised this on many an occasion.

'What will it entail, Ranulf?'

'Well, Wednesday is good for rat-catchers, Brother. We'll have Mass and bring our animals.'

'Which are?'

'Ferrets, cats, dogs, our traps and cages.'

'And how many will there be? I mean, rat-catchers?' Athelstan added quickly.

He glanced at Sir Maurice who was staring nonplussed at this strange parishioner in his black tarred jacket and hood. The belt round Ranulf's waist carried hooks, small traps and coils of wire, all the implements of a rat-catcher's trade.

'There'll be sixteen or eighteen. Afterwards we'll break our fast on a table in the porch. We will supply the food and ales. We'd like you to bless us and give a special blessing to our animals.'

'Agreed!' Athelstan said. 'But have a word with Benedicta. Now, clear the church, Ranulf, and lock the door! I've sent Crim the altar boy across to Sir John. When he returns would you help him with Philomel, just clean the stable. Afterwards, you may finish the oatmeal in the kitchen.'

Ranulf quickly agreed and sped out of the sacristy.

'A Guild of Rat-Catchers?' Sir Maurice asked.

Athelstan smiled. 'It's a wonderful life, Brother Norbert. Yes, it's time you changed. Put on the garb I gave you but wrap your cloak firmly around you.'

The knight hastened out and Athelstan walked back into the church. He knelt on the sanctuary steps to say a short prayer of thanksgiving followed by an invocation to the Holy Spirit asking for his help and guidance that day.

Sir Maurice had spent most of the night reading the tracts by St Bonaventure; Athelstan had woken to the young knight seated before the hearth, reciting to an owl-eyed Godbless and a rather feisty Thaddeus certain love poems he had learned. Athelstan, eager to begin his Mass, had simply cautioned the young knight on not being too impetuous.

He finished his prayer, crossed himself and walked down the nave. Huddle the painter was in the porch, a piece of charcoal in his hand. The artist was smiling at a bare expanse of freshly washed white plaster.

'I could do a lovely painting, Brother.' Huddle turned, his long, horse-like face wreathed in a smile. 'What about Christ in Judgement?'

Athelstan stepped back. The wall of one transept was now covered in Huddle's paintings, crude and vivid, full of colour, a constant source of wonderment to the parishioners. Athelstan often used them in his sermons, leaving the sanctuary to go down and stand before Huddle's depiction of scenes from the Gospel.

'It will cost you money, Brother. We'll need red and gold, vermilion, some black of course, and a nice scarlet.'

Athelstan was about to refuse when he remembered the silver John of Gaunt had given him.

'Do a sketch with the charcoal,' Athelstan agreed. 'One of your line drawings and then make an estimate for the paints.'

Huddle's smile disappeared. 'Oh, not the parish council, Brother! You know Watkin!'

'Watkin really admires your work,' Athelstan replied. 'But it must be agreed by the council.'

'But you'll support it? You'll see Christ in Judgement, the sheep to the right, the goats to the left. I remember your sermon from last Advent.'

'Very well, Huddle, but none of your jokes!'

Athelstan's eyes wandered up the transept. The artist had depicted the scene of Christ's birth, a brilliant lifelike scene just near the Lady Altar. Everyone had admired it except Watkin: Huddle, out of revenge, had painted the ox with Watkin's face.

'I'll support it.' Athelstan patted the artist's bony shoulder.

Huddle fairly skipped with joy. The Dominican left him and went out on to the porch. Godbless sat with his arm around Thaddeus. 'I'll clear the cemetery today, Brother. Weed some of the graves.'

'Good man, Godbless.'

'But they were back last night.'

Athelstan turned. 'The ghosts?'

'Yes, Brother, I saw them in the air, dark shapes against the night sky. I took Thaddeus into the death house and locked the door. I've never seen anything like that. Except when I was in Venice with a free company there. I saw a man who should have died but didn't.'

'You are sure you saw shapes?' Athelstan asked.

'Certain, Brother. They were hanging between heaven and earth.'

'Brother Athelstan!'

Sir Maurice came out of the priest's house, his military cloak around him. Athelstan would have loved to question Godbless but the day was drawing on, and the sooner he crossed the Thames and visited the nunnery at Syon the better.

They walked down the alleyway, stopping to buy a meat pastry at Merrylegs' pie shop. The stalls and booths had already been laid out for another day's trading. The Piebald Tavern was open for custom. Several of Athelstan's parishioners gathered in the doorway, tankards in their hands. Watkin and Pike were resting on their shovels and mattocks. Hig the pigman glowered out as if the world were against him. They shouted greetings and Athelstan sketched a blessing in the air.

Down near the riverside the bailiffs were also busy. Bladdersniff was there, his nose glowing red, watery-eyed, supervising the incarceration in the stocks of two drunks found sottish in an alleyway.

'*Caeci ducunt caecos:* the blind leading the blind,' Athelstan translated. 'Bladdersniff drinks as if there is no tomorrow.'

They reached the watery quay steps. Moleskin was there, his nut-brown face wrinkled into a smile. He bowed precariously in his wherry, gesturing at Athelstan to come quickly down.

'It will soon be busy, Brother.'

He helped Athelstan into his rocking boat and gazed curiously at Sir Maurice. He shrugged, bent over his oars and turned his wherry out across the Thames.

A morning mist still hung over the water but the river was busy with bum-boats, cogs of war, skiffs, the great gong barges bringing out the ordure and filth from the city streets and dumping it midstream. Some barges had bells and rang these as a warning to others on the river. Now and again Moleskin stopped to greet an acquaintance and once he pulled in his oars as a royal barge full of courtiers, officials and clerks made its way down the Thames to the Tower. Great blue and scarlet banners flapped vigorously from its poop and stern. A long, low, black skiff came through the mist, the bell on its prow tolling its funeral knell.

'In God's name!' Sir Maurice breathed.

Athelstan turned, pulling back his cowl. The skiff was long and low in the water. In the centre lay a wet, bedraggled corpse stretched out on a wooden platter. Around it crouched cowled, hooded men. The leader stood in the stern like the figure of Death himself, his hood pulled back to reveal his strange bony face and bald head. He glanced towards Athelstan as they passed.

'Good morning, Brother.'

Athelstan recognised the fisher of men whose task was to comb the Thames and pull out corpses for which the City Council would pay him a fee. Athelstan sketched a blessing in the direction of the corpse.

'A suicide?' he asked.

The fisher rapped out an order for the rowers to stop; his craft rose and fell beside Moleskin's skiff. The boatman glanced away, hawked and spat.

'No suicide, Brother, death by misadventure. This poor man was bitten by a rabid dog just near Dowgate. They threw him into the water thinking that would cure him. The poor man drowned so his soul's gone to God and his corpse to the City Corporation. Row on, my lovelies!' He raised his hand in salutation and his ghoulish barge disappeared into the morning mist.

'I hate passing him,' Moleskin observed. 'Combing the river for the dead.'

'A work of mercy,' Athelstan countered. And God knows, Moleskin, God eventually calls each of us to Himself.

In Fennel Alley just off Catte Street, Sir John Cranston, coroner of the city, would have agreed with Athelstan's conclusions. He pushed back his beaver hat, scratched his head and stared in disbelief at the chaos before him. The corpse of an old man, his hose pushed round his ankles, lay in the ruins of the stool-house which had collapsed bringing the poor unfortunate and the latrine he was sitting on crashing to the ground.

'Tell me again.' He looked up at the houses on either side.

'Very good, Sir John. The house on your left belongs to the victim, Elias Ethmol, once a trader in skins but now retired. The house on the right belongs to Humphrey

Withrington, a dyer by trade. Now, as you can see, Sir John,' the beadle continued mournfully, 'the two houses are very close together, or at least their top stories are. Now Elias and Humphrey were old men.'

'Where's Humphrey now?'

An old, rheumy-eyed man came out of the small crowd which had gathered and raised his ash cane.

'That be me, Sir Jack.'

'My lord coroner to you!' He stared up; the upper stories were at least twenty feet above the ground.

'What they did,' the beadle continued, 'was to build a house of ease…'

'You mean a latrine?'

'Yes, Sir John, between the upper stories.'

'And did you have a licence for this'?' Sir John glowered at Humphrey.

The old man shook his head fearfully.

'Continue!'

'Well, the latrine was wedged between the two stories. They could use it at night and, in the morning, empty the chamber pots. Last night poor Elias answered the call of nature and sat on the latrine.'

Sir John looked warningly at the beadle as he caught the humour in his voice.

'Now, from what I can gather,' the beadle continued, keeping his face straight, 'Elias was rather drunk. He used the chamber pot but then decided to dance.'

'I heard the noise.' Humphrey spoke up. 'The silly old bugger was always doing that. A real piss-pot he was, Sir John, I mean my lord coroner.'

Sir John studied the small door on the outside of each upper tier and the damage where the house of ease had broken away.

'The rest is obvious,' the beadle said. 'The whole thing collapsed, Sir John: boards, ceiling, chamber pot and small stool.'

'And poor old Elias?' Sir John added. 'Right.' The coroner pinched his nose at the smell. 'Does Elias have a family?'

'No friends except me.' Humphrey spoke up.

'Good, then you are responsible for the corpse. Don't whine, man. It was a stupid idea to build the place and against the civic regulations. I fine you one third of a mark.'

Simon, his scrivener, made the entry in the small calf-skin ledger he always carried.

'And who built this so called house of ease?'

'Michael Focklingham,' Humphrey whined, wiping his rheumy eyes.

'Ah yes, old Focklingham.' Sir John smiled. 'A man who builds wherever he wishes. Not the best carpenter in London. This is not the first time I've met his handiwork. He's fined one mark.'

The scrivener paused to dip the nib in a small inkpot he carried on his belt.

'And he's to pay it by Michaelmas: that's my verdict. Simon here will write it up.' The coroner turned away.

'Are we going to the Guildhall, Sir John?' Simon came hurrying up behind him. 'There are a number of cases...'

'I haven't broken my fast yet. I've been to Mass and I've just had to witness the stupidity of man. I need some ale and a juicy meat pie.'

'So, it's the Holy Lamb of God, Sir John?'

He brought his great paw on the scrivener's skinny shoulder.

'It's the Holy Lamb of God for you and me, Simon and, until then, the city of London can wait.'

Thankfully Sir John was just finishing his pie and ale when Crim, who'd already disturbed the Lady Maude, wandered into the tavern screaming for him.

'Over here, boy!' Sir John waved him over.

Crim tottered across, his mouth half-full of the freshly baked manchet loaf Lady Maude had given him. The honey she had smeared on it now covered the boy's face.

'It's Brother Athelstan.' Crim swallowed hard.

'What is it, boy?' Sir John got to his feet and towered over him.

'Brother Athelstan.' Crim closed his eyes, his hand on his crotch. 'Oh, Sir John, I want to pee!'

'Out in the garden!'

Crim dashed off then returned smiling with relief, still gnawing at the remains of the loaf.

'Brother Athelstan.' Crim closed his eyes. 'He has gone to the nuns at Syon. He says it's very important that you join him there. You'll find him at the tavern called the Jerusalem...'

'The Jerusalem Tree,' Sir John finished.

'That's right, Sir John.'

He dug into his purse and gave the boy a halfpenny.

'I'll go there. Simon.' He beamed at his scrivener. 'Go back to the Guildhall, write up my verdict on Elias Ethmol and sift through what's awaiting us. Deaths I deal with. The rest... Use your noddle-pate!'

'Very good, Sir John.'

Simon followed Crim out of the tavern. Sir John picked up his war belt where he had thrown it and strapped it on. He gave the taverner's wife a juicy kiss and, full of the joys of life, stepped out into Cheapside.

Philippe Routier was running for his life. He clasped the makeshift knife thrust in his belt and ran across the wasteland towards the copse of trees. He had some bread and a small water bottle wrapped in the bag he carried. He glanced up at the sky. The day was proving to be a fine one, the sun was growing hot and, if everything went according to plan, he'd be able to lose himself in the wasteland north of the city. And afterwards? Perhaps go back to the river? Or to the coast? Certainly, he could remain no longer at Hawkmere. Those grey, oppressive walls, the surly Sir Walter and the constant suspicion and tension among his companions. Routier stopped and threw himself behind a bush. He stared back the way he had come. He could make out the grey walls of Hawkmere and even catch a glimpse of the sentries on duty. Much good they were doing!

Routier had planned his escape well. They had gathered in the Great Hall to break fast and then, as usual, had been allowed to wander in the garden, 'taking the morning air' as Sir Walter sardonically put it.

Of all the prisoners Routier hated captivity the most. He was born and raised in the port of Brest. He was used to the open heathland and the sea: the feel of a ship beneath him; the wind on his face; the creak and groan of the canvas and the excitement of battle. A man who had never married because he could not be tied to one place, Routier had grown to hate Hawkmere, Sir Walter and even his own companions. He had no doubt there was a traitor among them. They had discussed it many a time: the *St Sulpice* and *St Denis* had been taken by treachery, so it must have been one of them. But who? Routier opened the water bottle and took a gulp. And Sir Walter? Was he the slayer?

Routier had discussed his plans with the others. He had even invited them to accompany him. Routier laughed quietly to himself. They, of course, had refused, believing it was impossible. Routier, however, had noted the garden wall could easily be scaled. Once into the yard beyond, it was a matter of just hiding in one of the outhouses and climbing through that unshuttered window.

Routier felt a slight pain in his stomach and gnawed at some of the meat he had taken. He wished at least one of the others had come with him; they had refused but agreed to quarrel volubly, which had allowed Routier to climb the garden wall and so make his escape. The Frenchman once again stared back. How long would it take before Sir Walter noticed he had escaped? Routier clambered to his feet and hurried at a stoop towards the copse of trees. As he ran his hand went to his stomach, where the pains were growing worse. Was he sickening? Had he eaten something? And then he recalled poor Serriem's corpse, grey and clammy. Had he, too, been poisoned? At last he reached the line of trees. The pain was now intense so Routier sat down. In the distance he could hear the barking of dogs and knew his escape must have been detected. He tried to pull himself up but he found he was unable to. His legs had lost their strength, the pain had spread from belly to chest and he was finding it difficult to breathe. His tongue seemed thick and swollen in his mouth.

Routier lay down, letting his hot face brush the cool, sweet grass. Above him a bird called and it brought back memories of the port at Brest and the sea birds skimming in. Perhaps he was already back there? There was a terrible pounding, like the crashing of surf against the harbour walls. Routier turned over on his back, his body jerking in spasms of pain. Who had given him the food he had brought with him? Routier tried to think, even as his mind slipped in and out of unconsciousness. He had eaten and drunk the same as the rest but of course the water, the food he carried!

Routier racked his brain. He had eaten nothing, surely? Nothing he had not seen anyone else eat and drink. Routier tried to lick his lips. The water he'd drawn from the butts outside the hall, but the bread? Hadn't Gresnay slipped him some of his? Routier's body arched in pain. He could hear the birds calling louder now and the roaring seemed closer. He tried to mutter a prayer, staring up through the branches at the blue sky, but the words wouldn't come. All he could think of was Gresnay, his girlish face twisted into that funny smile, offering him the bread and he, like a fool, had taken it!

Chapter 11

Sir John Cranston took one look at Sir Maurice Maltravers sitting beside Athelstan in the Jerusalem Tree Tavern and roared with laughter. He took his beaver hat off, slapping it against his thighs so the pedlars and tinkers who plied their trade along the waterside wondered if the lord coroner had lost his wits. Athelstan shook his head in mock reproval.

'Sir John,' he hissed. 'This is supposed to be done in secrecy.'

'I promise you, Brother. But do you think you can fool the hawk-eyed Lady Monica? This.' He took the tankard Athelstan had ordered and took a deep slurp. 'This,' he repeated, 'I must see. You are?'

'Brother Norbert of the Order of St Dominic' Sir Maurice spoke softly, pulling his face into what he thought was a look of piety.

'Oh, for God's sake! They'll think you are from Bedlam if you look at Lady Monica like that. What I suggest, Brother, is Athelstan speaks to Lady Monica and you'd best keep your tongue quiet until we meet Angelica.'

They walked up the steep, winding trackway to where the nunnery, nestling behind its grey curtain wall, overlooked the Thames. A porter led them through the postern gate and across the exquisitely laid-out gardens with herbers, smooth green lawns, flower beds, arbours and raised turf seats. The air was tinged with the heavy perfume of flowers. Sir John stopped to admire a luscious rose which dangled out over the path.

'The ladies of Syon are not sworn to poverty,' Athelstan noted.

'No, no, Brother, this is where the ladies of the court, who wish to retire from the glories of the world, can sit, reflect, meditate and pray.'

The nunnery buildings were made of honey-coloured stone. They passed the jewel of a chapel and entered cool, shady porticoes which wound past quiet cloisters and into the main building. Here the floor was paved and lined with boxes and pots of flowers. Gaily coloured tapestries hung on the wall displaying scenes from the Bible or lovely motifs such as a flaming rose beneath a golden crown. Now and again they passed nuns sitting in corners or in chairs, either reading from books of hours or talking softly among themselves. The porter, a wiry little man, turned a corner and knocked on an iron-studded door. Athelstan breathed a quick prayer. Sir John took one quick slurp from the wineskin and in they swept to meet Lady Monica.

Athelstan found her most forbidding. She was tall, elegant and more majestic than any queen. She was dressed in a snowy white habit with a cream-edged coif which framed an imperious face with sharp grey eyes, slender nose and thin, disapproving lips. She extended a bejewelled hand. Sir John went on one knee to kiss the long, ivory-white fingers. Athelstan and Sir Maurice bowed, the friar sketching a hasty blessing. Lady Monica sat down behind her desk while the porter, grumbling to himself, brought across three box chairs. Lady Monica nodded and all three took their seats. Athelstan felt as if he had gone back in time, to when he and his brother Francis were brought into the scullery to be reprimanded by Mother. Beads of sweat broke out on his brow and he wondered at the wisdom of what he had done. Lady Monica's steel-grey eyes studied them all. Athelstan caught a glimpse of humour in her severe face.

'It's been a long time, Jack.'

Sir John's face coloured and he shuffled his feet.

'Do you remember the tourney?' She sighed. 'You and my beloved, Sir Oliver, fought all comers: the King gave you the crown as champion of the tournament?'

'Grand days,' the coroner muttered, the tears starting in his eyes. 'I am older, my lady, and much fatter, but you haven't changed a whit. As beautiful as ever.'

'You were always one for flattery, Jack, and for wine. Would you like some?'

Lady Monica gestured to the porter still standing behind them.

'Cuthbert, some wine for our guests. The best claret you have.' Her face creased into a smile. 'Sir Jack has a partiality for that.'

The wine was served, the porter left. All the time Lady Monica threaded the ivory Ave beads which lay on her desk. She asked after Lady Maude and congratulated Sir John on the birth of the two poppets. She finally wrapped the Ave beads round her fingers and sat back in the chair. Athelstan couldn't meet her gaze so he looked at the beautiful devotional paintings, framed in black and gold, which hung on the brilliant white walls.

'Why are you here, Jack?'

Sir John coughed and rolled the small, intricately carved goblet between his hands.

'Sir Thomas Parr, my lady.'

'Ah, Angelica. Headstrong girl. Love is a terrible thing, isn't it, Jack? It turns the soul and dazzles the mind.' She gathered the Ave beads together. 'Did you ever love me, Jack?'

He kept his head down like a little boy.

'I asked you that once,' Lady Monica continued.

'My lady, you were betrothed. Sir Oliver was dearer to me than a brother.'

'But you did love me!' Lady Monica persisted.

Athelstan watched fascinated as tears brimmed in Sir John's eyes and, for once, this bluff, rough-spoken coroner seemed tongue-tied.

'You were always blunt, my lady. I think you know the truth. And, God forgive me if I gave any offence, but so did Oliver.'

'My lady,' Athelstan intervened, wanting to help his companion. 'Sir Thomas Parr has put his daughter in your care. He has asked me to visit her and give her spiritual comfort.'

'And does that need the three of you?' Lady Monica studied Athelstan carefully. 'I have heard of you.' She pointed a finger. 'I always listen to what happens to Jack. All your exploits. Anyway, why the three?'

'My lord coroner is here because he knows you,' Athelstan replied coolly. 'I am here because I am his secretarius while Brother Norbert has just returned from the Bridgettine Convent at Oxford.' Athelstan quietly prayed the lie would not be held against him. 'Where he provided wise counsel and spiritual comfort for the good sisters there.'

'And so why are you here?' Lady Monica now stared directly at Sir Maurice.

'I am here, my lady...' He fell silent.

Athelstan closed his eyes.

'You seem rather tongue-tied for one who gives spiritual comfort?' Lady Monica's voice was tinged with faint mockery.

'I am here,' Sir Maurice continued defiantly, 'to remind Lady Angelica of love, its true nature, function and purpose.'

Lady Monica squeezed her chin between her fingers and clicked her tongue.

'I've seen you somewhere before. Anyway...' Lady Monica picked up a small bell and rang it. 'I am charged with the Lady Angelica's care. Any spiritual comfort you give her is because Sir Thomas Parr wishes it.' She smiled thinly. 'He has written to me on this matter. But,' Lady Monica continued, 'it must be given in my presence.'

Athelstan's heart sank. 'Brother Norbert' leaned forward as if to protest but Athelstan quietly kicked his foot. The porter returned. Lady Monica gave him instructions and a few minutes later he was ushering the Lady Angelica into the room.

Athelstan could tell that this was a time of great danger. The Lady Angelica was dressed very similarly to the abbess. One look at her beautiful, heart-shaped face framed in the clinging, silken coif and Athelstan knew why Sir Maurice was so deeply infatuated. Lady Monica made the introductions. Athelstan was sure she must be able to hear his heart thumping but Lady Angelica did not betray them. She bowed at Sir John and Athelstan and, when Lady Monica explained their presence, Angelica's eyes, cold and hard, simply dismissed Sir Maurice with one imperious flicker.

'You say Father sent you here,' she began, taking a seat beside the Lady Monica.

'I know your father of old,' Sir John replied. 'He was determined that you be taken out of danger and not be pestered by an upstart knight.'

'And you are here to remind me of my duty to my father?'

'In a word, my lady, yes,' Athelstan said.

'And you brought this…?' Angelica paused, her brilliant blue eyes now on 'Norbert'. Athelstan caught a little softness as well as a sparkle of mischief. 'You brought this good brother but what does he know of love?'

'I know it's God given,' Sir Maurice replied quickly. 'I know it never ends. I know it's like the air we breathe and that we cannot live without it.'

'Prettily put,' Lady Angelica quipped. 'I love my father but I also love someone he does not like.' She clasped her hands in mock anguish to her breast. 'What am I to do? How can love be contradictory?'

In any other circumstances Athelstan would have laughed at this little minx who was playing the game so coolly and so cleverly. Her eyelids fluttered.

'If I must love my father, as I know you are going to tell me, then I must obey him. And, if I obey him, I must give up the love I have for this knight.'

'Very well put,' Lady Monica said. 'Angelica, you really should enter our house of studies. Our library here is well furnished…'

'But it's not contradictory,' said Sir Maurice.

'Why is that?' Lady Monica snapped. 'The Fourth Commandment says thou shalt obey thy father and thy mother!'

'In life,' he replied, 'there is a hierarchy, is there not? Even in this Order you, Lady Monica, are superior and the same goes for nature. Some horses are more fleet than others, some dogs more fierce. There is also a hierarchy in love, with God at its peak.'

'And beneath that?' Angelica asked. 'Surely love of father and mother?'

'That is not what Christ said,' he replied, warming to his theme, staring fully at Angelica who now blushed. 'He said that if a woman loves a man she should leave her kith and kin and go to him so that they become one flesh. That is God's will and, what God has joined together, no man should try to drive asunder.'

'Very well put,' Angelica teased back. 'But, Brother, I am not yet this man's wife. I am not even betrothed.'

'But marriages are made in heaven,'

'Norbert' countered.

'What is this?' Lady Monica asked.

Athelstan put his hands up the sleeves of his gown and glanced sideways. Sir John was already feeling for his wineskin. Had 'Brother Norbert' gone too far?

'Are you counselling the Lady Angelica to defy her father?'

'Oh no. I was simply discussing philosophy, the true value of love and its purpose.'

'But what is love?' Angelica quickly spoke up to divert the Lady Monica.

'It is the greatest of God's gifts.' He answered slowly as if aware that he had trodden unwarily. 'It means giving the heart, the soul, the body to the other. It recognises no obstacle; it is pure, eternal fire.'

Athelstan raised his eyes heavenwards. He wondered whether Sir Maurice was speaking what he had read from Bonaventure's writings or directly, from the heart. He was surprised at the young knight's intensity and, in a strange way, he envied his burning passion. Have I, will I, ever love like this, he wondered?

'Love has no end,' Sir Maurice continued. 'We are born like that, my child. I truly believe that every man and woman has two great loves: one for God and one for their spouse. Indeed, such a love reflects the life of the Trinity. As the great Bonaventure says, "As God loves the son and gives birth to the spirit which is love", so male and female, in holy alliance, become one and create a divine life, participating in God's creation.'

'And it knows no lies?' Angelica asked.

'None whatsoever.'

'Or division?'

'None whatsoever.'

'So, what shall Angelica do?' Lady Monica asked. Athelstan noticed her face had become slightly flushed.

'She should pray,' Sir Maurice replied. 'Pray with all her mind, her heart and soul that God's will be known. My lady, it will not be Sir Thomas Parr, nor you, nor this young woman, nor even that poor unfortunate, miserable, broken-hearted...' Athelstan kicked him on the shin. 'Woebegone knight who will decide but God. And God loves lovers.' He caught the steely glint in Lady Monica's eyes. 'His will shall decide.'

'And until then?' Angelica asked, drawing herself up, the laughter bubbling in her eyes. 'Am I to stay here and pine away? Not that the good sisters here,' she added hurriedly, 'are vexatious but I do wonder how this will end.'

'God will give a sign.' Athelstan spoke up. He put his hand out and gently squeezed Sir Maurice's knees, a reminder that he had said enough.

'Brother Athelstan speaks the truth,' Sir Maurice said, his eyes holding Lady Angelica. 'He will give a sign and His will shall be known. In the end all will be well; all manner of things will be well.'

'And will you speak to this young knight?' Lady Monica asked.

'Oh yes. I shall speak to him as soon as I leave here. I will seek him out.' He held a hand up. 'And I know what he will say, for I have met such young men before though, perhaps, none so smitten as he. He will be downcast, weeping copiously, be lost in his desolation. He will tell me that he loves this young woman more than life itself. That he will love her until death and beyond. He will say because of her, he'd storm the gates of hell and confront all the powers of darkness. How heaven and earth will pass away but his love will remain eternal. How he has given his heart to the Lady Angelica and that she will either heal it or break it!'

Lady Monica sighed noisily, her eyelids fluttering. 'That poor, poor, young man. I shall pray for him, too.'

'Brother Norbert. Tell him…'

'No, no!' Lady Monica grasped Angelica's wrists. 'You can send him no message, my child.'

Athelstan caught the look in the young woman's eyes and knew there was no need. He got slowly to his feet. Sir John did likewise.

'We must leave now,' Athelstan said firmly. 'But, Lady Monica, if it is agreeable to you, we will return?'

'Oh yes, oh yes.' The abbess wiped a tear from the corner of her eyes. 'Sir Jack, all this brings back sweet memories.'

Cranston nodded solemnly. 'We have seen the days, Lady Monica. Oh, we have seen the days!'

Once they left the convent of Syon, Athelstan had no objection to Sir John 'leading them into temptation', heading like an arrow to the welcoming darkness of the taproom in the Jerusalem Tree. Sir Maurice's face was saturated in sweat. Athelstan found that his legs were trembling a little while Sir John was chuckling. Indeed, by the time they had ordered three tankards of good, frothy London ale, this had turned into guffaws of laughter.

'I wouldn't have believed that.' He sighed. 'Trust me, Athelstan, Lady Monica, or Isabella Fitzpercy as she was known when I was thin as a beanpole, is a formidable woman.'

'I'll take your word for it.' Athelstan drank the ale rather quickly. 'I'm going to pray to St Antony of Padua, my favourite saint, that Prior Anselm never finds out.' He tapped his tankard against Sir Maurice's. 'But I warn you, if he does, you'll have to join the Dominican Order. You'll make a good preacher, Sir Maurice.'

'I feel sick,' the young knight moaned. 'Believe me, sirs, I've jumped from one ship to another. I have fought hand-to-hand in the most bloody mêlée but I have never been so terrified.'

'Did you love the Lady Monica once?' Athelstan asked.

Sir John ruffled his hair and twirled his moustache.

'In my day.' He slurped from the tankard. 'In my day, I was truly a lady's man, fleet of foot, sharp of eye and keen of wit. I could dance. Oh, I could dance, Athelstan! Those were the glory days when the great Edward held his court. I mean no offence, but men like Sir Maurice were as many as pebbles on the beach. Slim as a greyhound.' Sir John wiped the tears from his eyes. 'Fast as a swooping hawk!'

Athelstan gazed affectionately at this great mound of generous, laughter-filled man with a body as big as his heart.

'You did very well, Sir Maurice,' Sir John said approvingly, then bawled for another tankard. 'And the Lady Angelica is most beautiful. You could lose your soul in those eyes. If I were younger.' He tapped his fleshy nose. 'Never tell the Lady Maude but, if I were younger, Sir Maurice, I'd enter the lists against you. Oh the days!' he sighed. 'Oh, the passing of time!'

'One thing I did notice,' Athelstan said, putting his tankard back on the table. He watched a young boy sitting in the doorway, a pet weasel in his lap. 'Lady Angelica knew nothing of that business at the Golden Cresset. Now, if that had been the work of Sir Thomas Parr, he would have let his daughter know immediately.'

'I've been thinking about that,' Sir John said, nose in his tankard. He put it down and smacked his lips. 'I've asked my scrivener, Simon, a veritable ferret of a man, to seek out among the bawds and whores, the brothels and the courtesans, to discover if any young woman is missing.'

'Sir John?' A shadow darkened the door.

'It's magic. I speak the man's name and he appears! Simon, come here!'

His spindly-shanked scrivener tottered across. Sir John offered him his tankard, which the fellow drained in one gulp. Then he smiled at Sir John's glowering glance.

'A message arrived for you at the Guildhall. You are needed at Hawkmere.' He stared quizzically at Sir Maurice. 'Don't I know you?'

'Mind your own business!' Sir John snapped. 'What's happened at Hawkmere?'

'One of the prisoners has escaped and Sir Walter Limbright's beside himself with rage!'

They arrived at Hawkmere Manor dishevelled and dusty, hot and perspiring. Sir Maurice had taken off his Dominican robes and was now dressed in brown woollen leggings and white shirt, his military cloak slung over his shoulder. He had left his friar's robes with Simon who, for a penny, had agreed to take them back across the river to St Erconwald's.

Sir John had led them at almost a furious charge up through Farringdon Ward and across Holborn. Only now and again would he stop to catch his breath and loudly declaim, 'A French prisoner escape! Limbright has got a lot to answer for.'

Hawkmere Manor was in uproar. The yard was thronged with soldiers and archers. Huntsmen had great mastiffs which strained at their leashes, their barking echoing round the grey ragstone walls. Horsemen came and went. Sir Walter strode up and down shouting orders, wiping the perspiration from his face. On the steps of the Great Hall his moon-faced daughter sat, picking at the ground. The three French prisoners stood nearby, closely guarded by men-at-arms. Beneath a tree, which afforded the only shade in the sun-filled manor yard, Monsieur Charles de Fontanel sat with his back to the trunk, sipping at a cup of wine and eating from a small napkin laid out on his lap. Beside him his horse, held by a greasy-haired squire, cropped at the sparse grass. As soon as he glimpsed them, Fontanel jumped to his feet and strode across as if to reach the visitors before Sir Walter Limbright noticed that they had arrived. He took off his small cap and gave the most mocking bow.

'My lord coroner, Brother Athelstan. We meet again.'
He gestured round the yard. 'According to the rules of
war, Sir John, prisoners are supposed to be protected and
well guarded. I will protest most resolutely to my Lord of
Gaunt.'

'It is not my fault,' Sir Walter came up, his puce-
coloured face covered in sweat, 'that the prisoner has
escaped!'

'How do we know that?' Sir John countered. 'How do
we know the poor fellow isn't dead and his body hidden
somewhere in this benighted place?'

'Philippe Routier has escaped,' Sir Walter insisted, not
even bothering to glance at de Fontanel.

'Show me!' Sir John ordered.

Sir Walter led them through the manor and into the
small garden behind the main house. He pointed to the
far wall.

'If you notice, Sir John, there are footholds there. Two
soldiers were in the garden. A quarrel broke out among
the prisoners. Routier used this to climb the garden wall.'

He led them through the garden gate and into the dusty
yard beyond where he pointed to an outhouse.

'He went through there, unobserved by the sentries,
climbed through, loosened a shutter and escaped across
the heath.'

'Wouldn't the soldiers on the wall have noticed?'
Athelstan asked.

'No, they wouldn't,' Sir John replied, feeling rather
sorry for Sir Walter, who was so agitated. 'Sentries tend to
look in: their job was to ensure that no one left the castle
rather than broke in.'

'Thank you, Sir John. They were also lazy. In fact, they
were sitting on the parapet, Routier must have known

that. Once you're out, the land dips and falls and there are gorse bushes to hide behind.' He shrugged. 'But we are wasting time.'

They returned to the main manor yard. The three visitors, together with de Fontanel, joined Sir Walter and his men as they fanned out over the hot heathland. Ahead of them the grooms released the mastiffs which now ran about trying to detect the scent. Eventually one did and, followed by the rest, bounded over the sun-scorched grass towards a copse of trees in the far distance. The hounds stopped for a while where the land dipped. When Sir John reached the place, he squatted down, Sir Maurice with him. The grass here was scuffed, bread crumbs lay scattered about.

'He paused here for a while,' the coroner murmured. 'But then pressed on. He ate…'

A loud howling cut him short. The soldiers were now running towards the copse of trees where the mastiffs were bounding about. A sound of a horn rose above the shouts and yelps.

By the time they reached the copse the dogs had been whipped in, leashes attached. Sir Walter was kneeling beside the corpse sprawled on the grass beneath the tree.

'He's dead. The poor bastard's dead as a nail!'

The others grouped round. Athelstan knelt down. One look at Routier's corpse was enough. The man's skin was now a dirty white, the eyes rolled back, the open mouth stained, the tongue slightly swollen. Athelstan undid the leather jacket then the tattered shirt beneath. Purplish stains blotched the stomach and chest. The hands were cold and waxen to the touch. Beside the corpse was a water bottle and a linen cloth containing some bread and a little dried meat. Athelstan leaned across and picked them up and sniffed at them: he could find nothing amiss.

'He could have died of apoplexy,' Sir Walter said hopefully.

De Fontanel shook his head. 'Routier was an accomplished sailor. A man of good physique.'

'I am afraid I must agree with Monsieur de Fontanel,' Athelstan said, getting to his feet. He sketched a blessing over the corpse. 'Routier was poisoned before he left the manor.' He pointed back over the heathland. 'He would feel weak, perhaps the first early symptoms, so he paused where the land dips, and took some sustenance. But, by the time he reached the trees, the full effect of the poison made itself known. The poor man collapsed here and died.'

'It's disgraceful,' de Fontanel said. 'These are citizens of the French Crown. Prisoners of war, they honourably surrendered, they should be honourably treated.'

'They are pirates,' Sir Maurice broke in, pushing his way forward to confront the Frenchman. 'Pirates,' he repeated. 'They should have been hanged out of hand. You have no proof, Monsieur de Fontanel, that Routier here was not poisoned by one of his companions.'

A quarrel would have broken out but Sir John intervened.

'Enough!' he bellowed. 'Sir Walter, have the corpse removed. Monsieur de Fontanel, you are welcome to join us in our enquiries. I suggest these begin as soon as we return to Hawkmere.'

A short while later Sir John, Athelstan and Sir Maurice sat behind the table on a dais in the hall at Hawkmere Manor. Sir Walter had served some watered wine and pieces of freshly cooked chicken. Athelstan was grateful for the food and the refreshments as well as for the chance to wash his hands and face in a bowl of rose-scented water. The keeper also ushered in Aspinall the physician who had arrived just as they returned to Hawkmere. The physician had made a superficial survey of the corpse and agreed with Athelstan's verdict.

'No apoplexy,' he announced. 'Routier was murdered, the same death as poor Serriem.'

De Fontanel sat at one end of the table. He ostentatiously refused to eat or drink anything, as did the other three prisoners after the guards brought them in. Sir John ordered the doors to be locked and guarded, took one gulp of the wine and gazed darkly around. He had already taken advice from Athelstan and Sir Maurice both of whom had agreed that honesty was the best way forward.

'There is an assassin loose at Hawkmere,' he growled. 'Whatever these men were, whatever they did, they are prisoners of the English Crown and deserve honourable treatment. Two have been murdered. Serriem here and Routier out on that dry heathland. The questions are how and who is responsible? Sir Walter, when Serriem's corpse was discovered, nothing untoward was found in his chamber?'

'Nothing, Sir John. As I said, Serriem's corpse was found on the floor.'

Sir John turned to the three French prisoners.

'And, to the best of your knowledge, Serriem only ate and drank what you did?'

'Yes,' Gresnay lisped, looking rather bored by the proceedings.

'And the same goes for Routier!' Maneil snarled. 'This morning we came down to this damnable place.' He gestured round the hall. 'We had the usual mangy bread, smelly meat and foul drink.'

'And Routier ate all his?' Athelstan asked.

'Of course he did. He was planning to escape. He needed all the sustenance he could to keep his strength up.'

'But that's not true,' Athelstan replied. 'When we found his corpse he carried a water bottle, scraps of bread and meat.'

'I gave those to him.' Gresnay languidly lifted a hand. 'Why?'

'Because he was going to escape. He told us last night.'

'And that's why you agreed to quarrel in the garden to divert the attention of the guards?'

'Very perceptive,' Gresnay drawled.

'And why did he wish to escape?' Athelstan continued, ignoring the jibe.

'Because he fell in love with Sir Walter's daughter,' Gresnay grinned. 'They were going to elope, just like Sir Maurice here with the Lady Angelica.'

Both Sir Walter and Sir Maurice sprang to their feet but Sir John roared at them to sit down.

'And you, sir,' he pointed at Gresnay, 'will keep a civil tongue in your head or you'll be in a dungeon in the Tower!'

'Don't threaten me!' Gresnay screamed back, his face tight with anger. 'I am a citizen of France, a sailor. I'm kept in this fly-blown, rat-infested midden-heap and threatened. The Tower would be a welcome change!'

'Routier escaped,' Vamier intervened smoothly, 'because he could no longer tolerate being confined, trapped like a bird in a snare. He thought he had seen a weakness and could use it. He would have either gone into London or some other port. Sought shelter and succour from some captain. I cannot blame him.'

'Why didn't you go with him?' Athelstan asked.

Vamier shrugged. 'His chances were poor. The more who tried to escape, the more dangerous it became. Anyway, our ransoms will be paid soon.'

'Yes, I was going to ask about that.' Athelstan picked up his writing bag and put it on the table. 'Monsieur de Fontanel, these men are experienced sailors, as English shipping has discovered. Why doesn't the French Crown pay their ransoms and have done with it?'

Athelstan was not surprised to see the prisoners nod their heads in agreement. De Fontanel spread his hands.

'You have French prisoners at Hawkmere but you also have them in Calais, Dover, Winchelsea and Rye. The French parliament would be inundated with petitions.' He smiled crookedly. 'But you are right, Brother, I have pressed these men's claims with my masters in France; their ransoms will arrive soon.'

'But not soon enough for Routier!' Vamier spat out.

'I am not responsible for what happens in Paris. I do the best I can for your care.' De Fontanel then added something quickly in French.

Vamier sat back crestfallen.

'What was that, Monsieur?' Athelstan asked.

'I merely reminded him that I was not responsible for his capture.'

'Let us return to the matter in hand.' Sir John took a swig from his wineskin. 'Routier was poisoned before he fled Hawkmere. You, Monsieur Gresnay, were the last to give him anything to eat or drink, which could make you the poisoner.'

'It is also very obvious,' Gresnay sneered back, 'if I had given Routier poison, I would know he could not travel very far. I would expect to be accused, wouldn't I?'

Athelstan had to agree with the Frenchman's logic. He was about to ask further questions when the door to the hall was thrown open and a soldier clattered in, helmet in hand, his face white.

'Sir Walter, it's your daughter! You'd best come quickly!'

Chapter 12

'I think we'd best go with him,' Athelstan said.

Sir Walter was striding up the main staircase. In the stairwell a frightened-looking servant whispered in his ear and he stopped, grabbing the newel of the staircase. He rocked backwards and forwards and gave the most terrible moan.

'Oh my God!' he cried. 'My poor, poor daughter!'

He disappeared down the gallery. By the time Athelstan, Sir John and Sir Maurice reached it they could hear his lamentations through an open door. Inside the chamber they found him kneeling beside his prostrate daughter who lay sprawled on her back, head slightly twisted to one side. Athelstan grasped the girl's wrist and felt her throat for the life pulse but he could detect nothing. He turned the girl's face. The eyelids were almost closed, jaws slack, a drool of spittle on her chin; her face was livid rather than pale, her skin cold and clammy. Athelstan ignored Sir Walter's groans and quickly checked the girl's body but could see no mark, bruise or slash. Aspinall came in the doorway and crouched down. He held the girl's face between his hands and, ignoring Sir Walter's protests, took a small knife and cut the brown smock. Her neck and upper chest were already tainted with faint purplish blotches.

'She's been poisoned,' Aspinall said softly. 'Probably died within the hour.'

'Why?' Sir Walter clutched his daughter's hair, twisting it round his fingers. 'Why?' he moaned. 'She had no wits, she had no life!'

Athelstan whispered the '*Absolvo Te*' in the dead woman's ear, uttered a short prayer then blessed the corpse. He got up and helped Sir Walter to his feet. The knight's face was stricken with grief, tears streaming down his face, lips moving but no sound came.

'Sir Walter?' Athelstan made him sit down on a chair. 'Sir Walter, listen to me.'

The knight turned, bleary-eyed.

'Those bastards!' he grated. 'Those French bastards! They are responsible for that!' He clasped his hands together and rocked backwards and forwards. 'I'll kill them all!' he whispered. 'I'll kill every single one! You'll help me won't you, Cranston? The friar here can absolve them then we'll hang them from a bloody tree for the pirates they are: murderers, assassins, ravishers of women, killers of children!'

'Sir Walter! We have no proof of that.'

Sir John looked at the chamber. It contained a few leather chests, some faded cloths on the walls, an aumbry, two stools and a small writing desk beneath the window with a clerk's stool pushed alongside it.

'This was your daughter's chamber?'

Sir Walter nodded.

'And where was she before?'

'Why are you asking me?'

'Where was your daughter before?' Athelstan insisted.

'She went down into the garden. She just wandered around, like she always did. Brother, who would poison such a poor thing?' He wetted his lips. 'I need some wine,' he rasped.

Aspinall left and came back with a large goblet filled to the brim, but Sir John stopped him.

'Where did you get that?'

'From Sir Walter's chamber further down the gallery. It's packed with poison, Sir John,' he added wearily.

'Take a sip yourself,' the coroner ordered.

The doctor made to refuse but Sir John's hand fell to the dagger in his belt.

'Oh, for the love of heaven!' Aspinall complained and took a deep draught. He then went across and gave it to Sir Walter, who seized it greedily. He drained it in one gulp then gestured at his daughter's corpse.

'Pick her up,' he ordered. 'She's not a dog to lie sprawled on the floor!'

They lifted the young woman's corpse and laid it gently out on the bed, crossing the hands. Sir John opened his purse and put two pennies over the eyes.

'Leave me.' Sir Walter forced a smile, but there were tears in his eyes. 'Leave me for a while. You have business with those demons below.'

'Stay with Sir Walter,' Athelstan asked Aspinall. 'Sir John, Sir Maurice, we should go down.'

They returned to the hall and told the Frenchmen what had happened. De Fontanel quickly crossed himself. The prisoners, huddled together, looked frightened.

'It's not safe to leave us here.' Vamier spoke up. 'Sir Walter is our enemy already. He will blame us for his daughter's death.' He banged the table with his fist. 'I demand to be removed! To be given safer and better custody than this!'

'I can arrange that.' Sir John took a seat, tapping his hands on the table-top.

Athelstan sat down and took out his writing tray. He opened the ink pot, dipped the quill in but simply scratched the parchment, making strange signs and symbols. He had little to write; there was nothing about this affair which made sense. He glanced across at Sir John.

'*Semper veritas*,' he murmured. 'Always the truth. Perhaps it's time we were blunt and honest and told these gentlemen that they are, truly, in mortal danger but not from Sir Walter. Indeed, if we removed them elsewhere, or advised the Regent to change their keeper, it would look as if the finger of accusation were being pointed at Sir Walter.'

'He is, as you correctly say,' de Fontanel drawled, 'their keeper. He is responsible for their safety. I am truly sorry his daughter died but Vamier does speak the truth, Limbright is our enemy.'

'Tell me, gentlemen.' Sir John looked down the table at the three prisoners. 'Have you ever heard of Mercurius?'

Athelstan studied their faces. Was that a flicker of recognition in Gresnay's eyes?

'Mercurius?' de Fontanel sneered. 'Who is Mercurius?'

'He's an assassin,' Athelstan replied slowly. 'Employed by the French Crown. He kills people whom his masters in Paris want removed as quickly as possible. Do you know, sirs, you are probably safer in England than you are in France.'

'Don't talk in riddles!' Gresnay snapped.

'Mercurius is an assassin,' Athelstan repeated. 'The French believe the *St Sulpice* and *St Denis* were betrayed by an officer on one of those two ships. We think, indeed we know, Mercurius is in England. His task is to kill the traitor among you.'

'In which case,' Maneil replied guardedly, 'he has killed two.'

'No, no.' Gresnay spoke up. 'I realise what you are saying, Brother. Mercurius doesn't really care how many of us die.'

'As long as the traitor dies,' Athelstan declared, 'that's all that matters. Sentence of death has been passed against you.'

'But who?' Vamier sprang to his feet. He gripped Gresnay's shoulder. 'Is it you, Jean?'

'What do you mean?' Gresnay squirmed free.

'Vamier's telling the truth,' Maneil said. 'You were once a clerk! You're always boasting about your high-ranking connections in Paris.'

'And what about you?' Gresnay countered. 'Didn't you get preferment to the *St Denis* because of a relative at court?'

'This is preposterous!' De Fontanel got to his feet and walked down the table, sitting down next to Vamier. 'Sir John Cranston, I am an accredited envoy, a high-ranking clerk of the chancery. I have never heard of this Mercurius. I think you are trying to divide these men, frighten them into making confessions, make them watch each other.'

'It would certainly help,' Sir John said as he smiled back. 'If they watched each other more closely, perhaps they could discover the murderer?'

De Fontanel laid his hands on the table, spreading his fingers.

'Five men were here,' he replied slowly. 'Two are dead of the same poison but they only ate and drank what the others did. True, Serriem may have been tricked but Routier was alert to any danger. And why should Mercurius kill that poor girl who was a danger to no one? Don't you agree, Brother?'

Athelstan raised his eyes heavenwards. The murder of Sir Walter's daughter threw all these theories back into the melting pot.

'It could be an act of vengeance,' Sir Maurice said.

'Oh, come, come!' Vamier snarled. 'Sir Maurice, I would like to take your head and that of Sir Walter. We are soldiers, fighters. Why should we kill a poor wench? She had a woman's body but a child's mind.'

'Which is due to the French,' Sir Maurice added quickly.

De Fontanel got to his feet. 'I am not here to trade insults. Sir John, what are you going to do about the custody of these men?'

'They are going to stay here. Brother Athelstan, my secretarius, is correct. If they are taken elsewhere and Sir Walter is relieved of his duties, distraught though he is, that would look as if he were under suspicion.'

'In which case I shall send urgent despatch to France asking for the ransoms to be forwarded as quickly as possible. I ask my fellow countrymen to fall to their prayers and recite their Aves daily and be very careful of what they eat or drink.' He bowed. 'I shall return.'

His footsteps echoed along the gaunt, empty hallway, the door slamming shut behind him.

'We are finished here,' Athelstan said. 'There is nothing more we can do except speak to Aspinall. The business of Vulpina,' he added in a whisper.

Sir John nodded and, followed by Sir Maurice, left the hall. Athelstan sat sketching two parallel lines on a piece of parchment.

'You seem perplexed.' Vamier's tone was kindly.

'There is great evil here,' Athelstan replied slowly. 'I am right to call this the Devil's Domain.'

'I know of your Order in France,' Gresnay said. 'My father hired a Dominican as a chancery priest, a kindly man. Is there nothing you can do for us, Brother?'

Athelstan shook his head. 'Nothing. At least for the moment. Tell me now, on your oaths. Forget I am an Englishman, think of me only as a priest. Tell me, is there anything you saw or heard which provoked suspicion?'

The three men sat in silence then, one by one, shook their heads.

'Your two colleagues who have been murdered, you saw neither of them eat or drink anything extra?'

Again the shake of heads.

'Or did they say anything to you?'

'Brother.' Maneil spoke up. 'We have been down the same paths ourselves. We have no food or drink in our chambers. All our sustenance comes from Sir Walter's kitchens, paltry though it may be.'

'Does de Fontanel bring food?'

'Never. Sir Walter would not allow it.'

'I tell you this.' Gresnay pointed a finger. 'Yesterday morning we all took a solemn oath not to eat or drink what another didn't. We also searched each other and the shabby garrets which serve as our chambers. Nothing was found.'

'You did that?' Athelstan asked.

'Brother, a killer stalks us. We have to be sure.'

Athelstan got to his feet.

'One thing does intrigue me.'

'What's that?' Vamier asked.

'Well, Routier escaped this morning. He climbed the garden wall, crossed the yard and went through an outhouse. How did he know which path to take? How did he know that the outhouse was deserted, that the shutter was loose? You have never been allowed into that part of the manor, have you?'

All three shook their heads.

'Then I bid you good day, sirs.'

Athelstan left the hall and wandered out into the garden. He looked up at the parapets and realised that, if the sentries were less than vigilant, it would be easy for someone to cross the corner of the wall and climb the crumbling buttress. He now did this and let himself down the other side. The yard or bailey was deserted. A slight breeze was blowing up little clouds of dust. Built alongside, into the far curtain wall, were a line of wooden outhouses, probably used for storage. Athelstan crossed over and went in. Most of the doors were closed. Athelstan went through the one which hung ajar. Inside the walls were dirty and cobwebbed, and there was a smell of straw and horse manure. In the far wall the shutters were closed and barred. Athelstan lifted the bar, opened the shutters and looked out across the sun-scorched heath-land. He put his bag down, climbed out and began to walk, following the same path Routier had probably taken. He stopped and looked about him. Above him a crow circled, cawing raucously. Athelstan saw that there was no sentry on the rear wall while those along the side must not only have been lax but distracted by the supposed quarrel taking place among the prisoners. Routier would have run, heading for that distant copse of trees. Even if the sentries had glimpsed him they might have thought it was some chapman or peasant, not realising one of their prisoners had escaped. He looked back at the window whose shutters still hung open. Routier had probably closed them when he fled. Athelstan scanned the sky.

'There's something wrong here,' he said to himself. 'Something I've seen and heard but it's always the same: pieces in a puzzle!'

He walked back, climbed through the window, closed the shutters behind him and went out. His two companions were waiting for him in the hall. As Athelstan arrived, Aspinall came downstairs.

'Are you leaving now, Sir John?'

'Once we've asked you some questions, sir.' Athelstan smiled.

Aspinall peered at him. 'Why, Brother, what can I tell you?'

'Well, first, how is Sir Walter?'

'I persuaded him to go back to his chamber. He has fallen asleep. I will see to his daughter's corpse. Sir Walter will probably have it taken to the city and buried in the house of Crutched Friars; that's where Sir Walter attends Sunday Mass.'

Aspinall sat down on a bench and stretched out his legs. 'What other questions, Brother?'

'Does Sir Walter often go into the city?' Sir John asked. 'We know he was a customer of the poisoner Vulpina.'

Aspinall glanced up quickly.

'As you were, sir.'

'Vulpina's dead,' Aspinall said. 'She died in a house fire.'

'No, she was murdered.' Athelstan sat down on the bench next to him. 'She was murdered, Master Aspinall. Someone wanted to keep the secrets Vulpina held secret for ever.'

The physician shifted uneasily.

'What are you implying, Brother? Yes, I went to Vulpina. Her collection of herbs and poisons was well known throughout the city. An evil, ruthless woman,' Aspinall continued. 'She still had every herb and, yes, I bought poisons from her. Foxglove can be used to quicken the heart and stir sluggish blood. Arsenic, both red and white, can be administered to those who have pains in the gut. Just because a plant is poisonous doesn't mean it can't be used to heal. It all depends on the quantities you use.'

'Did you know Sir Walter purchased potions from her?'

Aspinall was about to deny this but then he shrugged.

'Yes. Sir Walter bought potions and poisons. I advised him not to but he followed Vulpina's advice.'

'Why?' Sir John asked.

'For his daughter,' Aspinall replied. 'I believe there was nothing that could be done for the poor girl. She was witless, her mind was empty. Vulpina advised Sir Walter differently. He bought herbal remedies to keep her calm and soothe her ramblings: St John's wort, a little belladonna. Such plants can have a soothing effect when the humours of the mind have been disturbed and are no longer in alignment. Nevertheless, I tell you this, Brother, the deaths which have occurred here are not the work of some common potion. I have never seen a poison with such an effect. You see,' he saw the puzzlement in Athelstan's eyes, 'if you want to poison a man, such potions take effect almost immediately. If I gave a man of Sir John Cranston's girth a cup heavily tainted with arsenic he would, within a short while, feel its effect. This is different. If you disbelieve me, ask any physician from the city. A man like Routier could take the poison but its effect is much slower to begin with; then it hastens up and the malignancy stops the heart.'

'So?' Athelstan asked. 'The murderer has chosen this potion because it works slowly?'

'Possibly,' Aspinall agreed. 'What I'm saying, gentlemen, is that most poisons kill quickly. If you reduce the grains, illness may occur but not death. This, whatever it is, acts in a simple way: it is prolonged yet still deadly. A good choice, because the assassin certainly doesn't want to be near when his victim dies.'

'But if that's the case,' Sir Maurice asked, 'how did the poor wench die?'

'I think it was an accident. I really do. Somehow or other, Lucy found this poison and ate it. You saw her yourself: she was constantly picking things up and putting them in her mouth. I have seen her in the hall after meals are finished, eating crumbs from the table.'

'It's possible,' Athelstan mused. 'I wonder if the assassin intended to kill Routier and one other? Perhaps a sweet-meat was left? A piece of cheese or bread smeared with a noxious substance? Master Aspinall, are the prisoners' rooms locked?'

'From what I can gather, at night they are but, during the day, no. They are allowed to take the air in the morning and evening but, for most of the time, the prisoners are kept here in the manor. They talk, sleep or play a game.'

'So Lucy could have wandered into one of their rooms?' Sir John asked.

'That's possible.'

'In which case,' Athelstan declared, 'those prisoners told me a lie. They said they had searched each other's rooms to clear any suspicions but nothing was found. Yet here's a witless maid who not only finds the poison but eats it.'

Cranston took a drink from his wineskin and glanced back up the stairs.

'It could still be murder,' he said over his shoulder. 'Limbright hates the French, the French hate him. The death of his daughter could be seen as a terrible act of vengeance. Master Aspinall, do you think that any of these prisoners have such malice?'

The physician shook his head.

'They strike me as soldiers, warriors. They might pillage and burn in the heat of battle but deliberately kill a poor madcap?' He pulled a face. 'No.'

Athelstan got to his feet. 'Lucy was found in her own room. The door was open. Is that not right?'

'So the soldier told me,' Aspinall replied. 'The door was open and she was lying on the rushes.'

'What is the longest time over which a poison can take effect?' Athelstan asked.

'In my studies,' Aspinall shrugged, 'certainly no more than an hour. However, if I follow your logic, it would be nigh impossible to see where Lucy had gone. She wandered this manor like a ghost.'

'So, it would be futile to investigate her death?'

'Yes, Brother, Lucy was frightened of both the French and the guards. She would take nothing from them and only heaven knows where she was in the time before her death!'

Athelstan glanced away. Lucy had certainly taken or been given the poison during the chaos caused by Routier's escape. Aspinall was right: God knows where she went but, Athelstan reflected, would the girl take something from this physician?

'Brother Athelstan, Sir John.' Sir Maurice, arms crossed, tapped his boot against the paved stones. 'Let us say for the sake of argument that the assassin is one of the prisoners. I know it's hard to believe but…'

'I know what you are going to say,' Sir John interrupted. 'Logic dictates that there will be two more deaths and the man left alive must be the assassin.'

'Not necessarily,' Athelstan said. 'God knows what de Fontanel will do. He may have the prisoners' ransoms ready and have them out of Hawkmere. For all we know Routier's death could be the last. What we should do before we leave Hawkmere is search this manor from top to bottom, and that includes the prisoners' rooms. Master Aspinall, if you would keep an eye on Sir Walter, my colleagues and I will begin our search. The guards cannot protest. I suppose Monsieur de Fontanel has left?'

'Yes,' Sir John replied. 'He left the hall and walked straight out of the manor.'

Athelstan rubbed the end of his nose. 'Let's begin in the garden.'

–

In the small garret which served as his chamber as well as his cell, Eudes Maneil pulled the bolt securing his door and sat at the small table placed just beneath the arrow slit window. He stared out at the blue sky. A bird whirled by and Maneil felt a pang of envy. The same sky, the same sun as in France. He half-closed his eyes. The Paris markets would be busy now. Its taverns and the cookshops full, the narrow streets a sea of colour, thronged with merchants, their wives, students from the Sorbonne, clerks and scriveners. How nice it would be to stroll those alleyways, flirt with the courtesans then sit in a tavern and enjoy a stew of fresh meat and vegetables, a cup of malmsey or some of the best claret Bordeaux could produce. Maneil's stomach grumbled in protest. He opened his eyes, his fingers tapping the table. Would he ever see Paris again? The *St Sulpice* and *St Denis* had been taken. He had resigned himself to a fairly lengthy and sordid imprisonment amongst the Goddamns, these tail-bearing Englishmen, but now it had grown dangerous. Maneil looked over his shoulder at the door. How on earth had Routier and Serriem been killed? He was sure that both his companions had been careful in what they ate and drank. There was no hidden supply of food. Sir Walter was a tight-fisted miser and the kitchen and buttery were kept under close guard. So was he the murderer? Maneil scratched his chin. Was that why the poor, witless Lucy had died? Had she gone into her father's chamber? Or was it someone else? There was something he had seen this morning, out there in the garden. He recalled Routier walking up and down then he had left, gone back into the hall. Someone had followed him, he was sure, but who was it?

Maneil went and lay down on his bed. Before he had run away to sea, Maneil's father had put him into one of the best church schools in Paris. Maneil recalled how he had been taught to collect evidence, sift it and draw a conclusion. So, if the assassin was one of them, that same person must be the spy in the pay of the English milords. But that seemed impossible. If there had been a spy among the French officers taking English gold, why should that spy now turn assassin? Maneil breathed in. Never once, and he had known the other four for a number of years, had he seen or heard anything suspicious.

Indeed, his companions had all lost kinfolk to the English and were fiercely committed to the bloody war at sea. So, if there was no spy, why should one of them now turn to murder? Maneil recalled Routier sitting at table breaking his fast. He had been against his companion's attempted escape. Routier, however, had whispered that he could stand Hawkmere no longer: he had to break out or he would become as witless as Limbright's daughter. He had refused to listen to Maneil. He'd eaten his bread and drunk the ale Sir Walter had provided. Maneil had been sitting by him all the time. True, Gresnay had saved some of his meal for Routier to take with him. However, this had been a spontaneous gesture while Gresnay had eaten some of the bread and meat. They had then left the hall and gone into the garden. The only time Routier had left them was when he went back into the manor.

Maneil heard a knock on the door.

'Who is it?'

Again the knock. Maneil sighed and swung his feet off the bed. He pulled back the bolt, opened it and the crossbow quarrel struck him full in the throat.

Chapter 13

Athelstan was still studying the garden; Sir John was taking some small refreshment in the arbour, mopping his brow, Sir Maurice was elsewhere when Simon Gismond, Sir Walter Limbright's captain of the guard, came out shouting for Sir John.

'What is it?' he demanded crossly.

'My lord coroner, one of the prisoners is dead.'

'Poisoned?' Athelstan asked.

'Might as well be. A crossbow quarrel full in his throat. The corpse is still slightly warm. You'd best come and see.'

They followed him back into the manor and met Sir Maurice on the stairs. All three followed Gismond up along the dusty, shabby gallery. The door to the chamber was open. Maneil was lying on his back, arms out, head slightly twisted. The front of his jerkin was soaked in blood which had splashed out to form a dark red puddle around his head. A soldier stood by the window gazing out.

'Who found the corpse?' Athelstan asked.

'I did.'

The soldier came over, cradling his helmet in his hand. He had a plough boy's face, open and honest, his cheeks chapped and red. He took one fresh look at the corpse and hurried back to be sick in the small latrine pot beneath the window.

Athelstan crouched down. He pressed his hand against Maneil's cheek. It was not yet cold. Aspinall came in. He took one look at the corpse, groaned and knelt beside it, pulling down the jerkin. Athelstan could see the great red angry hole around the crossbow bolt. He looked back at the door. The dead man had been flung at least two or three feet back into the room by the force of the quarrel.

'He would have died instantly,' Athelstan said. 'The crossbow must have been held only inches from his neck.'

Athelstan went through the dead man's wallet but he could find nothing except a few coins and a scrap of parchment. He walked over to the bed and looked down at the dirty, dishevelled blanket, picked it up and sniffed the sour, acrid smell of stale sweat. He threw it back and turned as Gresnay and Vamier were led into the room. Sir John dismissed the guard but told Gismond to stay. The two Frenchmen took one look at their colleague's dead face and went and sat on the bed, the most woebegone expression on their faces.

'We are going to die,' Gresnay announced. 'We are going to die in this awful benighted manor. Killed by some tail-bearing Englishman. Do you understand me?' He got to his feet, his face mottled in fury.

He turned to Sir John but Gismond stepped in between them.

'I think you'd best sit down,' he said softly. 'The coroner is not responsible for your friend's murder.'

'Well, who is?' Vamier expostulated. He flapped his hands around. 'Where's the arbalest? Where's the crossbow? Gresnay and I haven't got a pin between us!'

'Master Gismond,' Sir John barked. 'Take Maltravers here. I want this place searched for anything suspicious: knives, daggers, cross-bows, anything!'

Ordering Vamier to take the corpse by the feet, he shifted the body on to the bed. Athelstan knelt down, whispered the words of absolution and made the sign of the cross. He had barely finished when Sir Walter staggered into the room, clutching his stomach. He took one look at the corpse and crouched down just inside the door. His face was pale, flecks of vomit stained the corner of his mouth.

'Another one dead!' he grated. 'I've lost everything.' He began to sob quietly, head down, shoulders shaking.

Even the prisoners looked pityingly at their keeper.

'I swear to God I had no hand in the deaths of any of them. While my daughter's death is a punishment from God for my hateful heart!'

Sir John walked over and crouched beside him.

'Come on, man,' he urged. 'Take a drop of wine. It will settle your stomach, not too much.'

Sir Walter obeyed.

'Now, get to your feet.' Sir John pulled him up by the elbows. 'You are an English knight, you are distraught and, like us, you are in the Devil's Domain. A killer walks the galleries of Hawkmere. Now, it could be one of those.' He pointed across to the two Frenchmen. 'Or, indeed, anyone here.'

'It can't be the Frenchmen,' Sir Walter muttered, glancing shame-facedly at them. 'Not even my own men carry crossbows. They are locked away in the armoury and that's padlocked twice over. Gismond keeps one key, I keep the other.' He spread his hands beseechingly. 'Sir John, what am I to do?'

'I have a suggestion.' The friar spoke up. 'And it may save more lives. Our two French prisoners should be separated and locked in their chambers. A guard inside and one without. They are to be served food direct from the kitchen. They are not allowed to meet anyone except the soldier who is in the room with them.'

Vamier went to protest but Athelstan held his hand up.

'No, no, it's the safest way.'

'He speaks the truth,' Gresnay said. 'It should have been done before. I am sorry, Pierre.' He glanced at Vamier. 'But, until our ransoms are paid, even if the assassin strikes again, such measures might trap him.'

'But why be kept separate?' Vamier protested. 'Whoever killed poor Maneil there carried a crossbow and quarrel. Whoever killed him must have been a member of the garrison here or a visitor. And,' he added finally, 'Monsieur de Fontanel left long before poor Eudes was slain.'

Sir Maurice came back into the room.

'The armoury is still sealed and locked,' he announced. 'Gismond told me that no man carries arbalests, the guards have long bows and quivers.'

'Sir Walter.' Sir John snapped his fingers. 'Have these two men put in their chambers immediately! The guards must be posted. Care must be taken with their food.'

'I'll taste it myself,' Sir Walter offered, eager to assert his authority.

Sir John and Athelstan made their farewells and, a short while later, they and Sir Maurice left the manor.

The day was drawing on. Athelstan reckoned it must be close to Vespers time, for the blue sky was scored with red. A breeze had sprung up and clouds were massing over the city. He looked at the scorched grass.

'It will be good if there's a storm,' he remarked. 'The earth needs to drink and we, Sir John, need to trap an assassin.'

'I am not going back into the city. I suppose, Sir Maurice, you'll accompany Brother Athelstan. I am going to search out my friends the scrimperers,' the coroner said, swaying slightly on his feet. 'I wonder if they know about some poor whore who has gone missing?'

'Ah, the business of the Golden Cresset?' Sir Maurice asked.

'They'll be able to help,' Athelstan said. 'I know their reputation. But, Sir John, while you are busy with that could you seek someone else who deals in poisons?'

'Vulpina was the best,' he grumbled. 'But I'll search and see.'

They walked for a while towards St Giles, where Sir John left them. Athelstan felt tired so he and Sir Maurice hired a ride in a cart which made its way down through Portsoken around the walls of the city and down to the Tower. They then walked on to the Woolquay and hired a barge to take them across the now choppy waters of the Thames into Southwark.

By the time they reached St Erconwald's, the storm Athelstan had predicted was beginning to gather. The breeze had grown strong, the clouds, blocking out the setting sun, now massed low and threatening. They found Godbless in the church fast asleep with one arm round Thaddeus. Huddle had been busy on the wall and, in the fading light, Athelstan could make out the charcoal lines. He told Sir Maurice to wake Godbless and take him and Thaddeus back to the priest's house while he crossed the cemetery.

The ditch Watkin and Pike had dug was growing longer. Athelstan studied the hard-packed earth around the foundations of the cemetery wall.

'That was built to last,' he said to himself. 'There's nothing wrong with that wall.'

Still slightly suspicious, Athelstan was about to climb in to examine it more closely when the first large drops of rain changed his mind. He went back, closed the death house door and returned to the kitchen where Sir Maurice had already built up the small fire. The knight tapped the cauldron hung on a tripod.

'Someone has left you a stew.' He sniffed at it. 'The meat and vegetables are fresh.'

Athelstan knelt beside him.

'It's Benedicta,' he said. 'The widow woman.' He gestured round. 'She keeps the place clean as a pin. Where's Godbless?'

'He's still in church. He says he likes it there.'

Athelstan went to the buttery where he filled a bowl of water and washed his hands and face. He went up into the bed loft and found the Dominican robes Simon the scrivener had brought back. Below the door opened and Godbless came in.

'Stir the stew!' Athelstan shouted down. 'You'll find a ladle in the buttery! When it's piping hot, call me down!'

'I like stews,' Godbless called up. 'Master Merrylegs gave me a pie free but I'm still hungry!'

'Good.'

Athelstan lay down on the bed, staring up at the ceiling. He said a short prayer but, distracted, his mind went back to Hawkmere. How did those men die? Routier like some wretched dog out on the heathland. And Maneil with a crossbow bolt in his throat. Sir Walter and Aspinall had access to poisons but, although he had no real evidence, he believed that the physician's explanation was satisfactory. So, where did the poisons come from? And who had the

crossbow and the bolt? Surely not one of the French prisoners? He heard Sir Maurice laugh at something Godbless
had said. Was Maltravers innocent? Or, despite his protes-
tations, Limbright? Or was there someone else in the
manor? Some secret assassin hidden away? Was Mercurius
one of the guards?

'It's possible,' Athelstan whispered, his eyes growing
heavy. He fell into a deep sleep and woke confused when
the knight shook him by the shoulder.

Athelstan pulled himself up.

'Brother, Godbless has been cooking, it's ready now.'

Athelstan savoured the sweet smell wafting up from the
kitchen.

'I am starving,' he said and followed Sir Maurice down
the ladder.

Bonaventure had returned and was nestling up to
Thaddeus beside the hearth. Godbless had set the table
with three bowls, horn spoons, jugs and pewter goblets
and a jug of ale from the buttery. Athelstan, still half-
asleep, murmured grace and they sat down. He broke
the bread, blessed it and gave pieces to his companions.
Outside he could hear the rain drumming and the distant
rumble of thunder. He ate slowly, for the stew was deli-
cious but boiling hot. Godbless chattered like a squirrel
and Sir Maurice, rather bemused, just stared and listened
as this old beggar man described how he had fought in
the Low Countries, in France and even Northern Italy.
Athelstan was still distracted by what had happened at
Hawkmere. He could make no sense of it. Now and again
he stole a look at the young knight, who could speak so
elegantly about love. Was he as innocent as he claimed?

'What are you going to do about the ghosts, Brother?' Godbless put his spoon down and stared hungrily at the cauldron above the fire.

'Eat some more,' Athelstan told him. 'And there's another manchet loaf in the kitchen wrapped in a linen cloth.'

'What's this?' Sir Maurice asked as the beggar man hurried off.

'He believes that we have ghosts in St Erconwald's cemetery. Now, I believe in ghosts but not in Southwark. I think it's some game or a jest, or probably one of my parishioners up to mischief.'

'There are ghosts.' Godbless shook his head and returned to the table.

'You said something else,' Athelstan recalled. 'About a man in Italy who should have died but you saw him alive?'

Godbless looked bleary-eyed and Athelstan wondered how much he had drunk that day.

'Yes, yes.' Godbless scratched his chin. 'I don't really remember now. It will come back to me. Are you Dominican or are you not?' he asked Sir Maurice, abruptly changing the conversation. 'That smirking scrivener who brought the robe back, he said it belonged to you.'

'I was a Dominican for a short while,' Sir Maurice replied. 'And it's a great secret and you must not tell anyone, Godbless.'

They paused as the thunder cracked directly above them. Outside the window the lightning flashed, the rain now bouncing off the roof.

'I had best check on my death house,' Godbless said, putting his spoon down. 'No, no,' he said as Athelstan went to restrain him. 'I want to make sure there are no holes in that roof.' He grabbed his cloak, put it over his head and left.

'A strange fellow.' Maltravers filled his goblet. 'Brother, can we return to the convent tomorrow?'

'No. I am sorry, Sir Maurice, Lady Monica might become too suspicious. Perhaps Wednesday after I have celebrated the Guild of Rat-Catchers' Mass.' He jumped at a knock on the door.

'Who is it?' he called.

'Brother, for the love of God, please help us!'

At the door, a man stood in the darkness, supporting another, his head down, arm across his shoulder. Athelstan glimpsed an unshaven face and a brass ring glinting in an ear lobe.

'We've been attacked, Brother! For the love of God, can we come in?'

Athelstan stepped back. The man, grunting and groaning, brought his companion into the house. Athelstan was closing the door when he heard Sir Maurice's exclamation. He turned round to see both men were now on their feet, cowls back, the crossbows in their hands lowered and primed. They were both shaven-headed with lean, vicious faces, made all the more so by the brass rings hanging from their ear lobes. Athelstan glimpsed the sword and dagger belts beneath their cloaks.

'I am a priest,' Athelstan said, coming forward.

Both men stood back.

'You have no right to come here! This is God's acre and you commit the terrible sin of sacrilege!'

'It's years since I've been to church,' the taller one declared. 'So, no mealy-mouthed homilies though, if you wish, you may say a prayer.'

He gestured at Athelstan to move away from the door, to the far side of the table where the knight moved restlessly, his gaze straying to the inglenook where his war belt hung on a hook, the hilt of his sword glistening enticingly in the candlelight. The shaven-head leader followed his gaze.

'You may, if you wish.' He grinned, running his tongue round cracked, yellow teeth. 'You have eaten and drunk well. You'll not be as lithesome as you might like.'

'Why are you here?' Athelstan asked.

He could see both men were bent on murder yet there was nothing else he could do. He recognised the types, killers from the alleyways, professional assassins.

'Like you, Brother, we have a task to do.'

'And that is?'

The taller shaven-head pointed quickly at Sir Maurice.

'He has to die. I am afraid you must die with him because we cannot leave a witness.'

He glanced down at the fire where Thaddeus, crouched on his haunches, was basking in the heat; Bonaventure beside him had risen, back arched, tail up, as if he sensed these men were threatening.

'Who sent you?' Athelstan asked.

'Why, the devil himself.'

Athelstan gazed at the knight, who gestured with his eyes towards the fire. Athelstan swallowed hard. He knew the knight was asking that he cross between the two assassins and himself. Athelstan took a step forward.

'Where are you going, Brother?'

'I'm going to douse the fire,' Athelstan said. 'If I am to be killed, I don't want the house burned down. They are poor people I serve. The Bishop would expect them to build a new house for the next priest.'

He saw a flicker of puzzlement in shaven-head's eyes, as he went forward.

'Come on now, Bonaventure!'

Athelstan stooped, picking up the cat. He heard a movement and turned quickly, throwing the cat at the shaven-head's feet. Sir Maurice had moved, his speed taking Athelstan by surprise. A crossbow bolt whirred and smacked into the plaster at the far end. Athelstan felt himself pushed. He went staggering back and, by the time he regained his balance, Sir Maurice was among the killers. Both men had loosed their crossbows and that was their undoing, for they didn't have time to draw sword and dagger. The knight's sword sliced into the shoulder of one, sending him screaming back. The other threw his crossbow at Sir Maurice, hitting him on the arm as he turned. The knight stopped, flinching with pain, giving the taller shaven-head time to draw his weapons, throwing his cloak back over his shoulder. Sir Maurice moved in, sword cutting the air. The assassin was quick-footed and blocked the thrust with sword and dagger. The other assassin was now crouched near the door. The elder one yelled at him. He forgot his pain, and getting to one knee he drew his sword, glancing at the mêlée then at the Dominican. Athelstan picked up a stool. The assassin clambered to his feet. Athelstan threw it, the man ducked, the stool missed but then Godbless came in, throwing the door back. It struck the assassin and sent him staggering forwards.

Bonaventure was now on the table, hair up, spitting in fury. Thaddeus had got to his feet and fled to a far corner. Sir Maurice and the shaven-head were now in close combat, sword and dagger locked, each trying to seek the advantage. Athelstan picked up another stool but

Godbless snatched it from him. The wounded assassin turned and, as he did so, Godbless brought the stool down. Athelstan closed his eyes; the stool hit the assassin with a resounding thwack full in the forehead. The man collapsed. Before Athelstan could do anything, Godbless, dagger in hand, was standing over the man and in one quick swipe, he slit his throat from ear to ear. As he did this, Sir Maurice stepped back. Athelstan thought the struggle was still continuing. The shaven-head was crouched, a look of puzzlement on his face, his lips slightly parted. He came forward, sword and dagger still gripped. Athelstan saw the great dark patch under his heart; a froth of bubbles appeared at the corner of his mouth.

'In God's name!' the man gasped. His eyes rolled up as sword and dagger slipped from his hand.

Sir Maurice went in again, thrusting his dagger deep into the man's throat. The assassin fell to his knees, blood pouring from the wounds in his chest and throat, then he gave a groan and fell on his face.

Athelstan found he couldn't stop shaking. He picked up Bonaventure, took one of the stools and sat in front of the fire. He stroked the cat. Sir Maurice was speaking but he couldn't understand a word the knight was saying. Godbless came over and tapped him on the shoulder.

'Are you well, Brother? It's always like this after a blood spilling.'

'This is my house,' Athelstan replied, finding he couldn't stop the tears. 'This is my house. I live here with Bonaventure.'

Sir Maurice crouched down beside him. He filled a goblet with wine and Athelstan sipped from it.

'Of course it's your house,' the knight said quietly.

'Did you kill those men?' Athelstan asked.

'You know I have, Brother. And Godbless the other.'

'No, no.' Athelstan shook his head and put Bonaventure down. 'I mean those Frenchmen at Hawkmere. Did you kill them?'

'No, Father, you know I did not.'

Athelstan's body shook with a shiver. 'I am sorry,' he whispered. 'I have seen men die before but,' he took a great gulp from the wine cup, 'I wish old Jack was here!'

'I could send for him.'

'No, no.' Athelstan put the cup down. 'I am trembling like a maid.'

He got to his feet and, despite the objections of the other two, knelt before each of the former assassins and gave them the last rites. The men lay crumpled on the floor. They looked pathetic now, empty faces, sightless eyes, pools of blood around their heads.

'If God can forgive you, so can I,' Athelstan said.

The beggar man immediately went through the assassins' paltry possessions and found nothing but some coins which Athelstan told him to keep. They then wrapped the corpses in their cloaks and took them out. The storm had passed, the rain had stopped. They put both corpses just within the lych gate.

'We'll bury them tomorrow,' Athelstan said. 'We can put them in the ditch Pike and Watkin have dug.'

Sir Maurice now took over. He insisted that Athelstan, Bonaventura and Thaddeus go into the church.

'I can help,' Athelstan protested.

'No, no, Brother, those men came for me. The least I can do is clean your house.'

Athelstan unlocked the church and, followed by the two animals, went inside. He went up into the sanctuary and, taking some cushions from a chest in the sacristy, sat there, arms crossed, staring up at the red winking sanctuary lamp. He tried to pray for himself, for Sir Maurice, for Sir Jack and those two hapless souls sent into the darkness. He prayed they would not fall into eternal night. Thaddeus was still trembling and Athelstan had to put his arm round him. Bonaventure crawled into his lap.

'We are not a very brave trio, are we?' Athelstan said. 'But it was the speed, the savagery of the killing!'

Bonaventure purred.

'I'm sorry I threw you,' Athelstan apologised. 'But what could I do?'

The door opened. He saw a lighted candle and two dark shapes, Sir Maurice and Godbless, came up the nave.

'The house is clean, Brother. There wasn't much blood.'

Godbless was eating from another bowl of stew.

'Nothing like the cut and thrust to give a man an appetite.'

Sir Maurice stretched his hand out. 'Come on, it is time we slept. There's nothing more we can do.'

'Who sent them?'

'Ah!' The knight's usually handsome face turned ugly. 'Parr! I'll go down there tomorrow and challenge him.'

Athelstan shook his head. 'Don't do that, Maurice, please, for my sake!'

The knight crouched down, cupping the candle flame in his hand.

'You really don't think it was Parr, do you?'

'No, I don't,' Athelstan replied. He got to his feet. 'Those assassins. You see, if they had been captured and questioned, Parr would have lost his head on Tower Green or even hanged at Tyburn!' He sighed. 'I suspect it's Mercurius. And how could those villains lead us back to him? Ah well. In the end we'll know the truth. Come on, Godbless, you'd best sleep on the kitchen floor.'

Athelstan glanced at the knight.

'Won't my Lord of Gaunt miss you at the Savoy?'

'I'm in the Regent's favour. What I do, Brother, for two or three days, is of no concern to him.'

While Sir Maurice and Godbless, accompanied by Thaddeus and Bonaventure, went back to the house, Athelstan locked the door of the church. He then went and stood over the two corpses laid out on the wet grass. He sketched a blessing above them and returned to the house.

At Mass the following morning, St Erconwald's was well attended. The parish council turned out in force, thronging into the sanctuary. Athelstan realised that the news of the attack had somehow spread throughout Southwark. He gave the final blessing and turned to go into the sanctuary.

'Shall we hang them, Brother?' Pike coolly shouted, leaning on his shovel. 'Shall we hang them up by their heels as a warning?'

His words were greeted by a roar of approval from the other parishioners. Athelstan glimpsed Benedicta's pale face as she stared hollow-eyed at him, her lips moving as if she were quietly reciting a prayer.

'You'll leave the corpses as they are. What are their bodies now but poor husks? Their souls are before God, but you can help me.'

After he had divested, Athelstan went into the cemetery, his parishioners streaming around him. Hig the pigman stood on guard over the corpses, a thick cudgel in his hand.

'Crim,' Athelstan said. 'Go back to the sacristy. Bring a stoup of holy water and an asperges rod. Pike, over there, beneath the yew trees, you'll find an old wooden cross.'

'You are not going to bury them here?' Pernell the Fleming woman screeched.

'It's a Christian act to bury the dead,' Athelstan replied.

'Aren't you going to tell us what happened?' Manger the hang-man spoke up.

'They came here to rob. And my good friend Sir Maurice Maltravers heroically defended me! A true hero, a Sir Galahad!'

The knight was immediately mobbed by the parishioners.

'Your priest was brave as well,' he declared. 'And so was Godbless!'

The beggar man, too, received tribute. Athelstan glimpsed Benedicta slipping him some coins.

'We'll bury them here,' Athelstan announced. 'And they'll wait till the resurrection.'

'Aye, when the buggers wake up,' Watkin roared, 'the first thing I'll do is smack them in the ear!'

A chorus of approval greeted the dung-collector's words.

'Rats they are.' Ranulf the rat-catcher spoke up. 'And rats they died. Oh, by the way, Brother, you haven't forgotten our Mass tomorrow?'

'What's this?' Watkin asked.

'Ranulf will tell you,' Athelstan said. 'And I want no argument.'

Pike returned carrying the little wooden cross.

'Where are you going to bury them, Brother?'

'In that ditch along the cemetery wall.'

Pike's face fell. He glanced sideways at Watkin.

'It stands to reason,' Athelstan continued. 'They will be buried in consecrated soil but only just.' He scuffed the wet grass with his sandals. 'Despite the rain, the soil's too hard. It saves you digging an extra grave. Finally, no one ever asks to be buried next to the wall.'

'That's true,' said Bladdersniff. He was still swaying on his feet as the effect of last night's ale made itself felt. 'Best place for them,' he added.

Watkin and Pike reluctantly agreed.

'Very well,' Athelstan said. 'Lift the bodies up. Pike, you go ahead carrying the cross. The rest of you can be my witnesses. Say a prayer for their unfortunate souls.'

The strange procession wound its way across the cemetery. Athelstan loudly recited the *Pater Noster*. Pike carried the cross before him. Watkin trailed behind muttering, 'Bastards they were born, bastards they die!'

They reached the trench, most of it now refilled. The bodies were lowered, one on top of the other, Pike and Watkin ordering everyone around. Athelstan blessed the grave and muttered a prayer.

'Well,' he said to Watkin and Pike. 'Fill the ditch in!'

'Yes, fill it in,' Godbless added. 'What's the matter with you two? We can't leave two corpses out like that!'

Mumbling under their breath, Watkin and Pike began to shovel in the dirt. Athelstan looked up at the huge sycamore tree and then he noticed it. Part of the bark had worn away as if someone had tied a hempen rope around it. On closer inspection some of the branches were freshly broken, the sap still clean and white. A vague unease stirred.

'Ah well, we've buried them now.' He sighed. 'And that's the end of that matter!'

Chapter 14

Athelstan felt rather exhausted, tired and depleted, so he decided to spend the day in his parish. He went up on to the bell tower and stared out across Southwark, watching the plumes of smoke rise from the cottages and the tannery shops. The people in the narrow streets looked like colourful insects scurrying about. On such a clear day, though the sun was hazy, he could make out the Thames and the different ships and barges moving along it. He let the breeze cool his face as, crouching down with his back to the wall, he reflected on the previous day's happenings.

'What do we have here?' He addressed Bonaventure who had followed him up and now lay sunning himself on the trap door. 'We have a lovelorn knight but, in battle, he's a warrior who has taken two ships. Secundo, my dear Bonaventure, our beloved Regent may have a spy among the officers on those two ships. Whether that spy is still alive or dead we don't know.'

Athelstan watched the birds soar overhead. For some strange reason he recalled his sudden departure from St Erconwald's before Prior Anselm had abruptly ordered him to return. Was he pleased to be back? Yes, he was. For all the strife and blood, the petty annoyances of life, he loved this church and the people who thronged it.

'Even though some of them are villains,' Athelstan said loudly. 'However, back to the matter in hand, my dear

Bonaventure. Tertio, we know the French have a spy, Mercurius, in England. He is a bloody-handed assassin. He may be responsible for the deaths of those men and that poor girl at Hawkmere, although it doesn't make sense. He may have used some strange poison and probably bought this from Vulpina. He undoubtedly found out we had visited Vulpina so she had to die. Quarto.' He rubbed his hands. 'We have the death of that woman at the Golden Cresset. Undoubtedly the work of someone who wants to discredit poor Maltravers. Quinto, we have the death of the Frenchman Maneil but, this time, he is murdered with a crossbow bolt, not poison. However, none of the prisoners, or even the guards at Hawkmere, have crossbows. And who else had been in the manor apart from him, Cranston and Maltravers? Sexto, we have the attack on Maltravers last night. He believes it's the work of Sir Thomas Parr, I don't. Parr would not stoop so low or do something which would leave him so vulnerable.' Athelstan turned so his face caught the sun. 'What else do we have, my dear cat, my comrade in arms? Yes, that's right. The loose threads. How did Routier know how to escape?'

Both he and Bonaventure jumped as the trap door opened. Bonaventure immediately leapt into the friar's lap. Athelstan tensed but then relaxed as Sir John's great red face appeared, whiskers bristling, grinning from ear to ear.

'I thought you'd be up here.'

'Sir John.' Athelstan held a hand up. 'Do not try to get through the trap door. You are far too... well, you are far too large.'

For one moment he thought the coroner was going to ignore him. The friar had a picture of Sir John wedged in the trap door and having to be pulled loose by members of the parish. Sir John, however, had the sense to accept his advice.

'I've seen Maltravers and that good-for-nothing Godbless. They told me what happened last night.' The coroner's ice-blue eyes glowed fiercely. 'I wish I had been here, Athelstan, ferocious as a mastiff I would have been, striking swift as a swooping hawk. Maltravers still thinks it's Parr.'

'I know, I know, Sir John but, for God's sake, let's go down!'

Watching him fairly skip down the narrow spiral staircase, Athelstan was intrigued by how nimble-footed the over-large coroner always was. Holding Bonaventure, Athelstan followed. Sir John stood waiting on the church porch.

'Don't let's go into the house,' the coroner moaned. 'If that Godbless chatters at me again I'll hit him, while Maltravers appears to be more woebegone than ever.'

'The Piebald Tavern,' Athelstan suggested. 'I feel like a jug of ale, perhaps a pie. Yes, Sir John?'

He strode down the steps and was halfway along the alleyway before Athelstan caught up with him.

'You think those assassins were sent by Mercurius, don't you?' Sir John grasped the friar by the shoulder. 'Well, I've got news for you, but it will wait.'

They entered the taproom, Sir John shouting good-natured abuse at some of Athelstan's parishioners seated round the great wooden tables. Joscelyn, the innkeeper, waved them over to a window seat; the casements were open and the sweet smell of the flowers planted outside wafted through. The one-armed taverner brought black-jacks of cool London ale and a large pie cut up and quartered. He insisted on serving them himself, placing the slices on traunchers of hard-baked bread.

'Do you remember that girl?' Sir John began, smacking his lips. 'The one we found hanging by the neck at the Golden Cresset? Well her name's not Anna Triveter. She's better known along St Mary Axe Street, just near Pountney Inn, as Beatrice the Bawdy Basket. A quiet, rather gentle whore who sometimes dressed as a nun to please her customers.'

'I beg your pardon, Sir John?'

'Oh believe me, Brother. In that part of the city, if you have the silver, a whore can act any part you want: nuns, countesses, even Dominicans!'

'Don't blaspheme, Jack!'

'Dear Beatrice disappeared a few days ago,' Sir John blithely continued. 'Or so the scrimperers told me. Anyway, I've been to St Mary Axe Street and spoken to Peterkin the pincher. He's a pimp, a salacious rogue, who entices young women on to the streets and arranges for them to sell their bodies while he provides protection. Now Peterkin didn't want to speak to me. But, after I had banged his head a couple of times against the alley wall, he did recall two strangers approaching him. Hooded and cowled, he couldn't say who they were but they paid him good silver for Beatrice and took her away.'

'Two men?' Athelstan asked.

'Two. But, listen to this, Brother: their voices were disguised by mufflers but they were well accoutred, definitely English. Anyway, they took Beatrice away and that's the last Peterkin saw of her. After that I went to see my Lord Regent at the Savoy. I told him what had happened at Hawkmere. Do you know something, Brother? Gaunt held a hand over the lower part of his face. I am sure he was laughing at me.'

Athelstan leaned back against the wooden panelling and gazed out over the garden. He recalled his earlier suspicions about Gaunt. Was the Regent quietly rejoicing over what was happening? Was this all part of some game that subtle, wily mind was playing? Making him and Cranston dance like puppets?

'Is it possible, Jack?' Athelstan picked up his tankard and cradled it in his hand.

'Everything's possible, Athelstan. You said that.'

'No, I mean, could Gaunt be killing those prisoners to draw Mercurius out into the open?'

'Brother Athelstan! Brother Athelstan!'

The friar turned. Godbless, holding an arrow, came trotting into the taproom, Thaddeus behind him.

'Oh, Satan's tits!' Sir John growled. 'What does he want?'

Godbless looked at the tankards and licked his lips.

'Three more tankards!' Sir John shouted out. 'No, on second thoughts, make it four, one for the bloody goat!'

The arrival of Thaddeus caused a stir. A mongrel came in from the garden but when the goat lowered its head the dog changed its mind and disappeared.

'Where did you get the arrow, Godbless?'

The beggar man handed it over. It was just over a yard long, the wood smooth and white, the arrow head bright and sharp, the goose quills dyed a dark orange. Godbless waited until the tankards had been served and squatted on a stool. He drank from his while allowing Thaddeus to sup at the other.

'Goats are not supposed to drink from my tankards!' Joscelyn came over.

'I wouldn't say that too loud,' Godbless retorted. 'If that's the case, you wouldn't have any customers!'

Joscelyn looked at Athelstan.

'He's a clean goat,' the Dominican explained. 'I give you my word, Joscelyn.'

The taverner strode away, grumbling under his breath. Sir John leaned down, his face only a few inches from Godbless.

'Where did you get the bloody arrow? And why is it so important?'

'Well. Do you know the cemetery around St Erconwald's? Well, Thaddeus here likes picking things up. You know how curious he is.'

The little goat lifted its head and stared affectionately at the fat coroner.

'And Thaddeus found it there?' Athelstan asked.

'Yes, just near the sycamore tree.'

'Right. I've had enough of this!' Athelstan drained his tankard and got to his feet. The friar grasped the arrow and walked out of the tavern, a disconcerted coroner, Godbless and a slightly tipsy Thaddeus following behind him. Athelstan threaded his way through the alleyways and runnels of Southwark until they entered the small market area down near the riverside. Athelstan stood on tiptoe and gazed about.

'Ah, there he is!'

He went across to a stall. Its owner was a tall, thickset man with white hair, beard and moustache. The sign above the stall declared he was Peter the Fletcher.

'Good morning, Brother Athelstan.' The fletcher's cheery face lit with a smile. He came from behind the stall, wiping his fingers on his leather apron. He gazed mournfully down at his hands. 'It's the glue, it's always the glue!'

'Sir John Cranston, one of my parishioners, Peter Megoran, a Yorkshireman: arrowsmith, fletcher and carpenter, once a master bowman in the Earl of Salisbury's company in France.'

'I know you, Sir John.' The fletcher squeezed the coroner's hand. 'I was at Poitiers.'

'Were you now?' Sir John said. He took out his wineskin and offered it to the fletcher who took a generous swig.

'Halfway down the hill I was,' Megoran explained, handing the wineskin back.

Sir John's eyes took on a faraway look as he recalled the arrow storm which struck the massed French cavalry.

'Queen Mab's tits! And now?'

'I'm a carpenter, joiner. I make bows, arrows, but I have no licence from the city.'

Both he and Sir John damned the Guilds.

'Anyway, Brother, what can I do for you?'

Athelstan showed him the arrow. Megoran took it, his eyes squinting against the sun.

'This is good,' he said. 'The wood's not ash, it's a lighter wood, but the head's sharp and the tip is of good goose feather. If this hit you, Sir John, it would inflict a grievous wound. It also bears no mark. Most fletchers leave a mark, only a small one, on the arrows and bows they make.'

'So it was not made in the city?'

'No. I know all the fletchers and arrowsmiths.'

'So where?'

Peter's eyes took on a guarded look. 'Some arrows are made by poachers. Those who go hunting the king's venison where they shouldn't, deep in some forest glade.'

Athelstan breathed in. 'I think I know where it came from now. Peter, thank you.'

They moved away from the stall. Athelstan took a penny out of his purse and slipped it into Godbless's hand.

'Go swift as this arrow,' he whispered, 'into the city. Sir John, can I have one of your seals?'

Bemused, he handed across one of the small wax insignia he carried as a symbol of his office.

'I am sending Godbless to the Guildhall,' Athelstan explained. 'I want some of your bailiffs.'

'Search out Henry Flaxwith,' Sir John ordered. 'You'll find him near Ratcat Lane. He's got the ugliest dog God ever created, called Samson.' He grinned at the friar. 'How many men do you want, Brother?'

'Oh, a good half-dozen armed with picks and shovels.'

'Is this a mystery?' Godbless asked.

'Not for long,' Athelstan replied. 'Now, go!'

Godbless ran off, Thaddeus trotting behind.

'Watch out for that bloody dog!' Sir John shouted. 'It will eat the goat!'

Sir John and Athelstan returned to St Erconwald's. Athelstan walked into the graveyard where he looked across at the wall and the huge leafy sycamore rising above it. He was tempted to cross and investigate immediately but he was wary of arousing suspicion. One of his parishioners might wander in and they were always very curious about what their priest was doing. Strange, he reflected, he'd had deep suspicions that something unsavoury was happening in the cemetery and that Watkin and Pike were at the root of it. Thaddeus' discovery of a newly fashioned arrow had simply brought these suspicions out into the open.

They returned to the house. Sir Maurice was sitting on a stool, still poring over the writings of Bonaventure. He glanced up hopefully but took one look at the grim face of his host and stared quizzically at Sir John who just winked and put a finger to his lips. Athelstan went across to his writing desk. He took a fresh quill, sharpened it, opened the ink pot and wrote a short message, which he then rolled up and sealed.

'Sir Maurice, I don't want to use you as a messenger but would you please take this across to our mother house at Blackfriars and then come back here with the reply?'

'Of course, Brother, what's it about?'

'It's about poisons. We have no leech or physician at Blackfriars but Brother Simeon, our archivist, is a most knowledgeable man and knows exactly what books and manuscripts the library holds. I have asked him to make a search. It may take some time but the Brothers are very hospitable. And Sir Maurice.' Athelstan smiled. 'I am so grateful for your stout defence last night but your head is full of love and your wits are wandering. For the love of God, man! Don't forget your war belt!'

'Oh yes, of course.' The knight fetched it and strapped it round his waist.

'Take care, Sir Maurice!' Sir John eased himself down on the vacated stool.

'Oh, Sir Maurice!'

'Yes, Brother?'

'When you visit Blackfriars tell them nothing about the nuns at Syon or the visit of a certain Brother Norbert!'

Sir Maurice smiled. 'Of course!'

He left, closing the door behind him.

'That man,' Sir John declared, taking a swig from the wineskin, 'is so deeply in love, I don't think he even knows what day of the week it is.'

'It's Tuesday, Sir John, and we have villainy to pursue, the truth to discover and God's justice to carry out.'

'You are in fine fettle, Brother. Was it the attack last night?'

'No, not that. The business at Hawkmere will have to wait. It's more St Erconwald's, or some of its parishioners that concern me: a few strands are coming together and that arrow neatly ties them.'

After that the friar refused to be drawn. Instead he took his book of accounts and pretended to immerse himself in these. Sir John went off to get another pie, and probably also to renew his acquaintance with the Piebald Tavern.

Once the coroner had left, Athelstan checked on Philomel, his old war horse, and went into the church to prepare for the Mass for the Guild of Rat-Catchers the following morning.

By the time he came out, Sir John had returned, walking down the alleyway with his old friend, chief bailiff Henry Flaxwith, the ugly, squat Samson trotting behind them. Godbless, holding Thaddeus, trailed along looking rather tired. The attendant bailiffs were a brawny, stout group who carried mattocks and hoes, picks and shovels. Athelstan grasped Flaxwith's hand.

'I thank you for coming, Henry. I can't give you refreshment yet. However, I'd like you to dig a ditch for me.' He scanned the sky where fleecy white clouds floated. 'It's late afternoon,' Athelstan said. 'And probably the best time. Once we are in the cemetery, I want one of your men to guard the lych gate. No one is to be allowed in until we finish. Now, Godbless, go into the house and refresh yourself. Keep Thaddeus away from Samson.'

The rest all marched into the cemetery, Flaxwith leaving one of his men to guard the lych gate. Athelstan led them across to the boundary wall.

'This,' Athelstan explained, 'is a ditch dug by two of my parishioners, Watkin and Pike. At first I made no objection, as they said they only wished to check that the foundations of the walls were firm. They apparently dig it, fill it in later then continue the trench.'

Flaxwith scratched his balding head. 'What's wrong with that, Brother? It's often done. It's the only way to make sure the foundations of a wall are firm and secure, especially a place like this where the damp can seep in.'

'That's what they said. A small brook runs on the far side. Now and again it can flood and break its bank. However, I've become suspicious about their entire plan. Can you and your lads reopen the ditch? I'd like to see what you find.'

The bailiffs set to with gusto. The soil was soft, being freshly turned over and soaked by the previous night's rain. Sir John and Athelstan walked back to the priest's house where the coroner immediately became immersed in an animated conversation with Godbless about their warring days abroad and the depredations of the Free Companies in Southern France and Northern Italy.

Athelstan went up to his bed loft where he opened the divine office, crossed himself and began the psalms and readings for that day. Every so often he would stop and lift his head as if waiting for something. He wondered what would happen if nothing were found but then he heard the sound of running footsteps as Flaxwith burst into the house.

'Brother Athelstan! Sir John! You've got to come and see this!'

They followed him out across the cemetery. The ditch was now opened. The two corpses, buried earlier that morning, were back up, lying on the side of the ditch. Athelstan caught Flaxwith by the sleeve.

'I'm sorry,' he apologised. 'I should have told you about them.'

'Oh Brother, that's what cemeteries are for and we saw the cross. Anyway, Sir Jack and Godbless told us what had happened. However, this is what we've found.'

He led Athelstan and the coroner over to a pile of soil-stained canvas sacks. Two of them had been opened; one glance and Athelstan knew he was correct.

'Arrows! Freshly cut and barbed! I suppose it's the same with the rest?'

Flaxwith nodded.

'Lucifer's bollocks!' Sir John exclaimed. 'Henry, you'd better get the lot out!'

'Hide them over there.' Athelstan pointed to some gorse bushes in the far corner of the cemetery.

'You suspected this, didn't you?' Sir John asked.

'When Godbless brought me that arrow, yes. I've also been highly suspicious about those ghosts he saw.'

'Let me see. Let me see.' The coroner rubbed his hands. 'If old Jack's brain is as sharp as it should be.' He led Athelstan well out of earshot of the rest. 'Down the alleyway, Brother, and out of Southwark, we reach London Bridge. Once you are across that you are into the city.'

'Go on,' Athelstan said.

'Now. If the Great Community of the Realm, that bunch of snivelling, secret traitors, plot their rebellions and the peasant armies move on London, the city can be defended to the north, east and west by the old wall but the southern side is different. Whoever controls London Bridge will, in fact, control the city. If the rebels pour across they can lay siege to the Tower and cut it off from the rest of London. They'll also be able to swing west to control both banks of the Thames as well as capture Gaunt's palace at the Savoy. Once done, they can pour into the city with no one to stop them.'

'True, Sir John. We have been through this many a time.'

'Now the peasant army will be armed with hoe, mattock, spade and axe. Every peasant carries a bow and so they'll need a constant, fresh supply of arrows. By the time they reach Southwark their supplies could well be depleted as they clash with local sheriffs' posses, landlords, barons, the great seigneurs of the countryside.'

'Once the Regent and the Corporation know that the rebel army is marching, they'll seize all arms supplies and either destroy them or hide them,' Athelstan said.

'But the rebels come to St Erconwald's.' Sir John smiled thinly. 'A few yards from London Bridge, that precious pair, Watkin and Pike, have dug a deep trench, claiming they are checking on the foundations of a wall. No one objects and they can come and go as they wish... And then what, Brother?'

'At night the Great Community of the Realm bring their pack horses through the alleyways of Southwark, well away from prying eyes. All they've got to face are the likes of poor Bladdersniff who is so drunk he can hardly put one foot in front of another. They climb the wall, put a rope over the branch of the sycamore tree and lower themselves into the freshly dug trench. The sacks of arrows are hidden beneath a light layer of soil and off they go. Pike and Watkin will later come and fill the rest of the trench in and, heigh ho, the Great Community have almost finished the preparations for their march on London Bridge.' Athelstan stamped his foot in exasperation. 'May the Lord forgive me, Sir John, Godbless claimed he saw ghosts hanging in the air! What he saw were these messengers from the Great Community climbing the wall and going up and down into that benighted trench!'

Athelstan had heard a shout from the lych gate and hurried over. Crim the altar boy was arguing with the bailiff on guard.

'What's the matter, Brother?' The little boy's face was flushed and sweating. 'I only came to pick some flowers.'

'Go and fetch your father,' Athelstan replied. 'Don't tell him what you have seen, Crim. Just tell Watkin to collect Pike and bring him here. It's very urgent. Go on now!'

Crim ran off. Sir John went back to tell the bailiffs to guard the arrows then joined Athelstan in the priest's house.

'I am very angry,' Athelstan declared, sitting down at the table. 'Gaunt has spies in Southwark; Watkin and Pike could dance at Tyburn!' He banged his fist on the table. 'The whole parish could be fined. Now listen, Sir John, this is a matter for me.'

'According to the law, Brother...'

'According to the love of Christ!' Athelstan angrily interrupted. 'I am their parish priest!'

Sir John held his hand up in a sign of peace.

'Brother, Brother, I am not bothered about Watkin and Pike...'

'What's happening?'

Godbless poked his head round the door and stepped gingerly into the room.

'I have just put Thaddeus in the stable with Philomel. They seem to like each other.'

'Godbless.' Athelstan opened his purse and pushed across some coins. 'Take these to Master Flaxwith. Tell him to leave the bailiffs in the cemetery but go down to the tavern and buy some jugs of ale. You go with him, tell no one what is happening.'

Godbless disappeared.

'You were saying, Sir John?'

'I am not interested in Watkin and Pike. They are just noddle-pates.' Cranston played with the ring on his small finger. 'But the Great Community of the Realm, now Brother, they are different. I sympathise with them. Many of the peasants are driven to desperation but, when they invade London, they'll be traitors, rebels against the King. They'll have no compassion on people like me and the Lady Maude. It's a war, Athelstan. No pardon will be given and none asked.' He breathed in noisily. 'And the same goes for you, Brother. If you are not with them you are against them.'

'As you would say, Sir John, I couldn't give a fig! I don't care if they've got the solemn blessing of the Holy Father in Avignon! They don't use my cemetery as a place of war!'

He paused at a knock on the door. Watkin and Pike shuffled in, their boots caked with mud, their faces grimy and sweating.

'You sent for us, Brother?' Watkin licked his lips nervously.

'Yes I did. Close the door. Lock it behind you!'

Pike did so quickly. Athelstan took the small wooden cross which hung on a cord round his neck and held it up. His face was pale and tight as he glared at these two rogues of the parish.

'I am going to ask you questions,' he began. 'And, if you tell me one lie, I never wish to see you again this side of heaven!'

Chapter 15

Watkin and Pike did not take long to confess. They stood, hang-dog expressions on their faces, mumbling and muttering. Eventually the truth came out.

'It's like this,' Watkin said lugubriously. 'Everyone in Southwark knows the Great Community of the Realm. It's like autumn, everyone sees it coming. One day the rebels will march on London.' He spread his hands. 'What can we do? If we refuse to co-operate we will all die.'

'Co-operate?' Athelstan intervened. 'Do you know what it means?' He'd caught the stumble in Watkin's voice.

'That's what the Great Community of the Realm told us: co-operate or die.'

'They are bully boys,' Sir John broke in. 'And they used you two noddle-pates to store arrows in a churchyard. I suppose there are plots all over Southwark just like this. And, when the graveyard was full, I suspect you'd start storing them elsewhere.'

'Not in our houses,' Pike warned. 'You can't hide quivers of arrows in the hovels of Southwark.'

'Do you realise you could be hanged out of hand?' Sir John barked. 'Do you realise that, my buckoes? I could take you out, put a rope round that sycamore tree and hang you out of hand as rebels!'

'But my lord...'

'My lord coroner won't!' Athelstan said.

'They are coming back, aren't they?' Sir John continued. 'There was a storm last night so I suspect these envoys from the Great Community stayed at home. Now the soil is soft, they'll return tonight, won't they?'

'We don't know,' Pike mumbled. 'All they said was to dig the trench.'

'But you knew what they were hiding there?' Athelstan demanded.

Watkin nodded and dried his sweaty hands on his leather jacket.

'We dug the trench then we'd always leave it open. When we came back, we'd fill a part in and continue along.'

'Did you ever examine the arrows?'

'I did,' Watkin replied. 'I took a sack out one morning when you were saying Mass, Brother. I opened the rope at the top and shook them out.'

'That's how we discovered it,' Athelstan told them.

Both men were now shuffling their feet, wiping their hands and licking their lips.

'I want to pee,' Pike muttered. 'I am sorry, but...'

'Go outside,' Athelstan ordered. 'And, when you are finished, both go into the church and stay there. What time will these men return?'

'We don't know, Brother! After dark. One night Pike and I, well, we hid outside the cemetery and watched. There were two of them with sumpter ponies. They call themselves Valerian and Domitian. Yes, that's their names, or so they say.'

'Educated men.' Athelstan scratched his chin.

'What will happen to us?'

'Well.' Athelstan rubbed his hands. 'You two have helped the coroner with his enquiries. We will not betray you to the Great Community.' He glanced quickly at Sir John who nodded. 'Nor will we hand you over to the authorities. Nevertheless, you betrayed my trust. In the church you'll find some brooms and a little oil. They're kept in the basement of the tower. I'll lock you in and you'll clean the church till this matter's finished!'

'Can I have a pee first?' Pike moaned, jumping from foot to foot.

'Oh, get out! I'll unlock the church in a few minutes.'

Both men scampered out. Athelstan slammed the door behind them.

'They are stupid,' Sir John observed. 'Yet, they could be hanged.' He rubbed his face. 'But, there again, they are poor, their hovels are smoke-filled; they eat hard bread and drink coarse ale. What I'd like to know is who Valerian and Domitian really are? And, more importantly, I want to check on something.'

He hurried out across the cemetery. Athelstan went to the church, where Watkin and Pike stood in the porch. Athelstan gripped each of them by the wrist.

'Look at me!' They did so. 'Nothing is going to happen,' Athelstan reassured them. 'However, I want this church swept and I want you out of harm's way. You must never do that again!' He unlocked the door.

'Brother?'

Athelstan turned.

'We are very sorry, Brother,' Watkin said contritely. 'We truly are.'

'If you get really thirsty,' Athelstan told them, 'go into the sacristy, you can each have a little drink of altar wine.'

He closed the church door and locked it behind him. Sir John had returned to the priest's house, where he was refilling his jug of ale.

'There must be dozens of sacks there, literally thousands of arrows. I wonder who has the wealth to pay for that? Certainly not peasants.' Sir John clicked his tongue. 'You see, what your two noddle-pates said is true. There's a storm coming. Two or three years ago the Great Community of the Realm was a jest, a little demon who lived out in the countryside, lurking in the woods or the bottom of wells. A creature of the hedgerow and the hay rick: a figure of ridicule and scorn.'

'And now the demon's grown?' Athelstan asked.

'Yes, into a figure of fear and terror. The lords of the soil and the men of power no longer laugh but sit in their counting houses; they scratch their chins and wonder what will happen when this storm breaks.'

'I must see these arrows,' Athelstan said.

Both he and the coroner walked out. Athelstan noticed how quickly rumour had spread; some of his parishioners were congregating in front of the church: Ursula the pig woman, Pernell the Fleming, Mugwort the bell clerk, Amisias the fuller and others. They were pretending to talk to each other and looked guiltily up when Athelstan approached them.

'I know why you are here,' he said. 'But you must leave. You are not to come near the church nor the cemetery today and that's the end of the matter.'

'What about my painting?' Huddle cried from the back of the crowd.

'Huddle, my lad! Don't lie to your parish priest. The day is drawing on, the light is fading. It will wait until tomorrow.'

The crowd dispersed; Athelstan was at the lych gate when he heard his name called. Sir Maurice came striding across and thrust a scroll of parchment into Athelstan's hand.

'Your brothers at Blackfriars send you greetings.' He patted his stomach and grinned at Sir John. 'You should have come, my lord coroner: ale thick and rich and pastry soft in the mouth.'

Athelstan opened the letter.

'What's wrong, Brother?' Sir John caught his disappointed look.

'Simeon says it will take some time. However, he hopes that by tomorrow morning I can have an answer. I was going to look at these arrows but perhaps, Sir John, I've done enough for the day.'

'I think it's time,' Sir John declared, 'we prepared for our visitors tonight. If you don't mind, Henry Flaxwith and my buckoes will stay? The noddle-pates are locked in the church?'

Athelstan nodded.

'Good!' Sir John rubbed his hands. 'Maltravers, I'll explain later what's happening. Anyway, I am leaving you on guard. No one goes into that church or cemetery. You've had refreshment and it's time Athelstan and I did the same.' He clapped the knight on the shoulder. 'You can stay and write a love poem, Brother Norbert. And I'll be raising my goblet to you in the tavern!'

Darkness had fallen over Southwark when the two men, caped, cowled and hooded, sword and dagger clinking in their war belts, led the two sumpter ponies up along the trackway into Southwark. Valerian and Domitian had met the carter in the fields beyond the Tabard Tavern. The sacks had been taken from the cart and loaded on to the ponies. Now they made their way through the gloomy runnels and alleyways. The hovels, the dilapidated houses, rose dark and forbidding on either side, blocking out the night sky. They pulled their mufflers up over their noses against the stench from the midden-heaps and unclean sewers. Cats fought and screeched; rats slithered out from crevices in the walls. Beggars whined on corners. They thrust out their clatter boards but received little comfort from these two dark shadows. Now and again, from behind a closed shutter, faces peered out, eyes glittering, but Valerian and Domitian were known to the gangs who plagued Southwark, who were more terrified of these two men than they were of all Gaunt's spies and agents. Valerian pulled at the rope and glanced over his shoulder at his companion.

'It won't take us long.'

'How many more?'

'Perhaps another four or five nights' work and then we'll be finished.'

They walked on, the sumpter ponies docile, their hooves muffled in rags. Valerian and Domitian had also wrapped wool round their boots, so that they seemed to glide like shadows from one dark alleyway to another.

At last the line of houses ended. They crossed the barren wasteland which stretched to the cemetery walls of St Erconwald. Valerian stopped, his hand going to his dagger; he could make out the dark mass of the church, the tall tower soaring up against the starlit sky. He peered at the crenellated top but could see no flame or light which meant that the little friar was not gazing at the stars. He was about to go on but paused. Was something wrong? Last night the fierce thunderstorm would have prevented the friar going up the tower. Surely, on a clear night like this, he would seize the opportunity? Valerian licked his lips; he had to be careful, very careful.

'What are we waiting for?' his companion hissed.

'I don't know.'

'Is it safe?'

'Why shouldn't it be? We can't very well go back.'

Glaring into the gloom, Valerian led the sumpter pony forward. They crossed the small brook now drying up in the summer heat. They reached the wall. Valerian took a rope and climbed on. He flung one end of the rope round a branch of the sycamore tree, pulled it down, fashioned a slipknot and lowered himself into the trench. Was something wrong? Those fools usually dug to a certain depth; now it seemed shallower. He wished he had a cresset torch. Had the earth been disturbed? Did those two oxen-heads have the temerity to search for what was buried here?

'Come on!' his companion urged him.

A sack came over the wall. Valerian grasped it and put it into the pit. A second one then suddenly the darkness was seared with a light. Valerian scrambled out of the trench.

'What the...?' he exclaimed.

From behind the wall he heard the scrape of steel. Figures, shapes loomed out of the darkness. Valerian recognised the little friar. He drew his dagger, adopting the stance of a fighting man, and peered at the rest. These weren't soldiers! They were city bailiffs, beadles, men with families, timid as mice. Valerian tried his luck. He leapt forward and the bailiffs scattered. He looked over his shoulder. The wall was out of the question but if he could slip through the cemetery, he would soon be lost in the alleyways of Southwark. He was about to step forward again when a broad, massive figure moved out of the darkness. In the torchlight Valerian glimpsed a red, moustached face, cloak thrown back, sword and dagger in the man's hands.

'Out of my way, you tub of lard, and I'll not prick you!'

'I recognise that voice,' Sir John boomed. 'Put down your sword and dagger, my bucko, and surrender to the King's coroner, Sir John Cranston!'

'Piss off!'

Valerian darted forward. Cranston was old and fat, he'd prove no obstacle, but the coroner suddenly shifted. Valerian stopped and turned, lashing out with his sword. The coroner blocked this. Valerian drew away, prickles of cold sweat on the nape of his neck. Sir John seemed light as a dancer. In he snaked again, sword and dagger looking for an opening, locked in a whirling arc of steel. Valerian's dagger was knocked from his hand. He gripped his sword with both hands and came rushing in. Perhaps he could frighten the coroner? His sword sliced the air; Valerian knew he had made a mistake, only seconds before Cranston's blade dug deep beneath his heart. Valerian felt hot spurts of pain, blood bubbled at the back of his mouth. He fell to his knees; the night sky was whirling, the voices were like a faint roar and, spitting blood, he tumbled to the ground.

Sir John Cranston, chest heaving, wiped his sword on the dead man's cloak then sheathed it. He told the bailiff to come closer with the torch, turned the corpse over and pulled down the vizard.

'Satan's bollocks!' he swore. 'It's Ralph Hersham!'

Athelstan knelt down and pulled back the hood and cowl. He recognised the surly, close-set features of Sir Thomas Parr's henchman. He gave the man the last rites and, even as he felt for the pulse in the neck, realised the soul had gone out to meet its judgement. He rose at the cries coming from the far end of the cemetery. Sir Maurice and other bailiffs were bundling a figure across. The man's head was exposed, the vizard pulled off. As he was pushed into the pool of torchlight, Athelstan could see he was badly bruised and terrified out of his wits. The man took one look at Hersham's face and fell with a groan to his knees, hands extended in supplication.

'Oh, God have mercy!'

'What's your name?' Sir John barked. He came over and dragged the man's head back by the hair.

'Clement, Clement Margoyle!'

'And are you Valerian?'

'No, I'm Domitian. Hersham was Valerian.'

'You brought arrows to St Erconwald's?' Athelstan accused. The friar drew close and pressed his finger against the man's lips. 'Are you in a state of grace, my son?' Athelstan glanced over at the coroner and winked.

'Brother, I don't know.'

Sir John stood over the man and drew his sword, which he held up by the hilt.

'Clement Margoyle, you are a felon and a traitor. You have brought arms by night and the only reason must be that you plot treasonable mischief against our sovereign lord the King. You are also hooded and armed, travelling by stealth at night which is specifically condemned by the Statute of Treasons.'

'No! No! No!' Margoyle wailed.

'Therefore,' Sir John continued, his voice rolling like the peal of a funeral bell, 'I, Sir John Cranston, King's coroner in the city and its environs, do sentence you, Clement Margoyle, to death! Sentence is to be carried out immediately. May the Lord have mercy on your soul!'

He stepped back, refusing to meet Athelstan's eyes. 'Hang him!' he barked.

One of the bailiffs threw a rope over the branch of the sycamore tree. The speed at which they worked surprised Athelstan. One end was formed into a noose and put round the unfortunate Margoyle's head. Sir Maurice made to protest but Sir John commanded him to shut up. He rapped out an order. Immediately the bailiffs holding the other end of the rope began to tug. Margoyle, choking and coughing, was hoisted into the air, legs kicking.

'Sir John!' Athelstan implored him. 'For the love of God!'

'Oh yes, I forgot that. Let him down!'

Margoyle was dropped with a thud. He lay for a while on the wet grass coughing and retching. Sir John undid the noose.

'Maltravers, take him over to the priest's house. Henry.' He summoned Flaxwith forward. 'I want every single arrow removed from the cemetery and carted into the city. Take Hersham's corpse and give it to the Harrower of the Dead. He can find a burial plot for it. Tell him to send the bill to the Guildhall. Athelstan, let's adjourn elsewhere and question Master Margoyle.'

They left the confusion behind them and went into the priest's house. Margoyle sat on a stool, still shaking with fright from his rough handling. Athelstan poured him a goblet of wine and thrust it into his hands. Godbless and Thaddeus tried to enter, but Athelstan asked them to wait outside. He handed the beggar man the keys of the church.

'Go across,' he told him. 'And let those two miscreants out. Tell them to go straight home. There is nothing for them here.'

Athelstan locked the door behind him and sat down opposite Margoyle.

'Sir John, can this man hang?'

'He certainly will,' the coroner answered cheerfully from where he sat at the table. 'Either at Tyburn or Smithfield, it depends on the Justices.'

Margoyle took a deep sip of the wine.

'But what happens if he co-operates, Sir John?' Athelstan saw the hope flare in the prisoner's eyes. 'What would you do if Master Margoyle here made a full and frank confession?'

'That would depend on the song I heard. I do feel in fine fettle: that sword fight brought back memories of skirmishing with French pickets outside Dijon. Did I ever tell you that...'

'Thank you, Sir John,' Athelstan said hastily. 'You have, on many an occasion.' He studied Margoyle. A bully boy, he thought, but one with a weak face and watery, darting eyes. A bully and a coward, Athelstan considered, a man who certainly wouldn't die to protect someone else. 'Master Margoyle,' he offered, 'take another drink of wine, then confess. But I tell you this. If you lie, even a little one, Sir John will have you swinging from the branch of that sycamore tree.'

Margoyle drained the cup in one gulp. Athelstan refilled it.

'I am innocent of murder,' Margoyle blurted out. 'I never committed a murder.' He glanced fearfully at the coroner. 'I – I don't see why I should hang for that! Hersham's responsible!'

'What?' Athelstan asked. 'What on earth are you talking about?'

'The woman at the Golden Cresset.'

253

Margoyle was trembling so much he had to use two hands to grip the wine cup.

'Continue,' Athelstan urged him. 'You and Hersham were responsible for the death of that woman?'

'So, I was right!' Sir Maurice called out. 'Sir Thomas was involved!'

'Oh God help us, no he wasn't!' Margoyle moaned. 'I assure you, sir, he wasn't, that was all Hersham's idea! He hated you, Sir Maurice. He wanted to discredit you in the eyes of Sir Thomas. The rumours have now reached my master's household. He's already sent a messenger down to the nuns at Syon!'

If Sir John hadn't intervened, Sir Maurice would have thrown himself at the prisoner.

'For the love of God, sit down!' Cranston told him. 'The more this man talks, the better it is.'

'It was Hersham's idea,' Margoyle continued. 'He hired a whore from Peterkin the pimp and schooled her what to do. She was to go to the Golden Cresset, hire a chamber and lock the door till he came. It was Saturday afternoon. Hersham told me to go into the stable yard and stand guard there. I did so. He was gone a long time; the place was as busy as a beehive. I kept walking in and out of the gate. No one ever noticed me. Then the shutters opened up. I heard my name being called. Hersham told me that, when the yard became deserted, I was to whistle. I waited a while and, when the opportunity presented itself, Hersham cut through the shutters. He climbed on to the stonework, pushed the shutters close and dropped into the yard. He was almost dancing with glee. Only later did he tell me what had happened.'

Margoyle took another sip from the wine cup.

'Apparently Hersham, and he was as mad as a March hare, had stayed near the door and slipped up the stairs. He had a wineskin with him containing an opiate. The whore opened the door. I don't think she knew why she was there; she only acted out the instructions Hersham had given her. She must have thought it was some sort of game. Hersham gave her the wineskin, she fell asleep on the bed.' Margoyle put the goblet down and crossed his arms over his chest. 'I didn't know what to do when Hersham told me that he had taken a rope and hanged the poor wench. He said that no one would ever find out while Maltravers, who had been tricked to come to the tavern, would take the blame.' He glanced fearfully at Athelstan. 'Brother, I swear I had no part in it.'

Athelstan studied the muddy-brown eyes and accepted that he was telling the truth. Margoyle's gaze shifted to the knight now sitting at the table.

'He hated you,' he said. 'Not just because of the Lady Angelica but because you were everything he wanted to be!'

'And this mummery in the cemetery?' Sir John asked.

'That I am involved in,' Margoyle confessed slowly. 'The Great Community of the Realm, Sir John, is now well rooted in London. It has members among the Corporation, the aldermen, the merchants and the guilds. They make threats, unless these powerful men,' Margoyle stumbled on the phrase, 'assist and co-operate, they, their houses, their trade, their families, are all marked down for destruction. Now, or when the Great Community's army marches on London.'

Sir John tapped the table. 'Of course!' He drove his fist into one hand.

'Of course what, Sir John?' Athelstan asked.

'Nothing much. It's just that there's been the occasional fire in a warehouse, stores being broken into, property smashed. The Guild-hall thinks it's the work of night-walkers, footpads, but you, my little popinjay, say it could be the work of the Great Community?'

Margoyle nodded fearfully.

'Do continue, Master Clement. You sing like a linnet. What other little secrets do you hold? Are you a member of the Great Community?'

Margoyle lowered his head and muttered, 'Yes, Sir John, both me and Hersham. We were given the names of Valerian and Domitian. We were promised that, in the new commonwealth, we would hold high office.'

Sir John burst out laughing. 'When Adam delved and Eve span,' he taunted. 'Who was then the gentleman? So one set of laws are going to be replaced by another, are they?'

Margoyle nodded.

'Do sing on.'

'The Great Community recently held a council at St Albans. They believe their army will march within twelve months but they need to seize London Bridge. The men have bows but no arrows. If these were made in the city, Gaunt – I mean, His Grace the Regent,' Margoyle added hastily, 'would soon discover it.'

'And his guards at the city gates,' Athelstan observed, 'would hardly let cart-loads of arrows go trundling through.'

'The arrows were made by peasants,' Margoyle continued. 'In south Essex and Hertfordshire. They were then brought to an agreed assembly point and distributed. They were to be brought into Southwark. Valerian and I were to find a place as close as possible to London Bridge, and St Erconwald's was chosen.'

'Why?' Athelstan asked.

'Because it is a poor parish, Brother. None of the great ones live here.' Margoyle's eyes fell away. 'They say you are a good priest. Busy about the care of souls. Many in the council of the Great Community believe you are sympathetic.'

'I am not,' Athelstan said. 'And I object to men like you drawing simpletons like Watkin and Pike into your deadly game!'

'We were given their names,' Margoyle continued. 'We met them by night and told them what to do. They were to dig a trench and pretend to be examining the foundations of the cemetery wall. We put the arrows in, covered them with a layer of earth.' He shrugged. 'The rest you know.'

'But you are missing one important fact,' Athelstan insisted. 'Arrows cost money. Wood has to be bought. Sacks and carts provided. Arrow heads fashioned. Glue, not to mention goose feathers.'

'Sir Thomas provided that. Hersham was given bags of silver. Sir Thomas keeps a private account.'

'So he's a traitor?' Athelstan interrupted.

'He had little choice.' A note of defiance crept into Margoyle's voice.

'What do you mean?'

The man's eyes moved to Sir Maurice.

'Do you think the Lady Angelica was moved to the nuns of Syon just because of Maltravers?'

Sir John clapped his thigh. 'Of course! We thought she was there to protect her from Sir Lancelot here; but she had been marked down by the Great Community of the Realm, hadn't she?'

Margoyle nodded. 'I've told you the truth, Sir John.'

The coroner lumbered to his feet. 'Brother Athelstan, your church is locked and secure, yes?'

'Of course, Sir John!'

'And the windows are too narrow for anyone to crawl out?'

'Of course, my lord coroner.' Athelstan smiled as he caught the drift of the questions.

The coroner went over to Athelstan's writing-desk where he picked up two quills, an inkpot and a large square of rubbed parchment. He then went across and pulled Margoyle up by the scruff of his neck.

'Brother Athelstan,' Sir John said, beaming. 'Do open the door of your church. Master Margoyle is going into the sanctuary to sit at the small table there and write out his confession. When he has finished, if I am satisfied, I am going to let him run away. On one condition.' He turned the hapless Margoyle round to face him. 'If I ever catch you in London again, I'll hang you out of hand!'

'He'll implicate Parr,' Athelstan warned. 'Gaunt will have Sir Thomas' head.'

'No he won't. He'll write what I tell him to.'

'But the bailiffs?'

'Men like Sir Thomas are not easily impressed. Hersham's dead, Margoyle here won't mention the name Parr and Sir Thomas will simply say he had nothing to do with this villainy.' Sir John winked. 'But, he'll know that we know and that, my dear friar, is very important!'

Chapter 16

The following morning the parish was in uproar. News of what had happened in the cemetery had swept through the alleyways leading down to the Thames. St Erconwald's was truly packed, not just for the Guild Mass for the Rat-Catchers, but also by those eager to listen to the chatter and the gossip. Watkin and Pike looked woebegone. They stood on the sanctuary steps shuffling their feet. Athelstan, vesting in the sacristy, closed his eyes and quietly thanked God that things had gone well. Sir John had worked like a true soldier: the arrows had been removed, loaded on to carts and taken across London Bridge. Watkin and Pike had slunk away in the darkness while Margoyle had written a full confession, surrendered his arms and fled like a shadow in the night. Sir Maurice was beside himself. Godbless had danced like an elf shouting: 'I told you so! I told you I saw shapes in the cemetery!'

It had been long after midnight before Athelstan had quietened things down and snatched a few hours' sleep.

'Ah well,' he said, crossed himself and went into the sanctuary.

The Mass was a great success. The rat-catchers with their ferrets, cats, small dogs, cages, traps, mallets and spikes, nets and leather sacks were all piled together in the sanctuary. The ceremony was one of the liveliest Athelstan had ever conducted. One dog howled throughout the entire ceremony as if singing its own divine chant. Bonaventure slunk in and, if Crim hadn't intervened, the most horrendous fight would have broken out as this prince of the alleyways' one good eye alighted upon a rival. Two ferrets escaped and were pursued by a dog into the cemetery. One was caught but Ranulf came back, just as Athelstan finished the consecration, shaking his head and announcing in a loud whisper that 'the little bastard had gone for good'.

At the end of the Mass Athelstan preached a homily on all God's creatures being a delight in His sight. Ranulf stuck his hand up.

'Does that include rats, Brother?'

'Rats have their purposes, Ranulf,' Athelstan replied. 'But God knows why.'

'They clear away rubbish,' Ricauld, a rat-catcher from the priory of St Mary's, announced.

'You've got the makings of a theologian,' Athelstan told him. 'But, truly, you all do a great service for the community. I appeal to you to do it honestly and as kindly as possible.' His eyes caught Ranulf's. 'And not charge too much.'

After the homily Athelstan had blessed the different animals. On reflection this was very dangerous. Some of the ferrets lunged for his fingers. Bonaventure's rival curled its lip in protest. If it had not been for a well-aimed kick from Crim's boot, one of the dogs would have cocked its leg against Athelstan. The friar moved among the different pets, sprinkling them with water and afterwards blessing them with incense. The dog, which had been thankfully quiet during his sermon, now decided to renew his chant. Athelstan just thanked God Sir John wasn't there.

At the end of the Mass all the rat-catchers, together with the parishioners, thronged into the porch of the church and the open area in front. Stalls and booths had been set up to sell ales and cakes. Benedicta had cooked pies. Watkin's wife had brought fruit. Everyone announced it was a success and Huddle, ecstatic that the Rat-Catchers' Guild had hired him, loudly announced that soon he would be putting a fresco on the wall to honour the new confraternity.

Boso, a one-eyed cleric with a slit nose and one ear missing, who Athelstan secretly thought was a defrocked priest, set up a small table and unrolled the Articles of the Rat-Catchers' Guild. Each member signed their name or made their mark. A cat, a rat, a trap or a cage. Ranulf solemnly took out from his pouch the new seal of the Guild and Boso poured hot wax on the parchment. Ranulf sealed this and Athelstan did the same with the parish insignia. Fresh copies were produced and the same process repeated. Athelstan, feeling rather bemused by the whole affair, quickly conceded that a copy should be placed in a case and stored in the parish archives in one of the tower chambers of the church. He tried to catch Benedicta's eye but she just smiled, busy in making sure the revelry went smoothly. Watkin, Pike, Hig the pigman, Mugwort the bell clerk and others stood in a corner, heads together, whispering darkly among themselves. Athelstan was about to join them when he heard his name called. Sir Maurice, who had excused himself from the Mass, was standing in the doorway of the church holding a piece of parchment in his hand.

'Athelstan, it's urgent! It's from Blackfriars!'

The friar hurried across to take the parchment and walked into the house. It was cool and quiet after the frenetic activity of the church. He examined the seal, broke it and quickly read what Simeon the archivist had written. Athelstan smiled to himself.

'At last!' he said.

'Good news, Brother?'

'Good news, Sir Maurice.'

'Are we going to visit the nuns of Syon?' the knight asked hopefully.

'I think not.' Athelstan leaned over and grasped the young knight's wrist. 'Why should we go there, Sir Maurice?'

'Why, to see the Lady Angelica.'

'I do worry about you, Brother Norbert,' Athelstan teased. 'Sometimes I think that all you can think of is Angelica!'

'I love her. I go to sleep thinking about her. I dream of her. I see her face in crowds. Haven't you ever loved, Brother?' The knight bit his lip. 'I am sorry.'

Athelstan sat down on a stool. The knight stared at him.

'I – I didn't mean to embarrass you, Brother.'

Athelstan closed his eyes and thought of Benedicta.

'Is it hard?' Sir Maurice asked, intrigued by this olive-skinned little friar who seemed so sharp and kept his emotions under such firm control.

'Is it hard? When you are a priest, Sir Maurice, it's not the love act you miss, though the demands of nature do make themselves felt.' Athelstan laughed quickly. 'But that passes. It's the terrible loneliness, the feeling that you are watching the world go by and cannot become part of it. Sometimes, just sometimes, you meet someone! Thank God, not often, but you can see it in her eyes or face, the way she looks at you. Your heart beats quicker; your blood drums a little faster in the brain; your mouth becomes dry.'

'And what do you do?'

'You get on your knees, Sir Maurice, and you pray that you never ever fall in love. That you are never put to the test because, if you are, there's every chance that you'll be found wanting.'

'And do you envy men like me, Brother?'

Athelstan smiled up at the knight.

'You are a good man, Sir Maurice, you would have made a good priest, an excellent Dominican.' The smile widened. 'Particularly when it came to counselling young nuns.'

Sir Maurice laughed and fastened on his war belt.

'Believe me,' Athelstan continued. 'You will marry the Lady Angelica but keep praying! Pray,' Athelstan repeated, 'that your love never dies, never wavers but grows stronger by the day.'

'Oh it will.'

'Yes, I am sure it will. Now, go and find Sir Jack and tell him to wait for me at Parr's house but Sir Maurice, do not now or in the future tell Sir Thomas, or indeed anyone, what you learned last night.' Athelstan went to the door. 'I'm going to talk to Godbless about his adventures in Venice and a man who should have died but didn't.'

Maltravers left as fast as a greyhound. Athelstan went across to the death house, chattered to Godbless then returned to collect his writing-bag and slipped out of the house down to the riverside.

He found Moleskin with other boatmen on the quay-side watching the executioners despatch a river pirate from the gibbet which stood like a great black finger poked up against the sky. The felon had been pushed up the ladder.

A huge, burly oaf, he kept threatening the hangman and spitting out at the waiting crowd. Athelstan sketched a blessing in his direction. The pirate saw this and made an obscene gesture with his middle finger.

'Come away, Moleskin!' Athelstan called.

The boatman swaggered across, his cheery, leathery face dour, his eyes hard.

'You shouldn't watch such sights,' Athelstan said. 'It's terrible to see a man such as he about to fall into the hands of the living God.'

Moleskin looked over his shoulder at the gibbet.

'I couldn't think of a better place, Brother. That bastard is responsible for the deaths of three boatmen to the north of London Bridge. You know the marshes? Well, he kept a wherry there. He poled out, took their money and slit their throats.'

Athelstan followed his gaze. The rope was now round the felon's neck. There was a shout from the crowd. The executioners slithered down. The ladder was pulled away and the felon began his dance of death.

'It's over!' Moleskin said. He clapped the friar on the shoulder. 'Now come on, Brother, tell me what happened last night and where do you want to go?'

'I'll let the others tell you about all the excitement, Moleskin. I want you to take me along the Thames and find a Venetian ship.'

Moleskin led the friar down the green mildewed steps and into his stout wherry.

'Why a Venetian? Are you going to flee Southwark?'

'No, I want to ask the captain a few questions.'

Moleskin concentrated on manoeuvring his craft, for the river was busy with barges and fishing smacks. They reached the far side and Moleskin began to go slowly by the sterns of the moored ships: massive, fat-bellied cogs from the Baltic, merchantmen from the Low Countries and royal warships getting ready to put to sea. At last he found a Venetian galley which lay low and rakish in the water. Its raised, gilded red and gold stern was surrounded by bum-boats selling fruit, sweetbread and other items from the city markets. There was even a boat full of whores who stood shrieking up at the sailors, trying to entice them with their charms to get aboard. Moleskin, skilled in the ways of the river, managed to catch the eye of the officer responsible for maintaining order along the decks. The boatman jabbed a finger at Athelstan and, making a sign, asked to come on board.

The officer agreed. A rope ladder was lowered and Moleskin, his boat bobbing beneath him, helped the little friar up. Such attention provoked the jealousy of the others milling round the great Venetian war galley. There were shouts and imprecations, rotten fruit was thrown. Athelstan yelled at Moleskin to wait. The boatman took his craft away and sat watching the scene. Now and again a friend or acquaintance would pass in a hail of good-natured abuse and raillery. Moleskin undid the little chest in the stern of his craft, took out a linen cloth and gnawed on a piece of salted bacon, taking deep draughts from the water bottle which he had filled with ale. He sat wondering what the little friar wanted with a Venetian war galley, but there again he shrugged, for Athelstan was a strange priest. If he wasn't looking after those rogues at St Erconwald's, he was scurrying around after Sir John Horse-Cruncher, the great and high lord coroner of the city. Moleskin narrowed his eyes. He must remember that. He loved baiting the coroner, and next time Sir John hired him, Moleskin would charge him double because of his weight.

He finished his bacon, growing slightly impatient because the swell of the river was becoming more pronounced. Then he noticed movement on board the galley and glimpsed the black and white robes of his parish priest. Moleskin turned his craft and brought it in, using the oars to fend off rivals. At last he was beneath the rope ladder. Athelstan clambered down with a sigh of relief and took his seat in the stern.

'What was all that about, Brother?' Moleskin asked as he pulled away.

Athelstan smiled contentedly. 'Do you know, Moleskin,' he said, leaning back, 'there are certain pleasures in life one feels truly good about.'

Moleskin pulled a face.

'Oh, not that!' Athelstan laughed. 'I think I've just trapped a red-handed assassin! Moleskin, you are my champion among boat-men. Our next stop is the holy nuns at the convent of Syon!'

Moleskin bent over the oars. Nuns, assassins, Venetians, he thought. What on earth was this little Dominican involved in? It was all Sir Jack's doing! Everyone along the waterfront said where Lord Horse-Cruncher went, trouble always followed.

They swept upriver and Moleskin brought his boat along the quayside steps.

'Do you want me to wait, Brother?'

'No. you'll be pleased to know after this I am going to meet Sir John.'

Athelstan offered some coins but Moleskin shook his head.

'For you, Brother, it's free. Just remember me and my boat at Mass. I mean, if you can bless a collection of rat-catchers, cats and ferrets...' He looked hopefully up at the friar.

'I think it's a very good idea. Moleskin,' Athelstan replied. 'What we'll do is wait for the feast of some sailor, or a Sunday when the gospel mentions Jesus going fishing with His apostles, then I'll come down and bless you and your craft. Perhaps we can give it a name?'

Moleskin's smile widened.

'What about *St Erconwald*?'

Moleskin's smile faded.

'Or,' Athelstan added quickly, '*the Rose of Southwark*?'

'I like that, Brother. I knew a sweet girl called Rosamund. The only problem is so did half the boatmen along the Thames!'

'Then we are agreed.' Athelstan sketched a blessing in the air and walked up the steps.

A young novice ushered him into Lady Monica's presence. The abbess rose, as stately as a queen, though her face was slightly flushed.

'Ah, Brother Athelstan. Where's Brother Norbert?' Her eyes darted around. 'And Sir Jack?'

'They are not here, my lady. I have only come to collect the Lady Angelica.'

'I beg your pardon!' Lady Monica clasped her hands together, drawing herself up to her full height. 'My good Brother, you don't walk into a nunnery and demand that I hand over one of my girls!'

'Lady Monica, I am a Dominican friar. Holy Mother Church and my Order have entrusted me with saying Mass, preaching the gospel and looking after Christ's faithful. I am parish priest of St Erconwald's in Southwark where, as God knows, I have more precious charges than I can handle. I am also secretarius to Sir John Cranston, lord coroner of this city, personal friend of the late and glorious Edward. He is one of my Lord of Gaunt's most trusted counsellors and a personal friend of the young King. So, I believe I can look after a young maiden entrusted to my care!'

Lady Monica's shoulders sagged. 'I don't really...' she stammered and looked under lowering brows at Athelstan. 'Sir Thomas Parr will...'

'Sir Thomas Parr is a London merchant,' Athelstan continued forcefully, 'who has more wealth than he has sense. Now, my lady, do I have to go down to the King's Justices at Westminster and get a writ? Collect soldiers from the Regent's palace at the Savoy?' Athelstan held his hand up. 'I assure you, my lady, that the Lady Angelica must come with me to her father.'

'Very well, if you put it like that.' Lady Monica was now quite flustered. She picked up a small handbell and shook it vigorously. 'Tell the Lady Angelica,' she announced to the young novice who almost burst through the door, 'to get herself ready to leave. She's to wait in the guest house.' She waited until the door closed. 'Brother Athelstan, I would like you to sign that you have taken the Lady Angelica to her father and that you accept full responsibility.'

The abbess ushered Athelstan to a small writing-desk in the far corner of the room. Athelstan wrote out exactly what she wanted, signed it, waited until it dried and then handed it over. Then he rose and made to go towards the door.

'Brother Athelstan.' Lady Monica had retaken her seat. 'Please sit.' Her tone was almost wheedling.

Athelstan noticed Lady Monica's face had become more flushed, her eyes glittering. He sat down.

'How can I help you, my lady?'

The abbess sifted amongst the pieces of parchment on the desk.

'It's your Brother Norbert.' She kept her head down. 'I… I…' She looked up, blinking quickly. 'Brother, he spoke so eloquently of love. Since his departure, I have had strange dreams… fantasies…'

Athelstan quietly thanked God that Sir John wasn't here. Lady Monica had now picked up a sheet of parchment, using it to fan her face.

'I wondered if Brother Norbert would visit me, to continue his talks? To give me spiritual counsel?'

'My lady abbess,' he replied mournfully. 'Brother Norbert is no longer with us.'

Lady Monica let the parchment drop. 'Where has he gone?'

'It's a great secret,' Athelstan confided, lowering his voice. 'But he has gone to do God's work in another place. So, I ask you to remember him in your prayers.' Athelstan glanced away. The disappointment in Lady Monica's face was so apparent. 'However,' he added quietly, 'and I assure you of this, Brother Norbert thought as highly of you as you did of him. Indeed, until he received orders to go elsewhere, he could scarcely contain his eagerness to return here.'

'Oh, thank you, Brother.' Lady Monica leaned back in her chair. 'I shall remember him. Oh yes I shall!'

A short while later Athelstan, accompanied by the Lady Angelica, still dressed in the robes of a nun of Syon, her sandalled feet slapping on the cobbles, left the convent and took the road into the city. Athelstan had hardly bothered to glance at her, never mind explain, while the young woman had enough sense not to ask any questions until they were well away from the convent gates. At the corner of an alleyway she stopped and grasped Athelstan's arm.

'Brother, what on earth's happening? Where are we going? Why did Lady Monica release me? Is my father well? How is Sir Maurice?' She wiped a tear from her eye. 'I heard about that business at the Golden Cresset.'

Brother Athelstan grasped the young woman's smooth hands. He ignored the curious looks of two beggars crouched in a doorway.

'Lady Angelica, you are going back to your father's house. Sir John and Sir Maurice are already there. Sir Maurice loves you deeply. He is a valiant, noble knight who wears his heart on his sleeve and that heart is yours for as long as it beats.'

'You should have been a troubadour. Brother. But that poor woman?'

Athelstan swore her to secrecy then explained all that had happened. The change in Angelica's face was wondrous, reminding Athelstan of the old adage about the 'steel fist in the velvet glove'. Her face paled, her blue eyes became ice-cold, like hard pieces of glass, while her generous mouth tightened into a thin line.

'My father?' she asked.

'I believe your father is innocent. I do not think Sir Thomas would stoop to murder to blacken a man's name.'

'I believe you.' Angelica gazed over Athelstan's shoulder. 'I think we should walk, Brother, otherwise we might both be reported to the Bishop as a friar and a nun who fell in love and conducted their amour in public!'

They walked slowly up the street, Angelica asking questions, Athelstan doing his best to reply. Indeed, so engrossed was the friar that he hardly noticed the sights and sounds of the city, the busy frenetic cries of the market, the shouts of the apprentices, the clatter of horse and cart. Before he realised it, they were standing on the corner leading down to Sir Thomas Parr's mansion.

'I always despised Hersham.' Lady Angelica ran a finger round the rather tight coif about her chin. 'I used to catch him watching me. He reminded me of a cat stalking a pigeon.'

'Some pigeon, my lady. More like a hawk, as my good friend Sir Maurice will find out.'

Angelica grasped his hand and squeezed it.

'What you did, Brother, what you did was noble.' Her face relaxed into a smile. 'And when I marry Sir Maurice, I don't care what Father says, I want you to meet us at the church door and witness our exchange of vows.'

'I wouldn't recommend St Erconwald's,' Athelstan replied. 'Especially with a ferret on the loose.'

'A ferret?'

'I jest. Come on, Lady Angelica, let us first see your father before you arrange the marriage feast.'

The manservant who opened the door glanced at Athelstan then Angelica and his jaw sagged.

'Lord save us!' he gasped. 'Oh, what doings! What a morning! The bailiffs have been here closeted with Sir Thomas. Now, Sir John and Sir Maurice are kicking their heels in the parlour.'

'This is my house,' the Lady Angelica said. 'Richard, let us in!'

'Of course, my lady.' The manservant stood back and ushered them into the parlour.

Lady Angelica took one look at Sir Maurice and, in a manner that would certainly not have been approved by the Lady Monica, hastened across the chamber and threw her arms round his neck. Sir John, sitting in a window seat cradling a large goblet, shrugged and smiled.

'Sir Maurice!' Athelstan hissed. 'Lady Angelica! The waters are troubled enough!'

He heard footsteps along the gallery outside. Lady Angelica and Sir Maurice hastily stood away from each other and Angelica sat down. Sir Thomas Parr swept into the room. He scowled at his daughter and glanced angrily around.

'What is this nonsense? Angelica, who brought you here? And you sir!' He flung his hand in the direction of Sir Maurice. 'I'll have you driven from my home!'

'Father!' Lady Angelica sprang to her feet. 'I have told you not to scowl, it doesn't suit you. You are in very, very serious trouble! I think you should listen to Sir John and Brother Athelstan.' Angelica stepped forward, wagging her finger. 'Father, I am your dutiful daughter but I am very angry with you.' She turned. 'Sir Maurice, I believe we should adjourn. Don't worry, Father, I won't be ravished; I am taking Sir Maurice into the garden and I'll ask my maid to accompany us.' She glanced at Sir Maurice. 'Though not too close.'

She swept out of the room, Sir Maurice trailing behind her. Athelstan closed the door.

'Sir Thomas, I suggest you sit down.'

'This is my house, friar.'

'Sit down!' Sir John roared. 'Or I'll haul you off to the Fleet immediately!' The coroner lumbered to his feet. 'Hard of heart and hard of head Thomas, you were always the same. Never bending, never giving!'

Parr sat down.

'Are we here to discuss my character, Sir John? And, by the way, where're Hersham and Margoyle? Your bailiff, the one with the flea-ridden dog, he said both men had been detained?'

'He was lying. On my orders. Hersham is dead and Margoyle's in flight.'

Sir Thomas swallowed hard.

'Now, Thomas. I am going to tell you what has happened. And, before you interrupt me and start accusing Sir Maurice of being an assassin, don't!' He jabbed a finger. 'You know, in your heart, he's innocent of any murder.'

'I was mystified by the stories.'

'But you still told your daughter,' Athelstan interrupted.

'Enough! Enough!' Sir John picked up his wine cup. 'Sir Thomas, there was once a wealthy merchant of Cheapside...'

In stark, pithy phrases the coroner described exactly what he and Athelstan had discovered: the death of the young whore at the Golden Cresset; the fight the previous evening in St Erconwald's cemetery and the full and frank confession of Clement Margoyle. To give Sir Thomas his credit, he sat and heard the coroner out. Only occasional fidgeting, licking of dry lips and beads of sweat which appeared on his upper lip betrayed his fear.

'If we wanted to,' Sir John continued, 'we could take this full matter to my Lord of Gaunt. Believe me, he would love that! He would have you arrested, your wealth seized and he would take great joy in repudiating any debts he has to you.' Sir John drew out a roll of parchment from his pouch. 'Margoyle's confession is enough evidence, not to mention the witness of myself and Brother Athelstan.'

'What about Sir Maurice?'

'He does not know the full facts. And, to be quite honest, Sir Thomas, I don't think he really cares. You could tell him that the Pope is enthroned in Cheapside and it would fly over his head like a bird.'

'I had no choice,' Sir Thomas said. 'You don't know what it's like, Jack. The rebels are all over the city.'

'You could have come to me,' Sir John replied. 'In the main they are sound and fury. Think about it, Sir Thomas, they don't want to start kidnapping young damsels or burning a man's house. However, I tell you this: when these gentlemen, Jack Straw and the others, march on London, they won't give a fig for any promises made!'

'So, what will happen?'

Sir John got up and threw the pieces of parchment on to the weak fire burning in the grate.

'It's all over, Sir Thomas.' The coroner beckoned Athelstan to follow. 'We are leaving. Outside in the garden you have a daughter you should be proud of and a man I'd be delighted to call my son.' He sketched a bow. 'Goodbye, Sir Thomas; in all things remember honour!'

Chapter 17

Sir John was very pleased when they left Parr's house. He was confident that Sir Thomas would do the honourable thing and the betrothal of the Lady Angelica would soon be proclaimed throughout the city. His good humour, however, soon drained as Athelstan, lost in his own thoughts, wandered up and down Cheapside, along the alleyways and runnels, visiting one apothecary after another. He came out of each shop shaking his head and muttering to himself, clicking his tongue in annoyance. Eventually Sir John, exasperated beyond belief, seized the friar by the shoulders.

'Troublesome priest! What in the name of Satan's buttocks are you doing?'

'I don't really know yet, Sir John. Did you find me a seller in poisons?'

The other man shook his head.

'Well.' Athelstan winked. 'It really doesn't matter now!'

Cranston arched an eyebrow. 'So, it's Hawkmere is it? You little ferret. Oh bugger, here comes Leif!'

The beggar man, however, had espied his fat quarry and was hopping along as merrily as a grasshopper.

'Sir John! Sir John!' he gabbled. 'I have a new song!' He pointed back along the street. 'And a new friend. Rawbum can play the flute and accompany me.'

Athelstan stared in disbelief at the dishevelled beggar who stood a few yards away, a battered wooden flute in his hand.

'Rawbum?'

'He sat in a pan of boiling oil,' Sir John explained. 'And, ever since, he prefers to stand.'

'Can I sing you my new song, Sir John? It's about a law officer…'

Sir John dipped into his purse and thrust a coin into the beggar's hand.

'Just bugger off and leave me alone!' he growled.

'Very well, Sir John, and give my regards to the Lady Maude.'

Both he and Rawbum disappeared into a nearby ale-house, and Athelstan continued his mysterious pilgrimage. Eventually, in an apothecary's, just near the great conduit which served the hospital of St Thomas of Aeon, he came out, grinning from ear to ear.

'Come on, Sir John! It's the Holy Lamb of God for both of us!'

Soon they were ensconced in a small garden behind the tavern, admiring the fish which swam in the artificial carp pond. They sat in a shady arbour. Athelstan insisted on purchasing blackjacks of ale and a meat pie to share with his friend. He also described the conclusions he had reached. Sir John, at first ravaged by hunger, listened and nodded but eventually he swallowed hard and stared in disbelief at his companion.

'You can prove all this, little friar?'

'Oh yes, Sir John. But I haven't marshalled my thoughts yet. They are running round my mind like rabbits in a corn field. I have to impose some order and trap this assassin. What I want you to do is go down to the Savoy and ask the Regent to bring some archers. Seek out Sir Maurice and Aspinall, bring them to Hawkmere Manor.' He nodded at the empty tankard. 'I think you should go now, Sir John.'

The coroner was about to object but Athelstan grasped his podgy fingers.

'We'll meet again, Sir John, and celebrate the Lady Angelica's betrothal.'

Sir John got to his feet and turned his face up to catch the sun. This was happiness, he thought. He just wished Maude and the poppets were here. The brave boys would love the fish and Lady Maude would be out listing the flowers and herbs, loudly wondering whether she could have the same in their garden. A small cloud passed over the sun.

'I never asked this, Athelstan, but do you think they could still move you from Southwark?'

'They have,' Athelstan replied. He saw his friend's jaw drop. 'But,' the friar added hastily, 'I am here, Sir John, this is my life. Now, go please! We have an assassin to trap.'

The coroner, huffing and puffing, waddled back into the tavern. There was a squeal and Athelstan realised the coroner must have caught the taverner's wife and given her a kiss. The friar stared at the small, golden fish darting among the reeds. How was it to be done? The taverner's wife came out with another tankard. He drank it rather quickly and, before he knew it, he leaned back against the turf seat and fell into a deep sleep.

He woke refreshed and realised it must be mid-afternoon. Yet he was in no hurry. It would take Sir John some considerable time to organise the Regent.

In fact, Athelstan was quite surprised when he reached Hawkmere to find Gaunt's retainers had taken over the manor. Men-at-arms stood at the gateway while his archers patrolled the parapet walk. The Regent himself, Sir Maurice beside him, was lounging in a chair on the dais in the hall. The Regent was wearing brown and green velvet and looked as if he had recently come from the chase. His hair was ruffled, his smooth face bore slight cuts from branches and his muddy boots were propped up on the table. He slouched in the high-backed chair, slicing an apple, popping pieces into his mouth. Now and again he would turn and playfully nudge Sir Maurice; Athelstan realised that Sir John's prophecy had come true.

'I am betrothed,' Sir Maurice smiled as Athelstan came in. He welcomed the little friar with a bearlike hug. 'We'll be married by Michaelmas. In St Mary-Le-Bow. And you must be the celebrant.'

'A good day's work, Brother Athelstan!' Gaunt called out, beckoning him closer. 'How did you do it?'

'My lord Regent, God works in wondrous ways, His wonders to perform.'

'I'll take your word for it, Brother.' Gaunt's eyes hardened as his gaze moved to the small musicians' gallery at the far end of the hall.

Athelstan turned and looked but he could see nothing, since the gallery was hidden in shadows.

'What have we got here?' Gaunt asked.

'Why, my lord Regent, the truth.'

'Do you know something?' Gaunt pointed at him. 'You, my little friar, are a very dangerous man. Shall I tell you why?'

'If you wish, my lord Regent.'

'Because you see things, Athelstan. You have a love of logic, a hunger for the truth while people like myself can only echo Pilate and ask what is truth? So, do we have the truth here, Brother Athelstan?'

'I think so, my lord, but…'

'Ah, there you are!' Sir John, accompanied by Gervase, walked into the hall. 'I've just been up to see the prisoners. They are both frightened. Our other guests have not arrived yet.'

'My guards, where are they?' Gaunt asked.

'Everywhere but the mice-holes. And there are some men dressed in gowns and hoods. They must be your men, Gervase?'

'My lovely lads,' the Keeper of the House of Secrets simpered back. 'They go where I do and keep an eye on their patron. In fact, we are a most pleasing choir, be it a madrigal or the introit to a Mass.'

'Shall we begin?' Gaunt interrupted harshly.

'I think we should,' Athelstan replied. 'Sir John, if you could seal the doors?'

'Don't we need the prisoners here?' Gaunt asked.

'No, my lord, at least not for the time being.'

'Well,' Gaunt waved his hand. 'The truth, my good friar?'

'The St Denis and St Sulpice,' Athelstan began as Cranston closed the doors, 'were two French warships, pirates, marauders in the Narrow Seas. They were like cats among the mice, snapping up the English merchantmen. You, Sir Maurice, sank one and captured the other.'

'We know that,' Gaunt drawled.

'How did you capture them, Sir Maurice?'

'I told you, Brother. I was in Dover when news arrived by messenger from London that the wine fleet would be leaving Calais. We were to put to sea and ensure its safe passage across. You know the rest.' He spread his hands.

'It was luck, wasn't it?' Athelstan asked, staring at Gaunt. 'Absolute good fortune that the English ships came upon the St Denis and St Sulpice. My lord Regent, Sir Gervase, the English had no spies aboard either ship, did they?'

Gaunt smiled to himself, Gervase looked away.

'When the St Sulpice was brought into Dover,' Athelstan continued, 'and the prisoners taken ashore, the French officers were kept separate, weren't they?'

'Of course,' Sir Maurice said. 'It's common practice!'

'And you, Gervase, when they came here, visited them?'

'Naturally, they might hold information which would be useful to us.'

'And what did you find?'

Gervase now refused to meet his gaze.

'Nothing.'

'But you, my Lord of Gaunt, dropped hints, light as a feather, how this good fortune of war was really the result of treason among the French.'

Gervase glanced at the Regent; Gaunt picked up the apple core and chewed at it.

'Go on, friar,' he murmured.

'My lord, you couldn't believe your good fortune. Two of the most dangerous ships in the French navy had been destroyed or taken, their captains and officers either killed or captured. You had the prizes as well as the ransom money for the hostages but you decided there was more to win.'

Gaunt was now smiling to himself.

'The spy Mercurius, the professional assassin at the French court, what a marvellous way to trap him! Let it be known, and I am sure you could do this through our envoys at the truce negotiations, that one of the prisoners at Hawkmere was one of your spies.'

'Very good,' Gervase commented. 'Brother Athelstan, you really should work in the House of Secrets.'

'You were playing with men's lives,' Athelstan went on. 'The French court was furious that the spy, responsible for the destruction of two of their finest ships, could now look forward to honourable retirement as a pensioner in the Palace of the Savoy. Orders were issued and Mercurius began his bloody work.'

'Brother, Brother.' Gaunt shook his head in admiration as if they were playing chess or a game of hazard. 'You forget these were French prisoners, they were held for ransom. If they die, I lose the money.'

'A very small price, my lord. You invest one pound and recoup a treasure. The French would not use their deaths to break the truce. What would they care as long as the spy was destroyed?'

Sir Maurice looked bemused. He scratched his head and beat at the table-top.

'But, Brother, who is Mercurius, where is he? How could he poison so expertly? Why kill that poor girl? And Maneil shot with a crossbow bolt?'

Athelstan ignored him.

'My Lord of Gaunt, do I speak the truth?'

'You do, Brother. "Put not your trust in Princes," the psalmist says. Believe me, Athelstan, never were words so inspired. Outside of London the Great Community of the Realm conspires and plots. Across the Narrow Seas the French wait, ready to exploit any weakness. The St Sulpice and St Denis were captured by good luck and God's good fortune. But, as the House of Secrets knows, Mercurius has done terrible mischief to our cause both here and abroad. A spy and an assassin, I wondered if he could be lured out into the open? When the prisoners began to die I knew I was correct. The French would kill them all, or some of them, until they believed they had avenged the insult. But the deaths themselves?' Gaunt shook his head. 'They are a mystery to me.'

'Has Aspinall the physician arrived?' Athelstan asked.

'Yes,' Sir John replied. 'I asked for him to be confined in one of the upper chambers. He protested but he looks frightened enough.'

'Bring him down,' Athelstan ordered. He patted the table next to him. 'Ask him to sit here.'

Sir John left and, a short while later, brought in the physician. The man was visibly agitated, even more so when he realised whose presence he was in. He bobbed and scraped but Gaunt ignored him.

'Brother Athelstan,' he gabbled. 'Is there anything wrong? I mean...'

'When a man is poisoned,' Athelstan asked, 'how does the noxious substance work?'

'Why, Brother.' Aspinall swallowed hard. 'It goes down to the gut and seriously disturbs the humours of the heart and the brain.'

'And is there any poison that I can take which will not harm me but, if you eat it, would kill you?'

Aspinall wiped a bead of sweat from his upper lip.

'If there is, I have never heard of it, Brother.'

Athelstan took out a small leather pouch from his writing-bag. He opened it and shook a number of very small, hard peas out on to the table.

'This is the paternoster pea,' he explained. 'Also called the rosary pea. In Latin I understand they call it the Abrus precatorius. Master Aspinall, I would like you to take one.'

Aspinall sat, hands in his lap.

'Take it!' Gaunt urged.

Aspinall, trembling, picked up a pea.

'Now, put it into your mouth.'

'Is it poisonous?' the physician asked.

'What are you doing to do?' Athelstan asked. 'I mean, when you put it in?'

'I'll break it between my teeth.' Aspinall swallowed hard. 'But, Brother, I beg you, for the love of God!'

Athelstan smiled and took the pea back.

'Don't take it,' he said quietly. 'But, if you stay here, Master Aspinall, I am going to teach you something about medicine. Sir John. Bring the two prisoners down.'

They sat in silence, Aspinall moving further up the table. There were sounds of footsteps outside and the two prisoners were led into the hall. Athelstan scooped the peas up and put them back into the leather pouch.

'Ah gentlemen, I wonder if you can sit beside me. I wish to share some information with you.'

'Are we in danger?' Vamier asked.

'Pierre Vamier,' Athelstan said, 'Jean Gresnay, would you please sit down.'

The latter flounced down like a sulky girl. Vamier, his dark face wary, sat on the bench opposite. They glanced along the table. Sir John must have told them who was waiting in the hall but, apparently, they had both decided to insult Gaunt and his henchmen. Gresnay dismissed the physician with a contemptuous flicker of his eyes.

'You are both sailors,' Athelstan began. 'Monsieur Vamier, where are you from?'

'Originally my parents hailed from Rouen. My father owned a boat. I fought against the Goddamns. I found it easy to take their ships at sea, as well as raid their coastline. It's good to see towns like Winchelsea engulfed in flames.'

'And you, Monsieur Gresnay?'

Gresnay simpered. 'I was raised by the sea. A small village outside Montreuil. My father was a wealthy fisherman. The English sank his craft and I was raised to do two things: plough the sea and kill Goddamns.'

'But you were captured,' Athelstan taunted. 'Sir Maurice sank one of your ships and took the other captive, which is why you are here at Hawkmere.'

'Only through treachery,' Gresnay sneered.

'I am afraid not,' Athelstan replied. 'My Lord of Gaunt will take an oath that it was simply the fortunes of war.'

'That's a lie!' Vamier shouted.

'I am afraid, Monsieur, it's the truth,' Gaunt replied languidly. 'Your ships were taken in fair fight and you are prisoners here because the Goddamns beat you.'

'So, why murder us?' Gresnay sneered.

'But no Englishman murdered you,' Athelstan said. 'You see, both of you are sailors and probably very good ones but...'

He paused as the door opened and one of Gaunt's liveried servants hurried in. He bent over the table and whispered in the Regent's ear; he, in turn, called Sir John over.

'He's arrived,' Sir John announced.

'Tell him to wait,' Athelstan replied. 'We'll be with him shortly.' Athelstan waited until the door closed before picking up where he had been interrupted. 'Both of you are sailors, and probably very good at your trade: the trim of sails, scrutinising the sky, knowing the sea. You are probably stout fighters ready to run down an English merchantman, steal its cargo, slaughter its crew. God save us all!' Athelstan sighed. 'You're no different from those who live on the other side of the Narrow Seas.'

'What are you implying?' Gresnay's voice was strident.

'What am I implying? Why, one of you is a spy! Oh, not for the Regent here but for the court, the government back in Paris. A man who keeps an eye on his fellows, searches out mutiny, grumblings, any hint of treachery. After all, it's not unknown for ships, be they French or English, to enter into secret collusion with the enemy.'

'That's nonsense!' Vamier snarled.

'Is it?' Athelstan asked. 'You go to sea and you live in each other's pockets. You sleep, eat, do everything with your companions. However, when your ship returns to harbour, where do you go? To the taverns and the brothels or home to your loved ones? One of you also goes to Paris: to the Louvre Palace, or the Hotel de Ville, to deliver a report to his masters; scraps of information, morsels of news.' Athelstan glimpsed the uncertainty in Gresnay's eyes. 'Now your masters in France have a spy, an assassin called Mercurius.'

Neither man flinched.

'High ranking, very well paid. His task is to collect information and remove the enemies of France by fair means or foul.'

'Are you saying it's one of us?' Vamier asked. 'Even if you speak the truth, Brother, it could be one of those who have already died.'

'Oh, it's one of you,' Athelstan said. 'Your masters in Paris were furious to lose two warships, their cargoes and skilled crews all in one day. They reached the obvious conclusion that there must be treachery, as did you. You were brought from Dover and delivered into the hands of Sir Walter Limbright at Hawkmere Manor.' Athelstan sighed. 'An Englishman who has good cause to hate the French. He would keep you in straitened circumstances, deepen your bitterness. Make you drink the chalice of sorrow till the very last drop. One of you, however, secretly received information that the traitor who had betrayed the St Sulpice and the St Denis must be among the prisoners at Hawkmere. I suppose that man needed very little encouragement to carry out what he considered legal execution.' Athelstan picked up two of the peas.

'Messieurs, let me introduce the rosary pea, sometimes called a paternoster pea, an Abrin pea or, to those who are skilled in herbs, the Abrus precatorius. It's harmless enough. Monsieur Gresnay, there's two for you. Monsieur Vamier, the same for you. I will take two as well to show you that they possess no noxious qualities.'

'No,' Gresnay said. 'I am not taking them.'

The Frenchman walked down the hall towards the door.

'You killed my friends. You will not kill me!'

He started to run. Sir Maurice caught him, crashing into him and sending him flying across the hall. Gresnay stumbled but regained his stance and turned. Sir John seized him, grasping his arms and, assisted by Maltravers, brought the protesting Frenchman back to the table.

'I will not take it!' Gresnay's tongue came out, licking the blood at the corner of his mouth. 'Vamier, for God's sake!'

Athelstan turned. 'Why, Monsieur Vamier, you seem more composed?'

Vamier had the two peas in the palm of his hand.

'Go on!' Athelstan urged. 'Why not take them?'

'If you say so.' Vamier popped the peas into his mouth.

Gresnay's body went slack. Sir John pushed him back on to the bench.

'Please, for God's sake, what are you doing?'

Athelstan stretched his hand out. 'Monsieur Vamier, spit the peas back into my hand.'

Vamier did so.

'Now, sirs,' Athelstan said. 'Let me see the rosary beads you were given when you first arrived at Hawkmere.'

'They are in my wallet,' Gresnay replied. He took out his rosary beads and threw them on the table.

'And you, Monsieur Vamier, where are yours?'

He shrugged. 'They are in my chamber.'

'It can be searched.'

Vamier refused to meet Athelstan's gaze.

'I lost them,' he muttered. 'What's the use of prayer in a place like this? I threw them away.'

'You threw away rosary beads?' Athelstan persisted. 'Come, come, Monsieur Vamier, where are they? Down a privy? In the garden perhaps?'

The Frenchman folded his arms.

'Are you a prayerful man?' Athelstan asked. 'And, if not, surely like all sailors you are superstitious? Would you throw away Ave beads brought to you by the French envoy? Who now waits outside, to see what's happening. Ah well, I think I've seen enough! Sir John, Monsieur de Fontanel should join us. I would also ask for two of my lord Regent's guards to stand near the door, their swords drawn.'

A short while later de Fontanel swept in, cloak billowing about him, his high-heeled boots rapping on the wooden floor.

'My Lord of Gaunt.' De Fontanel slapped his feathered hat against his thigh. 'Why am I summoned here? To receive your apologies, your assurances?'

'Shut up!' Gaunt barked. 'And sit down!'

Gervase waved him to the stool beside him. De Fontanel obeyed. He sat opposite Gaunt, face impassive; now and again he glanced down the table at Vamier.

'You arrived at a most interesting time, Monsieur,' Athelstan began. 'I want to make certain things very clear. First, the English had no spy on the St Sulpice and St Denis: their capture and destruction were due to the fortunes of war.'

De Fontanel scraped the stool back.

'I swear,' Athelstan held his hand up, 'by the Mass I celebrated this morning that I speak the truth.'

The consternation on de Fontanel's face was apparent.

'Secondly, Monsieur de Fontanel, you are no more a Frenchman than I am. Your name is Richard Stilling-bourne, formerly an English clerk. You fled to France where you are known as Mercurius, an assassin and a spy.'

'This is nonsense!' De Fontanel made to rise but Gervase grasped his wrist.

He snatched the envoy's gold chain from round his neck and threw it to the floor. The Keeper of the House of Secrets' delight was apparent. If Gaunt hadn't stretched out a restraining hand, de Fontanel would have been struck as well as disgraced. The Frenchman placed his hands on the table, breathing heavily, eyes darting about.

'You are a traitor.' Gaunt picked up the small fruit knife, balancing it between his fingers. 'And you are in my jurisdiction, Monsieur de Fontanel.'

'Where's the proof?'

'I'll come to that,' Athelstan said. 'So, let's go at it hand in hand. Let's charge the truth, Monsieur de Fontanel, and grasp it with both our hands.' He picked up the Abrin peas and threw one down on the table. 'You know what these are?'

De Fontanel caught the hard pea.

'You do know what they are, don't you?' Athelstan persisted. 'After all, you have been to Italy and visited Venice.'

'I know nothing about gardens or herbs,' de Fontanel sneered, but his sallow face had paled. He kept glancing at Vamier.

'In which case,' Athelstan said, 'swallow it. Chew it carefully and swallow it. I assure you there's nothing wrong.'

De Fontanel threw the pea down on the table and let it bounce on to the floor.

'Of course you wouldn't.' Athelstan sighed. 'And I apologise for my lie. The Abrin seed is deadly. If a full-grown man took two, death would occur within the hour. From the little I know it has similar properties to hemlock. The Council of Ten in Venice use it to determine the truth. The accused is given two of these. If the prosecutor wishes him to die, he is made to chew. However, if the prosecutor, for his own secret reasons, wishes the man to be deemed innocent, he simply tells him to swallow them. The casing of the paternoster pea is very hard, rather like the pip of an apple. It goes into the gut and is discharged into the privy with no ill effects. Now.' Athelstan opened his wallet and took out his own rosary beads. 'Mercurius, Monsieur de Fontanel, whatever you wish to call yourself.' He waved a hand airily. 'You were sent from Paris to kill the supposed spy among these prisoners. You knew one of them was innocent, your own agent Pierre Vamier. Before you entered, I offered Vamier the seeds: he was quite prepared to swallow them because he knew their secrets. You came here and gave each prisoner a set of Ave beads.' Athelstan wrapped his own rosary beads round his fingers. 'Apart from Vamier! He can't find his now because, instead of ordinary beads, he was given a string of Abrin seeds, the wherewithal to kill the prisoners.'

Chapter 18

Confusion broke out as de Fontanel and Vamier protested their innocence. Gresnay, however, remained quiet, gazing intently at his companion. Athelstan realised that Gresnay himself must have seen something which he now judged suspicious.

'How could I do this?'

Only the presence of Gaunt's guards forced de Fontanel back into his seat.

'Oh, it was quite easy,' Athelstan replied. 'You visited the prisoners. You were allowed to talk to them, bring them gifts. Who would object to a set of rosary beads for men far from hearth and country? Vamier would be given secret instructions. You, of course, had been in the city and visited Mistress Vulpina who kept every known poison under the sun. You really didn't care if the prisoners died! You would be rid of a spy, no ransoms would have to be paid while the Goddamns would take the blame. What you didn't realise was that my Lord of Gaunt was deeply interested in these murders. Mercurius might come out of the shadows. His masters in Paris were both furious and frightened: two great warships lost. Mercurius, himself, would have to deal with the matter. A truce was arranged and you were immediately despatched to England as an official envoy. Your appearance has changed, you speak French fluently, and you have all the protection protocol dictates. My Lord of Gaunt, of course, did not know this but he suspected Mercurius was in England. So, he sent in his most feared investigator, the lord coroner, Sir John Cranston.'

Sir John bowed his head and beamed at the compliment.

'Questions were being asked,' Athelstan continued. 'So Vulpina had to disappear. You killed her and her two henchmen then burnt their infernal den to the ground. You also had other orders: Sir Maurice Maltravers had to be punished. You hired those two shaven-headed assassins.' Athelstan's voice rose. He felt a hot flush of anger in his cheeks. 'They crossed to Southwark to kill both him and me. Life to you, Mercurius, is very, very cheap!'

'This is nonsense,' de Fontanel rushed in. 'You have no evidence. Nothing but conjecture.'

'He has evidence.' Gresnay spoke up, his eyes fixed on Vamier. 'I was in your room, Pierre, a few days ago. I saw your rosary beads were broken; some of the beads were missing. You kept it well hidden, underneath the candlestick on your table.'

'That's how poor Lucy died,' Sir John said. 'Vamier here was careless. Some of the beads fell on the ground. Poor Lucy was always picking things up and putting them in her mouth.'

'A useless and futile death,' Athelstan said. 'A poor, witless innocent.'

Vamier dropped his gaze.

'Didn't you care?' Gresnay burst out. 'Pierre.' He spoke quickly in French but Athelstan could follow him. 'They were our friends. We fought back to back against a common foe. Aye, we burned and we pillaged, but murder like this? Of your own friends and companions?'

'Mercurius' real work,' Athelstan went on, 'was here at Hawkmere and it was quite easily done.' He pointed at the French envoy. 'You met Vamier and handed over the poisonous Ave beads. You convinced him how they were only noxious to chew. Vamier had no choice but to accept. After all, he wanted to return to France as quickly as possible.

'Serriem was the first to die. He'd be easy to persuade, especially after he had seen you swallow the seeds and suffer no ill effects. How did you describe them?' Athelstan asked. 'As a herb which would help? And was it the same for Routier? He would be the most gullible victim. He would need his strength, be ready to take any medication which might help his escape. Again, you showed him the seeds were not noxious, probably just before he climbed that wall and made his escape. Both men, even in their dying agonies, would never suspect the seeds were the cause of their deaths. Not from a friend who had eaten them himself and suffered no ill effects.'

'That's true, Vamier!' Gresnay's voice rose to a scream. 'You always were persuasive, a senior officer whose hatred of the Goddamns was well known.' He beat on the table. 'You were playing chess with Serriem the night he died! That poor bastard would take anything you offered, as would Routier!' Gresnay blinked back the angry tears. 'He trusted you completely. He was worried that he might not have the physical strength to make his escape. I offered him some food. You gave the poor fool those damn seeds. What did you do? Swear him, and poor Serriem, to secrecy? Tell them how you didn't have enough to share among the rest? I suppose,' he added bitterly, 'I was next.'

'Not necessarily,' Athelstan said. 'I suspect de Fontanel would offer to pay for your and Vamier's ransom from his own pocket, or take a loan from the merchants in the city. He would act all concerned. However.' Athelstan shrugged. 'Monsieur Gresnay, I do not think you would have survived long in France.'

'And Maneil?' Gresnay asked.

'Ah. Mercurius, or Monsieur de Fontanel, was very clever. Two men had died from poisoning but the death of Limbright's daughter, well, it muddied the pool a little. You see Mercurius wanted the blame for all these deaths to be laid firmly on the doorstep of the Goddamns. None of the prisoners were armed so, when Mercurius last visited Hawkmere, he probably came armed with a small arbalest for his own protection. However, in the confusion following Routier's escape, Mercurius decided to seize his opportunity. The arbalest and the bolts were hidden away. Vamier was told of their whereabouts, behind a chair, a bench or even a latrine. He was allowed to mix with you?'

'Yes,' Gresnay snarled. 'And he had a word with each of us.'

'That's true.' Sir Maurice spoke up. 'The manor was in uproar.'

'Mercurius simply exploited the opportunity,' Sir John added. 'Limbright was mourning for his daughter. The guards were still recovering from the hunt for Routier. Mercurius realised that death by a crossbow bolt would simply confirm suspicion that the assassin could not possibly be one of the prisoners.'

'Is that possible?' Aspinall asked. 'I mean, to dispose of?'

'There are privies here, aren't there?' Athelstan asked.

'Yes, yes there are, along the top gallery where Maneil had his chamber.'

'The arbalest would be small,' Athelstan explained. 'Like one ladies use when they go hunting. How long would it take Mercurius to tell Vamier that an arbalest was hidden in a certain place, a few seconds? Vamier acted quickly, exploiting the chaos: he collected the arbalest, concealed it beneath his doublet, knocked on Maneil's door and killed him. He then dismantled the crossbow and probably threw it down a privy where it would sink in the mud and ordure, never to be found.'

'You still have no real evidence,' de Fontanel screamed.

'Oh, we have evidence,' Athelstan replied. 'As well as the sheer logic of my conclusion. I began to suspect there were two killers. One inside and one out. First, let's take Routier's escape. Why did he choose that particular way? How did he know the shutters of the window in that outhouse weren't locked? The prisoners were never allowed to go there, so the information must have been given by someone visiting the manor. Secondly, Mercurius, on your last visit, you said something intriguing just before you left Hawkmere. You came here and sat beside Vamier. You told the prisoners to fall to their prayers. I recalled the gift of Ave beads and wondered if your words were a code, a secret message.'

De Fontanel got to his feet. 'I am an envoy of the French court,' he said. 'I know nothing of this Mercurius. I certainly have no responsibility for the terrible deaths which have occurred here or elsewhere.' He swallowed hard, glancing at the door. 'I have hardly left my lodgings! Why should I wander around Whitefriars?'

'Who told you Vulpina lived there?' Sir John jibed. 'You went there disguised as a priest; that was a mistake, strangers never visit Whitefriars.'

'And, as for your lodgings,' Gervase smiled, 'one of your retinue could act the part, especially with that ridiculous popinjay hat you wear. How did you leave there, disguised as a servant? Our intelligence is that Mercurius is a master of disguise.'

'My movements are my own concern! As are my conversations with my countrymen!'

'I saw you whispering,' Gresnay declared, hot-eyed. 'I saw you, Monsieur, talking to Vamier here on a number of occasions before the murders began!'

'Monsieur Gresnay, remember where you are,' de Fontanel snarled. 'You are a prisoner of the English but one day you must return to France.'

Gaunt stared at Athelstan: from the Regent's look, the friar realised that more proof would have to be given. He nodded slowly.

'We have all the evidence we need,' he said. 'It's here in this hall, so sit down, Monsieur de Fontanel!'

'What evidence?' The envoy looked shaken, nervous.

'First, we will search for Monsieur Vamier's Ave beads and we will find them. We know you gave them to him! Secondly, Monsieur Gresnay here is going to rack his brains, and he will start recalling the minutiae, helpful little details.'

'And?' de Fontanel asked.

'We have Monsieur Vamier. If we can prove, and we will, that his Ave beads are highly poisonous Abrin seeds then Vamier is a murderer. Be he French or English, my Lord of Gaunt will have him taken to the dungeons in the Tower where the interrogators will begin to work.

Oh, they'll piece the story together like I did. You don't know Godbless, do you? He's a poor beggar who lives in my cemetery; once he was a soldier and visited Venice. He talked of a man who should die but didn't. And then I visited a Venetian galley berthed in the Thames. The captain was a merry fellow. Of course he knew about the Abrin seed, how the Council of Ten gave it to their criminals. He simply confirmed what I had learned from our librarian in Blackfriars as well as the gossip of little Godbless. A short while later I visited an apothecary near Cheapside. He confessed it was one of the secrets of his trade; he told me all about Abrin's noxious properties.' Athelstan ticked the points off on his fingers. 'Venice, you have been there. Abrin seeds were on the Ave beads you gave to Vamier, he still has these.' Athelstan gazed straight at Sir Maurice. 'And, finally, one of those assassins, the shaven-heads you sent against us? He didn't die. He's lodged in the Tower. I suspect he will recognise you and your voice. It's wonderful what a man will do to escape the noose.'

'Both men are dead,' de Fontanel insisted. He closed his eyes at his terrible mistake.

'How do you know that?' Gaunt asked, getting up. He grasped de Fontanel by the shoulder. 'How do you know, Monsieur, about assassins who attacked a poor priest in Southwark?'

'I – I heard the rumours. My Lord Gaunt, I must leave here.' He broke free and walked towards the door.

Sir John looked helplessly on. The arrest of a foreign envoy was a serious matter.

'What about me? What about us?' Vamier shouted.

De Fontanel turned, his face pallid.

'You are going to leave me here to rot, aren't you? I tell you this.' Vamier strode forward. 'I'll not go to the Tower! I'll not dance on the end of a Goddamn's rope for you!'

'Hush man, keep your nerve!'

'Keep my nerve!' Vamier screamed. 'Here among the Goddamns! Have my flesh torn, my limbs racked!'

'Enough!' Gaunt looked up into the darkness of the musicians' gallery. 'Sir Walter, you have heard enough. Let sentence be carried out!'

De Fontanel whirled round. There was a whirr through the air like a bird beating its wings, then the goose-quilled arrows struck their targets. De Fontanel's neck was cruelly pierced, the shaft going through one side and out of the other. Vamier took two arrows, one in the shoulder, the second deep in his heart. Both men fell, legs kicking, choking on the pools of blood spilling out of their mouths. Gresnay sprang to his feet. He tried to run towards the door. Athelstan quickly seized him, shielding his body from the archers in the musicians' gallery.

'For God's sake!' Athelstan hissed. 'If you move away from me, you are dead!'

'Ah, he's safe enough,' Gaunt called out. 'Only the guilty suffer.' He held his hand up. 'Brother Athelstan, you have my word. Well done, Sir Walter, you may join us now.'

There was a movement in the music loft and, a short while later, Sir Walter, accompanied by three master bowmen, entered the hall. Before anyone could stop him, Sir Walter kicked both corpses and walked threateningly towards Gresnay.

'My Lord of Gaunt,' Athelstan protested, pushing Gresnay back on to the bench.

'I wondered what was going to happen,' the Regent said. 'I know you, little friar, you ferret out the truth! So, I placed Sir Walter and the bowmen in the shadows of the musicians' gallery.' Gaunt sighed and sat down in the high-backed chair. 'They were there if judgement had to be carried out.' He smiled bleakly. 'Moreover, if I am to meet Frenchmen it's best to be prepared, especially if Mercurius is in their midst. I wondered if de Fontanel would go for his dagger. The death of John of Gaunt would be a great prize for the French court.' He snapped his fingers.

The bowmen picked the corpses up by the legs and dragged them out of the door, leaving a trail of sticky, red blood on the wooden floorboards.

'They could have stood trial,' Sir John said.

'I don't think so,' Gaunt answered. 'Mercurius was a traitor and a murderer. Vamier no better. The evidence was there but hard to grasp. The French could protest, perhaps even threaten English prisoners in France. They would have certainly worked hard for Mercurius' return.'

'And so what will be your story?' Sir John asked. 'The French will appeal to the Pope in Avignon. You will have the cardinal of this or the cardinal of that knocking on the door of the Savoy Palace.'

'Oh, I'll tell them the truth.' Gaunt smiled. 'Well, some of it will be truth. I'll say that Mercurius was unmasked in my presence; that he and his accomplice Vamier drew their daggers and tried to kill me. I'll have his corpse searched while Gervase will scurry among the records. We'll point out that Mercurius and the English clerk Richard Still-ingbourne were one and the same person and, therefore, came under my jurisdiction. Vamier was just a casualty of war!' He gazed round menacingly. 'What can anyone say?

They were a threat to the Crown! Traitors and assassins! Lawful execution was carried out!'

'And how, my lord, will you explain your discovery of Mercurius?' Athelstan asked. 'By an angel come down from heaven?'

Gaunt laughed softly, clicking his tongue as if savouring a secret. 'What do you think, little friar? How do you think I'll explain it?'

'Oh, my lord, you'll let the dance continue. You and Gervase will suggest, both here and abroad, that not only did you have a spy on board the cogs of war but another one closeted in the most secret councils of the French court. You will let it be known, by whisper and rumour, that you knew who Mercurius was from the start and enticed him into your web. The Papal envoys will be informed about the true reasons for Mercurius' visit to England as well as the hideous murders he committed. You will insinuate how your alleged spy at the French court told you all this.' Athelstan sighed. 'You will be exonerated, a truly virtuous prince, while the French will tear themselves apart hunting for a traitor who doesn't exist.'

Gaunt threw his head back and roared with laughter, the tears sparkling in his eyes.

'Oh, I love this game. You are very good, Brother. Yes, that's exactly what Gervase will do.' His eyes slid to Gresnay, who sat transfixed like a rabbit before a weasel. 'And now, sir, we come to you.'

'My lord,' Athelstan broke in. 'He is an innocent man.'

'He'll be a dead one if he returns to France,' Gervase said. 'No one will believe or accept his story.'

'I have done no wrong,' Gresnay burst out, half-rising from the bench.

Athelstan pushed him back.

'Don't worry.'

Gaunt was now examining a spot on his hand.

'I'll tell you what, Monsieur Gresnay: you go to Monsieur Gervase here. Tell us all there is to know about the fortifications along the French coast. We'll send a letter to France saying that you, too, were a victim of this traitorous poisoner. You can change your name, take a reward from the English exchequer. Go down to the south coast and hide in one of our fishing villages. It's either that or back to France.'

Gresnay quickly agreed.

'In which case,' Gaunt concluded, 'all is in order, all is finished. Two French ships have been destroyed, Mercunus killed and further mischief planned for the French court. A good day's work, eh?'

He smiled at Athelstan, who stared coolly back. Gaunt stepped off the dais and clapped Sir John on the shoulder.

'Good work, Jack, eh? Sir Walter, this manor is yours, to do with as you wish. It's a reward, a little compensation for your sad loss.' He sketched a bow. 'Brother Athelstan, remember me in your prayers. Gervase, join me at the Savoy. Sing me that madrigal you've composed.'

And, with his arm round his spy-master, Gaunt walked down the hall. He turned at the doorway.

'Maurice, you'll join us? Or are you going back to see the Lady Angelica?'

'Sir Thomas Parr has invited me to supper, my lord.'

'Sir Thomas Parr is a most gracious man,' Athelstan observed.

'Aye.' Gaunt smirked. 'And pigs fly along Cheapside.'

'In which case, my lord,' Athelstan quipped, 'you'll find plenty of pork in the trees!'

Gaunt let go of Gervase's shoulder and walked back up the hall, striking his heavy leather gloves against his hand.

'And how are your parishioners, Brother?'

Athelstan looked over Gaunt's shoulder. Gervase glanced warningly and shook his head.

Gaunt pushed his face closer. 'And those arrows?'

'Hidden, my lord, by rebels but discovered by loyal subjects and reported immediately to the Corporation.'

'So, they are all hale and hearty?'

'My lord, they are in remarkably good health. They work hard, eat little and constantly pray for the welfare of the King.'

'Then pray keep them that way.'

'I do, my lord. I pray every day that, if they be not in the King's grace, they will speedily return to it and, if they are in the King's grace, God will keep them in it.'

'And when the revolt comes?' Gaunt asked, his face now drained of all good humour. 'Which side of the fence will you stand on, little friar?'

'Why, my lord, I'll be in my church, celebrating Mass, preaching the Gospel and looking after those in my care. That is the purpose of a priest, a member of the Order of St Dominic.'

'So it is, so it is.' Gaunt opened his purse and slipped some coins into his hand. He gave these to Athelstan, his blue eyes dancing with mischief. 'Well, buy a hogshead of ale, Brother. Let them drink my health and that of the King.'

Gaunt sauntered out of the hall, slamming the door behind him. Sir Maurice stepped off the dais and clasped Sir John's hand, then embraced Athelstan, squeezing him tightly.

'I cannot thank you enough, or you, Sir John.'

'Nothing to it, my boy.' Cranston took out the miraculous wineskin. 'You'll celebrate with me now?'

Sir Maurice spread his hands. 'A few pots of ale and a pheasant pie, eh, Brother?'

Athelstan put the coins Gaunt had given him into his wallet. He picked up his writing pouch.

'I have other duties,' he said. He turned and clasped Gresnay's hand. 'Do not worry, sir, the Regent will keep his word, you will be safe. Have nothing to fear from Sir Walter.'

He, Sir John and Sir Maurice then left the hall. Already it was becoming less of a prison, no sentries on duty, doors and casement windows flung open. They walked out and, as they did so, glimpsed Gaunt and Gervase, surrounded by their retainers, gallop through the gatehouse back towards the city.

'I knew Gaunt's father,' Sir John mused. 'And his elder brother, Edward the Black Prince, God bless and rest him. Gaunt is a cunning one. I think he plays the game for the sheer enjoyment. Come on!'

They walked down, through the gatehouse and on to the deserted heathland.

'Are you coming to the city, Brother?'

Athelstan shook his head.

'We should have made our farewells to Sir Walter.' The friar paused. 'Sir John, Sir Maurice, I am tired and not in the mood for rejoicing. You go into the city then, tomorrow, come to Southwark. We'll celebrate your happiness in the Piebald, perhaps tomorrow evening when the excitement has died down?'

He watched the coroner, arm in arm with the young knight, walk across the heathland towards the old city wall. Then he turned back and walked up to the gloomy entrance of the manor. He found a retainer and, after a short while, the servant brought Sir Walter down to where Athelstan stood just outside the doorway.

'Why, Brother?' Sir Walter looked more composed, as if the deaths of the two Frenchmen had purged something from his soul.

'I simply came to say farewell, Sir Walter, and offer the thanks and good wishes of Sir John.'

'A good man, the coroner.' Sir Walter beamed. 'And you, Brother.' He shook his head. 'A spider's game,' he added. 'But I am cleared of any wrong-doing though it's a pity that my daughter had to pay with her life.'

'She's at peace,' Athelstan replied. 'And so are you, aren't you, Sir Walter?'

'I confess, Brother. I was in the musicians' gallery. I enjoyed giving the order, watching those two traitorous murderers die.'

'But you knew, didn't you?' Athelstan asked.

'What do you mean, Brother?'

'Sir Walter, it's a question of logic. You sat here guarding those Frenchmen. I wager you watched them day and night. Oh, I am not saying you knew who the assassin was or how the murders were carried out. However, you must have seen Monsieur de Fontanel whispering, talking, perhaps more to Vamier than the rest?'

'I saw nothing, Brother.' Sir Walter held his gaze. 'I simply did my duty.'

'Oh, come, come, Sir Walter. You hired Master Aspinall the physician. You knew he was above suspicion. You also were aware of your own innocence. I wager you were only too pleased to see the French kill each other, men who slaughtered your own family?'

'I had no knowledge of who Monsieur de Fontanel really was, or how the murders were carried out.'

'No, but you had your suspicions and you did not share them with us and that, Sir Walter, is why your daughter died. You hated those men. And perhaps with good reason. You resented their arrogance, their whisperings, their quiet laughter. You knew you were innocent of any foul play. Let them kill each other, you thought; Sir Jack Cranston can resolve it, and the more who die, the better.'

'I hear what you say, Brother, but...' Limbright shrugged. 'That's why you let Routier escape, wasn't it? You told your guards to look the other way. I think you knew what he was planning and looked forward to the hunt. A way of releasing some of the bile in your own soul. Show these French who was the master?'

'I would have been blamed for Routier's escape.'

'Come, come, Sir Walter, a tired, dispirited Frenchman alone in England. You would have enjoyed hunting him down with your dogs.'

'Even if what you say is the truth, Brother, what is the use now?'

'The truth always matters,' Athelstan replied. 'Good day, Sir Walter.'

—

St Erconwald's was very quiet when Athelstan arrived back later that afternoon. Both church and house had been cleaned, Philomel was dozing in his stable. Athelstan took the second key he always carried and opened the church and stepped inside. Huddle had been busy drawing on the far wall with a piece of charcoal. Athelstan went over and crouched down to study what the painter had drawn: a stern Christ in Judgement. On his left, the goats, on his right the lambs. But, this time, Huddle had taken liberties with Holy Scripture: members of the parish stood among the lambs. Pernell, even Godbless holding a little Thaddeus, while others, whom Huddle disliked, such as Pike's sharp-tongued wife, were placed in the centre so people would wonder if they were a lamb or a goat.

'That will have to go,' Athelstan commented. 'Otherwise civil war will break out on the parish council.'

He crouched down, his back to the wall. Gaunt had said everything was neatly tied up but was it? He thought of all those souls thrust unprepared into eternity: the hapless prostitute hanged at the Golden Cresset, and those Frenchmen who never would see their families or homes again. Did Mercurius have a family? Did anyone grieve for Vulpina? Or those shaven-headed assassins?

'A long list of dead!' Athelstan whispered. Tomorrow he would say Mass for all of them, that Christ would have mercy on their souls.

The door swung open and Godbless came in, Thaddeus trotting behind him.

'God bless you, Father. All is well?'

'Aye,' Athelstan replied.

Godbless knelt before him, one arm round Thaddeus.

'What am I to do, Father?' he pleaded. 'I have got no home to go to.'

Athelstan dug into his purse and brought out one of the coins Gaunt had given him. He flicked this at Godbless, who deftly caught it.

'This is your home, Godbless. By the power given to me by Holy Mother Church,' he raised his hand in blessing, 'not to mention the provisions of Canon Law, I forget which clauses, I now make you *custos*, guardian, of God's acre, of our cemetery here at St Erconwald's. Your official residence will be the death house. I'll get those two reprobates Watkin and Pike to build a new one near the wall.' Athelstan rubbed his hands. 'Aye, the dead will be able to sleep in peace now. Your task, Godbless, and Thaddeus, will be to guard that cemetery with your life.'

The beggar chortled with glee, hugged Thaddeus and kissed the goat between its ears. Athelstan glimpsed a furry movement down near the porch, lithe and quick.

'Oh, and go tell Ranulf,' he said, 'I think I know where his ferret is hiding!'

Conclusion

The Abrin seed is not a figment of the writer's imagination. It contains a very toxic protein which causes nausea and very serious, and rapid, damage to vital organs. The seeds have a very hard coating and only become poisonous when they are chewed. This property was used in the past for trial by ordeal, particularly in Venice. The suspected persons were given paternoster peas to swallow: those whom the authorities wanted to escape were secretly warned not to chew them!